PRAISE FOR *S.T.A.G.S.*

'*S.T.A.G.S.* is a pacey and well-plotted young adult story that champions outsiders and questions out-dated viewpoints in a constantly evolving world.'

CultureFly

'M. A. Bennett .... er in suspense.'

Book Murmuration

'M. A. Bennett reinvigorates the boarding-school thriller ... This is a darkly compelling examination of the allure of privilege, and the unscrupulous means by which it preserves itself.'

Guardian

'*S.T.A.G.S.* is a thrilling and thoroughly enjoyable YA novel with dark undertones. A fun mystery thriller that sheds light on issues surrounding class and society. Highly recommend.'

Book Bag

'A gorgeous and compelling romp.'

Irish Times

90710 000 520 682

H.A.W.K.S.

Books by M. A. Bennett

S.T.A.G.S.
D.O.G.S.
F.O.X.E.S.
T.I.G.E.R.S.
H.A.W.K.S

The Island

H.A.W.K.S.

M. A. BENNETT

HOT
KEY
BOOKS

First published in Great Britain in 2022 by
HOT KEY BOOKS
4th Floor, Victoria House
Bloomsbury Square
London WC1B 4DA
Owned by Bonnier Books
Sveavägen 56, Stockholm, Sweden
www.hotkeybooks.com

A CIP catalogue record for this book is available from the British Library.

ISBN: 978-1-4714-0870-0
Also available as an ebook and in audio

1

This book is typeset using Atomik ePublisher
Printed and bound in Great Britain by Clays Ltd, Elcograf S.p.A.

Hot Key Books is an imprint of Bonnier Books UK
www.bonnierbooks.co.uk

For Mick Ward
who loved films too

An Eagle for an Emperor, a Gyrfalcon for a King; a Peregrine for a Prince, a Saker for a Knight, a Merlin for a Lady; a Goshawk for a Yeoman, a Sparrowhawk for a Priest, a Musket for a Holy Water Clerk, a Kestrel for a Knave.

The Book of St Albans, 1486

1

There were no curtains up in my study in Lightfoot, so I could clearly see The Invitation when it slid silently under my door.

It was quite near the end of the Hilary Term – summer term to you – and I'd almost begun to despair that the Order of the Stag would rear its antlered head before we left school. The sands of the STAGS hourglass were pretty much running out.

Heart thudding, I picked up The Invitation. It was completely square – a kind of thick ivory envelope folded over on four sides, just as before. And just as before, it was sealed with a blob of *Robin Hood, Prince of Thieves* wax, the red of our school stockings. On the wax was impressed a little pair of antlers.

I broke the seal, just like they did in the movies. Inside was a thick square card. There were just three words on it, right in the middle of the creamy card, embossed in red ink this time. The letters were slightly shiny and raised to the touch.

The Red Hunt

I turned it over. On the back, in neat italics, was printed:

You are invited to spend the weekend of Lammas
at Castle MacLeod, Isle of Skye.

Coaches departing STAGS at 5 p.m. Friday.

RSVP

The red embossed type jiggled in front of my eyes, and I suddenly had to sit down at my desk.

Shafeen was with me. He was with me most of the time, to be honest. Once we'd got to . . . well, home base . . . in India we'd become even closer, and it turns out that playing baseball (as we'll call it) is quite addictive, so we pretty much lived in each other's rooms now. Along with my girl Nel and the rest of our year, we'd spent the first part of the term doing revision for the Probitiones, so there hadn't been much time for baseball. Then the summer had been all ticking clocks and buzzing bees and individual tables spaced out in the gym and the rustle of exam papers being turned over and cramped hands and scribbling pens and the footsteps of the invigilating friars walking up and down the rows, their swishing habits stirring the pages we wrote on. But to be honest since the exams had finished it had been back to baseball, and by the time The Invitation arrived Shafeen and I were basically inseparable.

He read the wording over my shoulder. 'So,' he said, and I could feel his breath warm on my neck, 'this is all going to end as it began – with an Invitation.'

'I guess you're right.' But some things *had* changed. Two years had passed. Now I wasn't a newb, I was a Medieval myself. I no

2

longer thought the coaches would be real Cinderella coaches with actual horses. And this time I wasn't a dumb little bunny rabbit hopping unknowingly into a trap; I would be putting myself in harm's way willingly.

Because now, as then, I was going to accept.

That's not to say, of course, that I understood what I'd been invited to, any more than I had last time. 'What the hell is a Red Hunt?' I wondered aloud.

'No idea,' said Shafeen. 'But it sounds pretty sinister.'

'And what's Castle MacLeod?' The only time I'd heard that name before was in *Highlander*. You know, 'Conor MacLeod of the Clan MacLeod'. But I was pretty sure even the Order of the Stag weren't going to have immortals running around with samurai swords and quipping with Sean Connery.

'Never heard of it,' said Shafeen helpfully.

'And where on earth is Skye?'

Shafeen looked over my shoulder. 'It's an island,' he read.

'Wow, I'm so glad we had this chat,' I said sarcastically. 'And the biggest mystery, of course, is who sent it.' And to answer that question, we'd have to bring our *Inside Man* into play – the guy who had sent the first invitation two years ago. I looked up. 'We'd better tell Henry.'

From habit, Shafeen got out his phone.

'You're kidding, aren't you?' I said witheringly. 'We'll have to write him a letter.'

'Bloody Medievals,' said Shafeen, as I reached for my writing case.

3

2

Of course, what Shafeen didn't know was that I'd been keeping in touch with Henry ever since we'd returned from India. He'd been living at Longcross – not in the house, of course, because that looked like the burnt-out shell of Wayne Manor in *Batman v Superman*, but in Longcross Lodge, a rather pleasant little cottage near the estate's gates.

Before you judge me, I hadn't been lying to Shafeen. At least, not exactly. We'd actually written to Henry together the first time, to agree a plan of action, and read the first reply. When we'd all come back from India, Henry had told us where he'd been staying and to keep in touch with any developments. He seemed quite determined in his intention to help us bring the STAGS down, so we'd agreed, just as before, that we Medievals would keep our heads down, revise for our final exams and wait. The slightly awks thing was that, since that first exchange of snail mail, Henry's letters had come directly to me. I'd written back, and sort of forgotten to mention it to Shafeen. It was all a bit complicated, because of the small matter of Henry confessing his love for me in a hospital corridor in India, as if we were starring in *Junoon* or something.

I should just make it clear that Henry's letters weren't love letters. He hadn't ever mentioned love again, except for in his nonchalant scrawled sign-off:

Love Henry x

But.

Like some Jane Austen heroine, I'd spent hours studying his loopy signature – in ink pen, of course – and that casual cross that could mean nothing.

Or everything.

His letters had been chatty accounts of the building works, which sounded like a pitched battle between the staunchly Medieval Henry and the Savage contractors. 'They're trying to turn it into a bloody hotel,' he'd written. 'Power showers and Wi-Fi. I ask you.' He would also write hilarious accounts of how he'd have to hide away when Louis, visiting from his estate in Scotland and then from STAGS, came lording it around the manor, checking on the building works. Since the Longcross staff were well used to keeping secrets by now, the new earl would come and go with no notion that the true Earl of Longcross was alive and well and chilling in the lodge.

I'd asked Henry when we would have an opportunity to put our vague plan into action – that is, to end, once and for all, the death hunts of the Order of the Stag.

'The STAGS will move when they are ready to move,' he'd written. 'Trust me.'

Then I remembered that trippy snake in *The Jungle*

Book – Kaa – with the hypnotic eyes, lisping 'Trust in Me'. I *wanted* to trust Henry, but after so many years of him being slippery, it was a hard habit to acquire. And nothing – not even his declaration of love – made it easier.

Once I'd received The Invitation, Shafeen, Nel and I decided we would write to Henry together. We agreed to meet, out of habit, at the Paulinus well one balmy summer evening near the end of term. I was the first one there and I walked across the manicured green lawn to the ancient well. The well was in the dead centre of a quadrangle of heartbreakingly beautiful medieval buildings, all mullioned windows and climbing ivy, and as I waited in the lowering sun for the others I reflected that this might be the last time we would meet here. Oxford beckoned in the autumn, and I'd just received my reading list from Professor Nashe of Christ Church College this morning. I read it over while I waited for the others. It went like this:

Renaissance and Revolution – Joseph Anthony Mazzeo
European Theories of the Drama – Barrett Harper Clark
Youth Revolution – Anthony Esler
Notion of the State – Alexander Passerin D'Entreves
All's Well That Ends Well: The Problem Plays – Simon Barker
Rebel Women – Stephen Wilmer
Dramas of the Revolution – Mikhail Shatrov

At the bottom of this slightly scary list was a handwritten note from the Professor herself.

Greer – I think you'll find these books very revealing.
Regards,
Professor Nashe

It seemed like a lot of reading, but I couldn't think about that now. I folded the list away as Shafeen and Nel approached from different sides of the quad; Shafeen in his tiger-striped stockings and Nel in her hot-pink Chanel knee socks. I don't know if they too had figured out that this might be the last time, but we all met together in a three-way hug.

We agreed that Henry should come to the school while he still had the chance. 'Term ends in a week,' I said, 'then we'll be leaving STAGS.'

'Never to return,' said Nel dramatically, placing the back of her hand to her forehead.

'Well, not *never*,' said Shafeen. 'There's a big leavers' party back here at the end of August.' As he'd been at the school forever, and as Aadhish – his father – had been before him, Shafeen knew about all the traditions.

'You mean like a prom?' I asked.

'*God* no,' he said in mock shock. 'That would be *far* too American, darling. No, they call it the Surroyal Ball.'

'The *Surreal* Ball?' I echoed, thinking of some nightmarish *Pan's Labyrinth* party with people dressed as fish and lightbulbs.

He laughed. 'No. S-U-R-R-O-Y-A-L. The surroyals are the topmost branches of a stag's antlers. We're the top of STAGS school. See?'

'Clever,' said Nel. 'When did you say it is?'

'End of August. Bank Holiday usually, so people can get back here.'

'OK – so this is really our last chance to get Henry to STAGS during term time,' I concluded. 'Problem is, if he comes here Louis will definitely find out he's alive.'

'Well, he's got to know sometime,' said Shafeen reasonably.

'Yes, but I rather think Henry wants to use the timing of that particular revelation to his advantage,' I said. I couldn't admit, of course, that I knew from Henry's letters that he'd been playing 'Hide the Heir' with Louis.

'Let's get him here in the dead of night then,' said Shafeen. 'I don't know how they do it in movies, but that's when conspirators always meet in books.'

'Good idea,' said Nel. 'It has to be here, because there's an added dimension this time.'

'Don't tell me,' I said, because I knew her well by now. 'Something to do with your dreamboat, Abbot Ridley?'

'Yes,' she said defiantly, her cheeks colouring slightly. 'But not just him. Have you forgotten about the FOXES?'

Incredibly, we had.

'I'm just saying,' she went on, 'that if there's a whole secret society of people hell-bent on destroying the STAGS, we'd be foolish to ignore them, no?'

'She's right, you know,' I said to Shafeen. 'It's time for the Avengers to Assemble. So that means inviting Ty too.'

'Definitely,' he said.

'And what about Cass?' Nel said.

I hesitated. I was still, after all this time, not at all sure what the deal was with Louis's twin. 'No,' I said eventually. 'There's no doubt she's devoted to Henry. But she's too close to Louis. Safer not to.'

'OK,' said Nel. 'So, secret meeting to defeat the Order of the Stag. Place: STAGS. Time: Dead of night. Dramatis personae: Us, Henry, Abbot Ridley and Ty. Let's set it up.' She snatched The Invitation from my hand and grinned cheekily as she flounced away across Paulinus Quad, her Tudor coat flapping in the evening breeze. 'I'll tell the Abbot.'

3

We met, in the dead of night, in a place I'd never been before in the whole of my two years at STAGS.

It was called the Crypt, and it was a sort of underground burial chamber below the chapel. God knows – actually, he's probably the only one who *does* know – how old it is, but since the chapel dates from 673 I'm guessing it's even older than that. It was gloomy and candlelit, and had a few hard dark-wood pews where we sat while blank-eyed saints watched us from little niches. It had those arching things over your head – I think they're called cross-ribs or something – and that old-stone smell that all churches have. All in all, it was the perfect setting for a conspiracy.

Shafeen, Nel and I sat on the front pew, with Ty on the other side of the little aisle, as if we were at a wedding and she knew the bride and we knew the groom. I smiled at her and she smiled back, a little tightly. I always felt sorry that after a promising start to our friendship a distance had grown between us after all that business of the Boxing Day hunt at Longcross, after which we'd sort of learned not to trust each other. I hoped that all that was set to change – now we were on the same side.

The Crypt had been the Abbot's idea. He stood before us now, tall and hooded as if he was about to lead a service, but that whole dynamic – of priest, headteacher, authority figure – had dissolved now. We, the conspirators, were equals and I spoke to him as such. 'How did you know about this place?' I said.

He took down his hood and ruffled his curls, looking far more human. 'I got a pretty thorough briefing before I took this job,' he said.

'From Reynard, the mysterious leader of the FOXES, I suppose,' I said, fishing.

He grinned. 'Among others.'

'I don't suppose you're going to tell us who Reynard is?' I said.

'Not just yet,' he said. 'But perhaps you know already.' He looked pretty pleased with himself.

I didn't, so I ignored his teasing manner and cut to the chase. 'So what about these "others"?' I probed. 'Can you tell us about them?'

'Jesus, Greer.' Nel rolled her eyes. 'I know this *looks* like the HQ of the Spanish Inquisition, but you don't have to play the part.'

'*Thank* you, Nel,' the Abbot said to her, with an intimacy to his tone I hadn't heard before. I wondered just how close they'd got while Shafeen and I were in India. 'Is your fifth columnist coming, I wonder?'

He meant Henry, of course. He was changing the subject, but I let him – I didn't want Nel getting all pissy with me again. 'We told him in the letter,' I said. 'Midnight on Tuesday in the Crypt. I assume he knows what a crypt is.'

'Oh, he'll know,' said Shafeen. 'You couldn't exactly get more Medieval than this, could you?'

And as he said this, Henry de Warlencourt walked down the stone stairs, stirring the candle flames as he came.

The Abbot walked forward to greet Henry. Henry was wearing mustard cords, an open-necked shirt, brown boots and a Barbour jacket, and he looked, as always, like a Burberry model. The two good-looking dudes shook hands guardedly, like two dogs sizing each other up in that split second when you're not sure if they're going to fight or start sniffing each other's bums.

'Nathaniel Ridley,' said the Abbot.

'Henry de Warlencourt. How d'ye do?' said Henry, an archaic greeting which suited him well. He nodded at the rest of us, and I saw Ty staring at him like a deer in the headlights. I remembered that the last time they'd met he'd been hauling her out of a burning Longcross Hall.

'Get here all right?' asked the Abbot, as if Henry was some party guest.

'Perfectly,' said Henry. 'Terribly obliging man of mine named Perfect drove me up in the estate car. You all remember Perfect, don't you?' He looked at us with a smile. I swallowed. I certainly did remember man-mountain Perfect, willing slave of the de Warlencourts since he was no more than a hillock, who'd stalked us around the estate with a shotgun. The mention of his name made it even more impossible to believe that Henry was now on the side of right.

'Let's sit,' said the Abbot, obviously sensing some tension, and Henry and he sat at the end of two different pews, facing us, and we scooched up so we were all in a sort of circle.

Henry, who looked comfortable everywhere, threw his arm casually along the back of the pew and waited, looking faintly amused, for what was coming next.

'As I understand it,' said the Abbot, addressing him, 'you have agreed to help end, once and for all, the heinous practices of the Order of the Stag.'

I don't know if I'd expected denial, or excuses, but Henry offered neither. 'You understand correctly,' he said.

The Abbot nodded once. 'We were hoping that an opportunity would present itself before this current cohort of "Medievals" – ' he nodded at Shafeen, Nel and me – 'leave the school. And it seems as if that opportunity is at hand. Greer?' He shot a green-eyed glance at me. I brought the thing out from the sleeve of my Tudor coat, like someone cheating at cards, and handed it to Henry.

Henry read the front of The Invitation, then turned it over in his scarred hands and read the back. He raised one eyebrow like Roger Moore's James Bond.

The Abbot said, 'What can you tell us about it?'

'Everything,' said Henry. 'Where do you want me to start?'

Shafeen leaned forward. 'Let's begin at the beginning,' he said. Whatever had happened to improve things with Henry, he still couldn't make his voice sound totally friendly when he addressed his old adversary. 'What's the Red Hunt?'

'It's a big deer-stalking event that takes place every August in Scotland. Always the principal stag of the herd, known as the Monarch of the Glen. The Monarch is always an Imperial, that's a 14-point stag, the biggest size there is.' He looked at Abbot Ridley. 'It's a hierarchy thing. The alpha male is

13

dispatched each year so the young bucks can come through. It's common throughout the animal kingdom.' This was definitely a burn for Nathaniel. Henry knew, by now, all the gory details of the Abbot's part in his family's lives. Or rather deaths. Henry's grandfather, Monty de Warlencourt, had been pulled from his horse by Nathaniel as the old soldier rode out from the Tiger Club in Jaipur. Then Henry's father, Rollo de Warlencourt, had been thrown from his horse when the animal had been spooked by the same man, dressed as Guy Fawkes at the Boxing Day hunt at Longcross. I'd half expected Henry to do that Inigo Montoya thing from *The Princess Bride* – '*Hello, my name is Henry de Warlencourt. You killed my father. Prepare to die.*' But that wasn't strictly true. The Abbot may have knocked Rollo from his horse, but it wasn't the fall that killed him. Rollo had been poisoned by an unknown hand. But I could still sense the tension between Henry and the Abbot. Which de Warlencourt alpha male would be the next to be lopped off? And would it be Nathaniel Ridley who did the deed for a third generation in a row? I got the feeling I wasn't the only one heading for a dangerous summer.

'And what makes the hunt red?' asked Nel, who was still, understandably, a bit nervous of Henry since he'd once chased her down with a pack of dogs. 'Blood, I suppose.'

For the first time Henry looked vaguely uncomfortable, and I knew he was feeling uneasy, because he was playing with the gold signet ring on his finger, the one with the deer antlers, the one *they* all wore. He looked at Nel, almost apologetically. 'The deer,' he said kindly. 'They're red deer.'

'So far so standard,' I said. 'Huntin' as usual. So what's Castle MacLeod?'

'A big old pile on the Isle of Skye, just off the west coast of Scotland,' he said.

'And it's an actual castle?' asked Nel.

'Oh yes,' he said. 'Considered to be one of the finest examples in Scotland.'

'I'm sure the de Warlencourts would expect nothing less.' Shafeen couldn't help himself – his tone was decidedly acid.

'Naturally, old boy,' said Henry, all pleasantness. 'But the castle actually belongs to the twins' mother, Lady Fiona.'

'Was she a MacLeod of the Clan MacLeod?' I asked.

Of course, as a Medieval, Henry didn't get the *Highlander* reference. He just looked vaguely impressed. 'Yes,' he said. 'She is. And she married Peregrine, my father's younger brother.'

I glanced at Shafeen. When we'd read Aadhish's diary in Jaipur, the teenage Rollo had mentioned the birth of a younger brother. That must have been Peregrine.

'Well, now we know who the castle belongs to, that probably answers my biggest question: who sent The Invitation?'

'I would think, almost certainly, Louis,' said Henry, shifting slightly on the hard pew. 'He still thinks he is the head of the family, and as such he will be invested into the Dark Order of the Grand Stag. My guess is that the DOGS know you know too much and can't let you go off into the wider world with the knowledge you have. Remember, Piers and Cookson as well as Lara, Charlotte and Esme all ended up at Oxford. The Order can't take the risk of you exposing them there.'

15

I felt a sudden chill, which seemed to be almost seeping from the ancient stones of the Crypt. At the Paulinus well I'd felt almost sorry to be leaving STAGS. Now I knew the ancient order which had founded this school was still out for my blood I couldn't wait to get out of here. But then, as Henry had reminded me, the Order had a foothold at Oxford too. No, the only way forward for me was to destroy them utterly – that's the only way I'd ever be safe. My fear made my voice more flippant than ever. 'Well, it's always nice to know where and when you'll be hunted to your death.'

'But we *don't* know when,' said Nel. She turned to Henry. 'The Invitation says "Lammas weekend". What's Lammas?'

'Lammas is an ancient Scottish pagan festival,' he replied. 'Lammas Eve is quite the party. Feasting, bonfires, folk music – you get the idea.'

'Sounds a bit *Midsommar*,' I said.

'Well, it is the Scottish midsummer, pretty much,' said Henry.

'It's a film about . . . never mind,' I said. 'Is Lammas always the same date, like Christmas?' I asked. 'Or does it jump about like Easter?'

'It's always on 1st August,' he said.

'OK,' I said, doing the maths. 'So the Friday the "coaches" leave must be 31st July.' I goggled. 'That's *this* Friday.'

'End of term,' said the Abbot.

'So what do we do? We can't just let Greer go on her own,' said Shafeen.

'No, indeed,' said Henry.

'But no one else has been invited,' said Nel. 'It's not like last time, when Shafeen and I were there too. Then we had each other's backs.'

'I'll go,' said Henry.

'But Louis doesn't know you're alive,' I said. 'So presumably this Scottish branch of the family don't know either.'

Henry smiled. 'What better time for the big reveal?'

I could see that Shafeen wasn't very happy with this idea, but he couldn't exactly tell Henry he couldn't go to his own uncle and aunt's house. 'Great. Now we just need a way to protect her from *you*,' he said pointedly.

Henry laughed, which seemed to make Shafeen even madder. 'And how do you propose to do that?'

'Last time we had tech,' said Shafeen stiffly. 'Nel's dad's Saros phone. At least there was some way of keeping track of Greer's movements on the fishin' day, when *someone* tried to kill her.'

'What about the FOXES?' I suggested, trying to deflect from this dangerous subject. I addressed Abbot Ridley. 'Isn't this where your lot come in? If you're the anti-STAGS, you should have the tech side of things sorted, shouldn't you? They're Medieval, you're Savage; that's it, isn't it?'

'Oh, we do have the tech side of things "sorted", as you put it,' he said confidently. 'Or, at least, we know someone who does.'

He looked to Ty, who'd been so quiet all this time that I'd almost forgotten she was there.

'Ty?' I said. 'Well, there's no doubt she's the Girl with the Dragon Tattoo when it comes to hacking.'

She spoke for the first time. 'He's not talking about me,' she said. 'He's talking about Ratio.'

4

'What's Ratio?'

We all wanted to ask, but Shafeen was the first to get in there.

'Not what. Who.' Ty spoke clearly and distinctly, and I remembered the power of her performance as Queen Cynthia in *The Isle of Dogs*. 'He's someone I've been in contact with online. He's very anti-STAGS – the school *and* the Order – and he's been helping me in my attempts to bring them down.'

'Could be a fifty-year-old creep,' said Nel.

Ty ran her fingernail along a groove on the back of her pew. 'I don't think so. He sounds like an insider. He knows an awful lot about this school.'

'Could still be a fifty-year-old creep,' I said. 'That's how they groom kids, isn't it? They find out a lot about your world.'

'Well, he, she or it helped me loads last year,' insisted Ty. 'Surveillance is his thing. He seems to have eyes everywhere. In fact, he seems like an inside man. I wouldn't have known half of what I knew, about the FOXES, or the de Warlencourt family, or what happened to my great-uncle, Leon, without him.'

'Wait,' said Henry, looking slightly discomfited for the first time. 'This character knows *my* family?'

'Inside out,' she said. 'He seems to be holding quite the grudge. And that's what I mean about being an insider. He was one of you. Us.'

'How do you mean?' said Nel.

'I mean he doesn't just know a lot about the school. I think he *went* to the school.' She looked round at us all. 'Here. STAGS.'

'*The call is coming from inside the house*,' I mused. 'How do you know?'

'He told me.'

'*What?*'

Ty nodded. 'He said he was expelled.'

'You keep calling him a him,' Nel said. 'How can you know he's male?'

'Oh, I'm pretty sure,' said Ty. 'You see, he was expelled for watching porn.'

'I heard that story when I first came here!' I exclaimed. 'So it must have happened relatively recently.'

'I remember something about it,' said Shafeen. He turned to Henry, almost friendly. 'Do you?'

'Vaguely,' said Henry. 'Some big scandal in the senior school, when we were still in the juniors.'

'I don't know if it was the school that turned him or what,' said Ty, 'but he's the most Savage of the Savages. I bet he'd know how to keep track of you up in Skye.'

'But you've never met him?' I asked.

'All messaging,' she said. 'Never clapped eyes on the guy.'

'Nor me,' said the Abbot. 'But he is one of the FOXES. He's verified as one of our hacktivists. But like most hackers, he remains anonymous.'

'Could we meet him?' asked Shafeen.

Ty sucked her teeth. 'I could try to locate him from his IP address.'

'What on God's green earth,' said Henry, 'is an IP address?'

'Internet Protocol address,' said Nel, who was also a Savage. 'It's a unique location that identifies a device on the Internet or a local network.'

'Can you find it on a phone?' I asked. We all still had our Saros smartphones, courtesy of Nel's lovely dad.

'Probably,' said Ty. 'But it's easier to use this.'

From under the skirts of her Tudor coat, she produced a sleek rectangle – mean and metal and thin, it was covered in decals and had an apple logo. We Medievals were so unused to these things that we stared, mouths agape. I swear it took me a good few seconds to recognise the thing for what it was.

A laptop.

As she opened this ark of technology in the candlelit chapel, the screen backlit her face like Marsellus Wallace's briefcase in *Pulp Fiction*.

'How did you smuggle that in here?' asked Nel admiringly.

'I gave her permission,' said the Abbot simply.

'OK,' said Ty. Then she went all *Girl with the Dragon Tattoo*, just as I'd said, her fingers a blur on the lighted keyboard. She muttered under her breath, 'Ratio, where are you?'

I watched her proudly. 'How did you find him, anyway?'

'He found me,' she said, without looking up. 'When I started using the username **mrs_de_warlencourt** he just popped up in my DMs.'

'And why is he called Ratio?' asked Henry.

'It's a Twitter thing,' Ty replied, just as if he was one of us. 'When your replies outnumber your posts. Also, *this* is his username.' She turned the screen round and we peered at the brightness.

:

'A colon?' I said.

'Remember your maths?' asked Ty.

It had been a while, so I was relieved when Shafeen spoke up. 'That's the symbol for a ratio. The colon separates the two relative values. You know, 1:1, 2:1, etc.'

'I became pretty familiar with that little symbol last year, I can tell you,' she said. 'It was popping up the whole time. Look.'

She called up her chat history. There were pages and pages of messages and replies, as Ty, planning her spy mission to Longcross as Louis's guest, had accepted the help of her mysterious ally.

: **The back stairs of Longcross lead directly to the kitchen.**

: **Remember the secret passage to Longcross church is located behind the portrait of Esmé Stuart on the mezzanine of the library. Might be useful if you** want to get in and out at night without using the main door.

: On Boxing Day the hunt will stop for lunch at the Trip to Jerusalem, a pub on Longcross land. They'll be there for about an hour. The hunt servants will bring second horses, but Rollo will stick with his favourite hunter, Harkaway.

: The hunt will pass through Huntsman's Covert to Longacre. Longacre leads into the east side of Longwood. There's a beck where you can hide and intercept the hunt.

'This Ratio seems to know Longcross inside out too,' said Henry grimly.

'Yep. He gave me –' Ty looked to the Abbot – '*us*, lots of maps and directions and coordinates to intercept the Boxing Day hunt.' She threw a glance at me. 'That's what I mean about helping to keep Greer safe. Ratio seems to have eyes in the sky. But he's not the only one with a few tech tricks up his sleeve.'

She turned the screen around again and began to tap away at the keyboard, a concentrated look on her face.

'What are you doing now?' Shafeen asked. Ty was typing reams of incomprehensible code onto the screen.

'I'm initiating a keystroke recorder,' she said, as if it was the most natural thing in the world. 'The messenger is telling me he's online right now. The keystroke recorder will tell me what he's typing.'

'Who's up at this hour?' said Henry.

She smiled. 'Geeks,' she replied. 'I'm actually hoping he's internet shopping.'

'Why *shopping*?' Nel asked.

'Because we need his address,' said Ty. 'Midnight to 2 a.m. is a spike time for online purchases.'

'Jeez,' I said. 'Don't nerds sleep?'

'It's not late everywhere, Greer,' she smiled. 'There's a whole world out there. *Yes!*' She sat up. 'Looks like he's on an auction site – like an eBay-type portal – in the Far East. My guess is Japan.' She looked up briefly. 'Computer geeks like manga. Anime. Figurines. And it seems he's no exception.'

We all crowded round the glow of the laptop like people would have huddled around a fire in medieval times. 'What's he buying?'

'A rare Funko POP! figure of the Joker. It's costing him £49.99.'

'For a *playing card*?' asked Henry.

'No, Henry Tudor,' I said, feeling safe enough to take the piss out of him now. 'The Joker's a baddie in the DC Universe. He's Batman's half-brother and nemesis. Funko POP! toys are those plastic action figures with big heads.'

Henry shrugged elaborately but didn't seem to mind me burning him.

'We just have to hope he's not bought from this seller before,' said Ty to the screen, ignoring us.

'Why?'

'Because if you buy repeatedly from somewhere like Amazon, your browser remembers your address. It's only

23

for new places you have to input it. Never mind – we're golden. He's typing it in.'

We leaned over her as the precious information appeared word by word:

Flat 8, Drumpellier Street
Blackhill
GLASGOW
G33 1BX

'Bingo,' Ty said softly, and sat back.

'OK,' said Nel, eyes shining. 'We've got an address. What do we do now?'

'We go and see him,' said Henry. 'Glasgow's on the way to Skye.'

'It is?' I said. My Scottish geography was sketchy at best.

'Yes. You go up the west coast – Glasgow, Glencoe, Skye.'

'But how do I get out of going on the "coaches"?' I waved the embossed card at him. 'That's what The Invitation tells me to do.'

'It tells you something else too.' He pointed with his little finger, and the golden nugget of his signet ring gleamed softly in the candlelight. 'It says RSVP. So you should just RSVP – by letter of course –'

'– of *course* –' I mocked him gently.

'– and say that you accept the kind invitation, but you'll be making your own way there.'

'Is that . . .' I searched for the words, 'the *done thing?*'

'Absolutely,' said Henry. 'It's quite commonplace, particularly for an August invitation when one might be summering at several great houses in one season.'

'Like you do,' muttered Ty under her breath.

'It just means that your host doesn't have to lay on transport,' said Henry, as if she hadn't spoken.

'I don't know where to write *to*,' I protested.

'But I do,' said Henry. 'And I don't need a . . . personal computer, or whatever you call it.' He tapped his head. 'Mine's in here.' He took out an old-fashioned pocketbook and pencil and wrote down the address. The directions appeared on the page in his flourishing handwriting; the Medieval version of Ratio's address appearing on the screen in Savage bits and pixels.

Henry gave me the piece of paper. It said, in his now-familiar script:

The Hon. Lord Peregrine de Warlencourt
Castle MacLeod
Dunvegan
Isle of Skye
SCOTLAND

It was quite a different address to the mysterious Ratio's. 'Write to my uncle here,' said Henry, 'and say you'll be making your own way, but will arrive on 30th July. We'll leave here tomorrow, be in Glasgow by the afternoon to meet this Ratio character and go on to Skye on Thursday.'

'We?' I queried.

'You and me,' said Henry.

'And me,' said Shafeen. He was looking daggers at Henry

again, and was clearly not going to be left behind while Henry and I went on a romantic Highland sojourn.

'And me,' said Ty. 'I'm not missing the chance to meet Ratio at last.'

'What about you, Nathaniel?' said Nel. The name, far too familiar for a headmaster, slipped out.

But he didn't seem to mind. 'I have a school to run,' he smiled. 'But if you want to go, I'll come up at the weekend and find you.' He looked around at the rest of us, suddenly serious again. 'If this is truly the last act in the STAGS drama, someone from the FOXES should be there.'

'That's settled then,' said Shafeen, setting his chin with determination. 'We'll *all* go.'

Ty sat forward suddenly and began typing again.

'What are you doing now?' I asked.

'I'm just adding a delivery instruction to Ratio's order.'

'Why?'

She smiled a secret smile. 'You'll see.'

Abbot Ridley turned to Nel. *'Ye'll take the High Road and I'll take the Low Road,'* he said fondly, *'And I'll be in Scotland before ye.'*

He was quoting from something, but as the Abbot always did that, I ignored him. I had bigger things to think about than literary flirting.

We had a plan.

5

On the day before the end of term Shafeen, Nel, Ty, Henry and I took the train from Alnwick to Glasgow.

I left STAGS without a backward glance – for one thing I was now, once again, afraid of the place, and for another, we'd be back for the Surroyal Ball at the end of August.

We travelled to Edinburgh Waverley and changed to Glasgow Central. We'd all decided to wear our own clothes, instead of looking like some weird cult, so in Henry's case that meant an immaculately cut Savile Row tweed suit and in everyone else's case jeans and T-shirts. The journey was odd but guardedly friendly – we all chatted for a bit, then there was another interesting division of Medieval and Savage. Shafeen, Nel and Ty went on their phones. Henry read a book, which seemed to be, of all things, about St Albans. I mostly looked out of the window and watched the gorgeous summer scenery roll past, as Northumberland turned into Scotland.

At Glasgow Central station we queued for a taxi, which took us through a grand and grey Victorian city centre to Blackhill, where dark, towering tenement buildings blocked out the light. The pavements were crammed with plastic bins full to bursting, and scrawny cats ran between our legs as loud music sounded from open windows. It was quite the contrast to the genteel STAGS. 'We're not in Kansas any more,' I remarked, as I had once at Longcross.

We found Drumpellier Street and Ty rang the bell for flats 7–15. The intercom crackled into life and a distorted female voice said, 'Hello?'

Without hesitation Ty leaned into the doorway. 'Hermes delivery,' she said.

After a second of silence the door gave a deafening buzz and clicked open. We all looked at Ty admiringly, and we walked into a hallway that had a sticky carpet and an odd smell. Dark patches of damp stained the walls and piles of post littered the floor. To my surprise Ty stopped to sort through it and picked up a square brown box. It had some Japanese characters on the front. 'What's that?' I asked.

'The Funko POP! figure Ratio ordered,' she said triumphantly. 'I added a delivery instruction to leave it in the hallway. I thought it might be our golden ticket inside.'

My admiration for Ty grew as she led us all up the stairs, over an obstacle course of bikes and pushchairs, to Number 8. She rang the bell and the door opened a suspicious crack. A pair of dark eyes looked us up and down. 'You're not from Hermes,' said the voice we'd heard on the intercom.

'No,' said Ty, 'but we do have a package for Ratio. We're friends of his.'

The door opened a little more. A woman stood there – dark-haired and slight, in a tracksuit and slippers, with a face you could tell used to be beautiful but was now lined and worn.

'Well, I know that's not true,' she said, smiling a little sadly. 'My son doesn't have any friends. Not In Real Life, anyway.' She had a soft Scottish accent, which was very attractive.

'Madam,' said Henry, piling on the de Warlencourt charm. 'You don't know us, but –'

Her reaction to him was startling. She took a step backwards and placed a hand on her heart as if afraid. The beauty that she still possessed sort of shone through from somewhere and she spoke as if in a dream. 'I believe I could almost put a name to you. You *must* be Rollo de Warlencourt's son.'

'Yes,' he said, visibly astonished. 'How did you . . . ?'

Now she took two steps forward and held out the hand that had covered her heart, almost as if she was about to touch Henry's face. 'You're very like your father.'

Now Shafeen stepped forward, almost impatiently. 'Do you know where Ratio is?'

The sad smile returned. 'Always the same answer to that,' she said. 'In his room.' She opened the door all the way. 'You'd better come in.'

The flat was very small and very shabby. Paint was peeling from stained walls, and the sofa was threadbare. A tiny and ancient telly was showing *Cash in the Attic*. I wondered what Henry thought of these living conditions – I'd bet he'd never been in a home this small in his life. The woman led us through the room – which took all of two seconds – and knocked on a connecting door. The door had a sign on it featuring a skull wearing a German stormtrooper helmet. The wording said: *Achtung! Nazi Zombies!*

29

The woman knocked on the door but there was no reply. 'He never hears,' she said fondly. 'Just go in.'

We filed into the room, which was bigger than the rest of the house. Someone in a top-of-the-range gaming chair – one of those with speakers in the headrest – was facing away from us playing *Valorant* across three massive flat-screen computer monitors. The someone wasn't wearing headphones and the sound was at full blast – clearly he hadn't heard us come in, so that gave us a chance to look at the room.

I could see why he never left it. It was quite different to the other room. It was clean and sleek – cluttered but achingly modern, a nerd-paradise tech palace. Framed Marvel posters covered three walls, a shelf groaned under the weight of an army of Funko POP! figures, from Batman to his naughty descendant Deadpool. A luminous fish tank hummed calmly in the corner, with rainbow-coloured iridescent fishes flicking back and forth – the only natural things in the room except for a carefully trimmed bonsai tree. The fourth wall was covered in photographs connected by red strings, just like you see in films like *Kiss the Girls*, when some maverick detective is trying to solve a heinous crime.

But the most remarkable thing about the room was its occupant. After finishing a round in which he'd blown away all his opponents, he spun around in his chair like a Bond baddie and regarded us.

He looked at us in turn. 'Tyeesha Morgan. Greer MacDonald. Chanel Ashton. Shafeen Jadeja.' He was going to say it. He said it. 'I've been expecting you.'

It was the classic supervillain greeting, but he didn't look all that villainous. Even though he didn't get up – not for this

Savage all that bobbing up and down when ladies entered the room – we could see that he was bigger than any of us; he had that stretched look of the very tall. He was wearing ripped jeans and a T-shirt with a fox on it and the words 'OH, FOR FOX SAKE'. He looked older than us too by a few years – maybe he was twenty-three or so; somewhere in between us and Abbot Ridley. He resembled Sick Boy from *Trainspotting*, with his soft Scottish accent, handsome face and cropped hair. Most bits of his face were pierced, including his nose, lip and ears. In one ear he had a distinctive antler earring, not delicate and dangly but one of those that goes right through your earlobe and makes the hole really big. One arm was entirely covered in a sleeve tattoo, which seemed to be some sort of hunting scene of a deer in a forest. His fingernails were painted black, and his eyes were a rather startling blue. They reminded me of someone else who I couldn't quite place. But the most notable thing about him was his hair colour – it was Joker-green, as if Astroturf was growing out of his head, and it suited him admirably.

Ratio looked up at Henry. 'And Henry de Warlencourt. I certainly wasn't expecting *you*.'

'He's on our side now,' said Ty. 'He saved my life.'

'Aye,' said Ratio. 'I know.' He directed a rather attractive smile at Ty. 'I suppose that was you logging my keystrokes the other night, was it?'

She smiled back. 'Guilty.'

'Did you use Hypervisor or Kernel?' he asked.

'Kernel,' said Ty. 'A root-access device driver.'

'Thought so,' said our new friend. 'I knew what you were up to, but I let it play out.'

31

'Why?' said Ty.

'I thought it was time we met,' said Ratio candidly. 'We're in the endgame now.'

The way he said that gave me a chill – it sounded so final. Hopefully not for me.

'Did you really go to STAGS?' I asked.

'Yup,' he said. 'For a while.'

'No offence,' said Shafeen, 'but how did you possibly afford it?'

Ratio didn't look offended. 'Someone paid. A benefactor.'

Nel was impressed. 'Must have been a very kind person.'

Ratio laughed a bitter laugh. 'I doubt if he's ever been described that way. It was Rollo de Warlencourt.'

We all registered shock. Henry walked right up to him, so he was actually between the splayed-out bejeaned legs, and addressed him directly for the first time. 'My father paid for *you* to go to STAGS?'

Ratio looked up at him, unmoved and insolent. 'Yup,' he said again.

'How come?'

'It was guilt money. My mum worked at Longcross Hall in the nineties. Lorna Rennie, a young Scottish girl, a long way from home, no family around her, no protection. She was a sitting duck.'

I glanced at Shafeen. This was just like the story of Ina, the kitchen maid from County Durham who had befriended his father Aadhish when he'd been at Longcross. That had been in the sixties, but this story from thirty years later sounded depressingly familiar. 'What happened to her?' I said, with a sense of unease.

'What d'ye think happened to her?' he said, suddenly very Scots, eyes suddenly very blue. 'She was the prey for Rollo's little Hunger Games. She ended up being hunted, and terrorised, and almost broken.' He spat the words. 'But we're a hardy clan, the Rennies. My mother survived, and she had the balls to turn the situation to her advantage. She decided to blackmail your father –' this to Henry – 'and make sure her young son got some of what he had. And it would have worked too, if I hadn't fucked it up.'

Henry flinched at the swear word. 'And how did you manage to do that?'

Blue eyes met blue eyes. 'I pissed it away deliberately,' said Ratio, precisely. 'Smuggled my laptop into STAGS and logged on to the noughties equivalent of Pornhub. Made sure I got caught, made sure I got kicked out.' He shifted his angular shoulders in the gaming chair. 'I didn't want to take anything from your father. I decided to do something more useful with my life than being pampered at some privileged school.'

'Which was?'

'Go to a Glasgow comprehensive. Get my Highers. Get a first-class computer science degree. And dedicate my life to taking down your father and the rest of the Order of the Stag, for what they did to my mother.' He looked at Shafeen. 'And your father, Aadhish.' Then Ty. 'And your great-uncle, Leon.' Then me. 'And Gemma Delaney. And all the other poor saps who were treated like electric bunnies at a greyhound race.'

Nel was walking round the room looking at the hardware. 'You've got a lot of kit here. How d'you make a living?'

'YouTube,' he said briefly. 'You can make good money gaming online. My channel has millions of subscribers. One day I'm going to get my mum a house, make up for all the shit she got from the de Warlencourts. And,' he said, 'I do a bit of cyber-surveillance as a side-hustle. For big companies. Governments. That's why it's quite good to have a name like Ratio. No one believes it's my real name.'

'And it is?' Nel said in surprise.

'Oh yes,' he said. 'Christened and everything.'

I looked at all the pictures on the wall, connected by the CSI red thread. 'The cyber-surveillance – is that how you got all these?'

'Yup,' he said, a syllable that was obviously his catchphrase.

Henry looked at the CSI wall more closely. 'These are all of Longcross,' he said in a voice of outrage.

I joined him at the wall. There was the hunt from above, gathering at the Trip to Jerusalem. There was Longwood, and Longmere, and Longcross church. There was the hall from above, all those silvery leaded roof tiles, where Henry had kissed me the one and only time. 'How *did* you get these pictures?' spluttered Longcross's Lord himself. 'This is trespassing.'

'No,' said Ratio coolly. 'Your family may own a lot, but they don't own the air above our heads.'

'But it's a total violation of privacy.'

'I hardly think,' said Ratio dangerously, 'that your family are in a position to talk about violation.'

Ty was looking at the pictures too. 'It's like you have eyes in the sky,' she said, just as she'd done in the Crypt of STAGS chapel.

'I do,' said Ratio. Finally, he rose from his chair, towering over us. He walked to a black Peli case in the corner and tapped in a code on a keypad. The lid popped open to reveal a sleek black machine, about the size of a laptop, nestling in black foam. It was neat, and constructed on flowing aerodynamic lines, with four rotary blades like a quartet of mini helicopters. Ratio lifted the thing out, closed the lid of the case with his elbow and laid the thing tenderly on the top.

'Meet the HAWK,' he said.

6

Henry peered at the strange tech creature. 'What on earth is that?'

'A drone,' said Ratio. 'It's called the HAWK. The Hovering Airborne Wing Kite. Especially designed for surveillance.'

Henry narrowed his eyes. 'By whom?'

'Me,' Ratio said simply. 'I made it. It's a quadcopter with a high-definition camera, which records high-quality 4K video. Three-axis camera gimbals give it perfect 3D aerial coverage. I developed bespoke noise-cancelling technology, so it doesn't spook wildlife too much, and I've built in collision avoidance – you can key in customisable flight-pathing options. The whole thing's controlled by my iPhone.'

Henry looked at him as if he was speaking another tongue – but instead of one of those ancient dead languages with which Henry was so familiar, this was an entirely new, modern jargon.

'It's simple,' said Ratio. 'You need to take the HAWK with you. That way you can keep an eye on Greer at all times.' It was odd to be spoken of by someone who clearly felt like they'd known you for years when you didn't know them at all. Ratio patted the drone as if it was a living thing, and addressed me directly. 'The HAWK has 'box acquisition' which means, in simple terms, that it draws a box around you and follows you wherever you go. This one takes into account your biometrics and your unique heat signature too, which means it won't lose you as long as you're outdoors. But it can't track you in a vehicle.' He turned to the rest of his guests. 'The only way to expose this cult is to shine a light on it. You record the Order of the Stag chasing Greer at the Red Hunt. And you share it with the world.'

Ty touched the winged creature delicately, and one of the rotator blades began to spin gently. 'Who will operate it?' she asked.

'I will,' Ratio said, in a Savage echo of what Henry had said in the medieval STAGS Crypt. 'I'll come with you.'

We all looked at each other. This felt a bit weird – first there'd been the three murderers – Me, Shafeen and Nel. Then Ty had joined us. Then the most unlikely ally of all – Henry de Warlencourt. Now this tall young geek, a guy we didn't know at all, was joining our band of brothers. Everyone looked doubtful except for Ty, who was beaming. She'd obviously found a kindred spirit, a social-justice warrior to join our platoon. 'Excellent,' she said.

But Henry was not so keen. 'No,' he said. 'Not on any account. I'm not joining forces with some overgrown tennis ball who's been spying on my family for years.'

'Fine,' said Ratio, fronting up to him. 'Then you won't have the HAWK. And this thing will never end.'

Medieval and Savage glared at one another, clear dislike on both sides.

'Look,' I said, turning to Ratio, 'you've got the drone. You can record the hunt, and cover whatever happens outdoors. And Henry's got access to the family. He can get us *into* Castle MacLeod. He's a proper Country Gent.'

Ratio sneered. 'More like a proper Gentry C—'

'NO!' I blurted, drowning out the terrible word. 'You need to put aside this shit and work together. You both need each other. You can't do it alone.'

Neither one moved. I wasn't getting through to them. Clearly I had to speak in a language they understood. 'Ratio,' I appealed to him. 'It's like the Justice League. Batman and Superman were mortal enemies, but they teamed up to fight Lex Luthor. And Henry,' I searched my mind for some reference he would get – this was harder for me. But I found the answer deep in my memory banks: the first time Henry's cohorts had threatened Shafeen it had been in a history lesson at STAGS about the Battle of Hattin. 'The papacy and the Holy Roman Empire were ancient enemies, but they joined forces on the Crusades to kick Saladin's butt.'

Ratio looked convinced, Henry less so.

'Henry.' I laid a hand on his tweedy arm and played the only card I had left. '*I'm* asking you.' It was unfair; I was exploiting his feelings for me, and I could feel Shafeen's suspicious eyes upon us, but this was too important.

'All right,' Henry grunted. He held out a hand to Ratio. Ratio looked at it as if he didn't know quite what to do with it; for a moment I thought he was going to refuse the gesture, but then I clicked that it was more likely that he just didn't get a lot of handshakes.

Finally, Ratio clasped the proffered hand with his long fingers and the two young men shook.

We had a deal.

We stayed the night in Glasgow, at a hotel near Central Station. Henry wanted to pay for everybody, but of course Shafeen wasn't having that, so he and Henry split the cost of one room and Nel, Ty and I shared another. To our relief Nel quietly paid in the morning. Ratio hired a people carrier from Hertz, as he was the only one who was old enough, and picked us up first thing.

The black Peli case containing the HAWK nestled safely in the boot. Ty sat in the front seat next to Ratio and the two of them chattered about Savage things all the way through the Highlands. I sat in the back, in a rather uncomfortable Henry/Shafeen sandwich, but at least I was free to admire the scenery, which was, frankly, breathtaking. The hedgerows were studded with yellow blossoms and the hillsides carpeted with purple heather, which gave off a sweet, heady scent. I may have drifted off to sleep a couple of times but other than that I did a lot of thinking. The drive gave me plenty of time to go over what had happened in India. It had been a life-changing trip. I had slept with Shafeen for the first time, on a Jaipur rooftop, and then Henry had declared his love for me in a hospital corridor. Drifting in and out of consciousness, I lolled against one shoulder and then the other: I'd wake to see Shafeen's dark hair stirring in the breeze of the open window, then the next time I looked he'd been exchanged for Henry, blond hair glittering in the summer sun.

We stopped for breakfast in Loch Lomond and for lunch in Glencoe. I watched the two young men interact with each other. They were civil, even guardedly friendly, but there was no doubt that they were deadly rivals. Shafeen instinctively disliked Henry but was grateful to him for saving his beloved father's life, and Henry instinctively liked Shafeen but couldn't forgive him for being with me. I felt Henry watching us too and knew he'd divined what had happened between me and Shafeen – that our relationship had ratcheted up to the next level. I knew then that the best thing I could do for Shafeen and me would be to stay as far away from Henry as possible – but since Henry and I were destined to attend the Red Hunt together that was going to be difficult.

By the afternoon we were on the ferry from Mallaig to Skye and we all got out of the car, tacitly spreading out as much as we could to enjoy some fresh air and space after so many hours in the car. The sun was shining and the ferry was picking up speed over the silvery water as the gulls dipped and cried. I went to the very front of the boat and, of course, threw out my arms, Leonardo DiCaprio-in-*Titanic* style. 'I'm the king of the world!' I yelled into the breeze.

'Are you?' said an amused voice.

I whipped around, feeling foolish. Henry was beside me.

'It's a quote from . . . never mind.'

We both leaned on the rail. He did look a little Leonardo DiCaprio actually, with his blue eyes narrowed against the wind and his blond hair flopping in his eyes. I didn't quite trust myself to look at him, so looked ahead into my uncertain future. A lump of land lay ahead of us. 'Is that Skye?'

'Yes,' he said. 'Land of your fathers.'

'Of *my* fathers?' I said, confused.

'Yes. Skye is the ancestral home of the Clan MacDonald.'

'My spelling? Or McDonald like the golden arches?' It was suddenly really important that it was mine.

'Your spelling,' he said. 'You're going home.' He gazed at the misty isle. 'You'll like it. It's beautiful.' He shot me a glance. 'Like you.'

As ever when Henry gave me a compliment, I didn't know what to do with my face. The conversation was getting dangerous, so I edged away along the rail a bit. I studied the island as it grew gradually closer and searched for something to say. 'Where's Castle MacLeod? Will we be able to see it from the boat?'

'No,' he said. 'It's at the far north of the island. Quite remote.'

I could see the dark shoulders of hills hunching up from the landmass. 'What are those mountains?'

'The Cuillin.'

'Coolin?' I repeated.

'Close enough,' he smiled. 'That one closest to us, he's Sgùrr nan Gillean.' My gaze followed his pointing finger. 'That big fellow in the middle, Sgùrr Alasdair, the highest peak in the Cuillin.' I noticed he talked of them like they were people.

'And what about that broad peak in the distance?'

His face shuttered. 'That's Ben Horneval.'

Something about his voice when he named that particular mountain made me look at him again, however dangerous that might be. 'And what's special about that one?'

41

'It's where the Lammas Eve celebrations take place.' He seemed reluctant to say any more, so I looked back at the mountains.

Even though it was a sunny day, the rock looked black as night. 'Why are they dark like that?'

'They're formed of black volcanic rock, so they actually absorb the light. They're known as the Black Cuillin.'

No wonder they looked so ominous. The thought of being in an isolated castle, and the sight of the mysterious black mountains, invited a feeling of foreboding to creep over my skin. It was a nice day but still I shivered.

Henry stroked my goosebumpy forearm with the back of his scarred fingers. 'Don't worry. I'll be there with you the whole time.'

I gave him a tight smile. I could feel eyes on us, and turned to see Shafeen, standing at the bows, watching us like a hawk.

7

Shafeen didn't say anything when we got back in the car.

Ty surrendered the passenger seat to Henry, because Henry knew the island, and Shafeen sat in the back with me, arm firmly clamped round my shoulders. I nestled into his neck and kissed the edge of his rigid jaw, just to let Henry know where things stood. He saw us in the wing mirror and smiled slightly, as if he knew exactly what I was doing.

Nel, oblivious to these undercurrents, took charge. 'Right. The rest of us need to find somewhere to stay before we drop Greer off at her castle.'

'I think I have that covered,' said Henry. 'There's a peel tower on the castle land. It belongs to the family but it's disused.'

'What's a peel tower?' asked Ty.

'It's a small, fortified keep – sort of a free-standing mini castle,' said Henry. 'Lords – or lairds as they're known in Scotland – would build them on their land for defence. They were essentially watchtowers where you could light signal fires on the roof if anything untoward happened. Of course what happened was that disaffected rebels captured them, set up camp and sulked there until they could move against the nobles.'

43

'Sounds ideal,' said Ratio pointedly.

'Cass and I did it up one summer when we were younger,' said Henry, as if Ratio hadn't spoken, 'as a little den for us. We'd stay there overnight sometimes. It's got hot water and electricity – quite comfortable really.'

'And you just happen to carry a key around with you at all times, do you?' asked Shafeen waspishly.

'No,' said Henry calmly. 'But I know where one is.'

We drove through the incredible scenery of Skye, and the Black Cuillin towered over us. I kept my eye on them and wondered what the 'Lammas Eve celebrations' entailed, and why Henry seemed so reluctant to talk about them. Ben Horneval wore a black cape of scree that looked as if it were made of glittering chips of jet. I imagined trying to climb up it – or run away down it. But halfway up the hill I could see some people moving about; they were building something with sticks, probably some sort of bonfire.

We saw quite a bit of wildlife too. A deer bounced across the road, causing Ratio to brake, and then a fox slunk along the hedgerow. It was as if all our greatest hits had come back for one last appearance as this saga of ours came to an end. No tigers, but at one point I did see a bird of prey hovering above the heather, somehow holding himself almost still in the air.

'Look!' I pointed.

Henry glanced upwards. 'There's the medieval version of your HAWK, Ratio,' he said drily. 'A sea eagle. Keep your eye on him, he'll stoop in a minute.'

'Stoop?' I echoed.

'It's the breakneck dive they do when they go in for the

kill. He's spotted something he wants; he's just waiting for the right moment.' He might have been talking about us. I watched the sea eagle out of the window and, sure enough, the bird stopped hovering and seemed to hang in the air for a fraction of a second, before folding his wings and seeming to dive to earth. He fell from sight, but I imagined him sitting on the grass, munching some poor mouse who hadn't even seen him coming. 'Skye is great for spotting birds,' said Henry comfortably, as if he was some sort of tour guide. 'And flying them.'

'You do that?' I said.

'Falconry? Yes. We do it at Castle MacLeod.'

'Of *course* you do,' muttered Shafeen.

'I bet you do too,' said Henry, amused, flicking him a glance over his shoulder. 'I've heard of the shikra hawks in India. I reckon your father taught you too. Tell me I'm wrong.'

Shafeen was silent, and Henry smiled at the ribbon of road unravelling in front of us, shaking his head slightly. 'When are you going to understand that you and I are not that different?' he said, like some supervillain in a movie. 'I'm surprised you didn't teach Greer while you were out there.'

'We were kind of busy,' snapped Shafeen.

Henry looked at me in the mirror, his blue gaze very direct. 'Don't worry. *I'll* teach you, Greer, when we're at the castle. It'll be *my pleasure.*'

I could feel Shafeen fuming beside me – despite our new intimacy, Henry had got one up on him.

'You keep saying when *we're* at the castle,' I said, trying to get away from this dangerous duel. 'When are you going to do

45

your back-from-the-dead bit? I know you planned it for Boxing Day at Longcross, but that got sort of interrupted.'

'Well, I thought I'd let you settle in for the first night, so it doesn't look like a big conspiracy,' said Henry comfortably. 'They can't know that we are on the same side. Then I thought I'd make an appearance at The Gathering, tomorrow night, and attend as your partner.'

I could feel Shafeen bristling.

'What's The Gathering?' asked Ty.

'A ball,' said Henry. 'The ladies wear lace, and the gentlemen wear their clan tartans. The Gathering opens the weekend on the Friday night – all the guests and some local families. Then the Red Hunt will be on the Saturday, on Lammas Day. Then it's the Lammas Eve festivities that night.'

'Wait,' said Nel. 'Isn't Lammas Eve the night before, like Christmas Eve?'

'No. Here it just means the evening of Lammas Day. That's when the festival is.'

'And what happens at the festival?'

'All manner of things,' said Henry mysteriously, but once again he shut down, as if there was something he wasn't saying.

We drove ever northward until we passed a road sign saying DUNVEGAN. 'Nearly there,' said Henry. 'We're on MacLeod land.' We looked around us at the fantastic scenery – golden shafts of godlight breaking through sullen clouds to brighten the silver sea and the pewter mountains. There, in the middle of the landscape, was a lone tower, tall and crenellated like a rook on a chessboard. I half expected it to start sliding around, like

Howl's Moving Castle, but it stayed still long enough for us to pull up the short gravel drive to the front of it. It was a tall and skinny building, with one door and two windows above it, and it looked like it had stood on this spot for hundreds of years. 'This is the Peel Tower,' said Henry.

We unfurled ourselves from the car, stretching and yawning, gulping the salty island air. Henry hunted around by the little white door, dislodged a stone from the wall, and a silver key fell into his hand. 'Ah,' he said. 'Just where we left it.' He put the stone back carefully and fitted the key into the little arched door.

Inside was a comfortable-looking living room, with a fireplace, threadbare sofas with tartan cushions, and the inevitable stags' antlers on the wall. No telly, of course, because we were in Medieval-land, but a bookcase crammed with ancient-looking tomes. It was chilly, as the walls were bare stone, but you could see that the Peel Tower could be cosy in the evening when the fire was lit. 'There's a little bathroom and kitchen through there,' said Henry, pointing to a side door, 'and the bedrooms are upstairs.'

He took us through a stone arch up a rickety staircase to a bedroom with a double bed covered with a tartan throw. A second bedroom, and a second bed, was just above the first. 'Cass and I had a room each when we camped here,' said Henry, 'but I'm afraid you'll have to share.' Then he climbed further, pushing open a little trapdoor leading to the roof. We emerged, gasping and windswept, and stood there slack-jawed as we gazed at the incredible scenery – the mighty mountains, the rain-swollen clouds and the sunlight playing on the heather. The four sides of the square of battlements looked out to the four points of the compass. 'MacLeod land as far as the eye can see,' said Henry matter-of-factly. As usual, the de Warlencourts were masters of all they surveyed, even if it was only by marriage.

'This was your childhood den?' said Ty incredulously. 'It's quite the Wendy house. We played in a run-down maintenance shed on the Limehouse Estate.'

'You think this is good?' said Henry, pointing. '*That's* Castle MacLeod.'

We looked towards the coastline to see an enormous grey edifice, a sprawling complex of towers, battlements and ramparts, which almost looked like it was carved into the very cliffs themselves. My stomach flipped over. I couldn't believe that by nightfall I would be a guest in that ancient pile – alone, without any of my rebel allies.

As we headed back to the staircase, we passed a wrought-iron cradle that looked a bit like a medieval barbecue. 'What's that?' asked Nel.

'That's the fire basket for the beacon,' said Henry. 'The castellan would light it to give the alarm if there was danger.'

'Better spark it up now,' I said.

I was joking, but I meant it too.

8

I felt almost jealous as the others began discussing where they would sleep.

It was decided that Ty and Nel would share the top bedroom, and Shafeen and Ratio the lower one. Henry, for the one night he would be in the Peel Tower, would sleep on the couch in the living room. I wished heartily that I could stay in the little castle with them, instead of going off to the big one.

It was decided that Ratio should be the one to drive me to Castle MacLeod, as he was the only one who would be unknown to the twins, should they be there to greet me. Invitation in one hand, wheelie suitcase in the other, I went out to the car. I hadn't brought much – just jammies and underwear, because I knew very well by now that great houses dressed you up like a doll. Ratio, in his role as my taxi driver, was already in costume – Henry had found him a battered old Barbour jacket and a flat tweed cap. With the green hair and slacker clothes covered he looked refined and oddly aristocratic. 'You almost look like one of them,' I joked, still slightly shy of this tall young stranger. Ratio smiled and rolled his eyes, reassuring me. 'God forbid,' he said, as he opened the back door for me to get in.

I thought the journey might be slightly awks, since we didn't really know each other, but Ratio was clearly a really lovely guy. He spent the whole of the short journey reassuring me. 'The first thing I'll do when I get back will be to fly the HAWK over the castle, to map the flight path and get an idea of the terrain. The top of the Peel Tower is an ideal launchpad. I'll be keeping an eye on you all the time.' He checked the mirror. 'And you know what they're like – nothing will happen to you until the Red Hunt. They're all about the sport, and it's a team sport too – they want to provide a fun day out for all the other monsters. And by the hunt day Henry will be with you.' He paused. 'If that's any reassurance. I'll be keeping an eye on him too,' he murmured, almost to himself.

'Don't you trust him?'

'Do you?' he shot back.

I thought about this. 'Yes, I think so. He's had plenty of opportunities to screw us over. He could have let Ty die in the fire at Longcross, but he rescued her. He could have let Shafeen's father die in Jaipur, but he rescued him too.' It was refreshing not to have to explain all this to Ratio – he probably knew as much about those instances as I did. 'I think he's changed.'

He flicked a blue glance to me in the driving mirror, just as Henry had on the road to Dunvegan. 'I don't know what they say about stags,' he said cryptically. 'But I do know what they say about leopards. They never change their spots. Be aware that he's been on their side for nineteen years, and on ours for about five minutes. Has it ever occurred to you that he might be a double agent? That he might be serving you up on a silver platter as the ultimate prize, to bring himself back into the fold?'

I knew this wasn't true, because of Henry's declaration of love for me, but I wasn't about to tell Ratio that. Despite him seemingly having eyes everywhere, there were some things he didn't know, shouldn't know. I wasn't about to tell him about my twisted little love triangle, but I thought I could tell him a little – not too much – about something else he couldn't possibly know. 'Henry's not always had it easy, you know. His father – well, presumably you know a bit about how evil he could be, from your own mother.' The blue eyes flickered. 'But let's just say that Rollo terrorised Henry too, when he was a little boy.' I couldn't break Henry's confidence by telling Ratio about the 'fox in the box' story – the time when Rollo had locked young Henry in the boot room at Longcross with a feral Reynard – but I wanted him to know that Henry hadn't always been bad. 'Henry was all right once,' I said. Then I thought about Aadhish's diary, and the love that there once had been between Shafeen's father and Henry's. 'And, actually, so was Rollo.'

'I find that hard to believe,' said Ratio, and by then the car's wheels were crunching on the gravel of the castle's drive. The castle and the Peel Tower were so close I evidently could have walked if I'd known the way. As we snaked up to the entrance through acres of beautiful parkland Ratio passed a purple Scottish £20 note over his shoulder.

'What's this for?'

'Give it to me when you get out,' he said. 'I'm a taxi driver, remember?'

The drive ended at a long, broad sweep, and Ratio stopped the car in front of a grand, baronial entrance. He got out of the front seat and opened the door for me. I clambered out of the car as elegantly as I could, imagining eyes watching me from the arrow slits. I passed Ratio the banknote. 'Keep the change,' I said.

He touched his cap and nodded. 'Thank ye, mistress,' he said, very Scots. And then with a last reassuring glance of the blue eyes, he got back in the car and drove away with a spin of wheels and a scatter of gravel.

I turned to the immense stone pile, looking at the studded oak doors, the immense buttresses, the battlements and towers soaring above.

I took a deep breath.

I was alone at Castle MacLeod.

I was not alone for long. Cass streaked out of the door like a blonde bombshell and enfolded me in a bone-crushing hug. 'I'm *so* glad you could come.'

I studied her. She looked absolutely right for the castle – she was wearing a beautifully cut tweed suit like the one Henry had travelled north in, and with her cropped gamine hair and blue eyes she resembled him closely. 'We're going to have the *best* weekend. It will be *such* a larf.'

That was almost exactly what Henry had said, two years ago, when he'd invited me to Longcross for the first time. It didn't exactly inspire confidence in me. 'Come and meet Mummy and Daddy. You're the first one here. That's all right, Compston –' this to the butler who had appeared belatedly at the door. 'I'll take Miss MacDonald through.' She led me across a huge, wood-panelled atrium. Castle MacLeod was clearly the daddy of the Peel Tower – the decor was exactly the same, but on a bigger, posher scale. A fire burned merrily in a huge stone fireplace, the inevitable stags' heads stared glassily from the walls, and plump tartan cushions balanced on their points on chaises longues. But there were some next-level touches too, like old gold tapestries on the walls and hollow suits of armour standing sentinel at the doorways. One of these baronial touches looked familiar to me – a pair of duelling pistols hanging on the wall, one above the other like a mirror image.

Cass saw me looking. 'They're from Longcross,' she said as we passed. 'After the fire Daddy agreed to store some of the artefacts that were saved, while Longcross is being renovated. Handy if any of our guests has a grudge they want to settle,' she joked. Then she turned to me. 'Speaking of grudges, I don't know if you know this, but the MacDonalds and the MacLeods are ancient enemies. Such a jape! Nice that you're here as our honoured guest now. Quite the turnaround.'

I smiled but was actually thinking that if they were planning to murder me at the Red Hunt in two days, then that would be exactly in keeping with the ancient feud.

Cass opened a door. 'They're in here, having tea.' She smiled at me. 'Don't worry. They won't bite.'

9

Cass led me into a beautiful drawing room, walls panelled to within a foot or so of the ceiling. Even though it was July another fire burned in the grate. Round the walls were pictures of tartan-clad aristocrats – most probably all the dead people who used to hang out in this beautiful room – and the floors were covered with Persian carpets, threadbare but obviously priceless. Tall windows, framed with that red creeping ivy, gave onto a breathtaking view of the sea – the castle was obviously on a peninsula right in the north of Skye, and I was so busy gawping at the view that it took me a moment to notice the three other people in the room.

Louis was lounging in an overstuffed chair, feet dangling over one arm, holding a teacup but not by its handle. A man who looked like a younger version of Rollo de Warlencourt was standing by the fire, warming his bottom in that aristocratic way. And a stout woman sat very straight in a hard chair, her feet planted firmly on the ground. There were at least four fat Labradors in the room, black and blond, and although they listlessly thumped their tails when Cass and I walked in, they couldn't be arsed to get up.

Louis did get languidly to his feet as we entered and kissed me on both cheeks. 'Ah, Greer,' he said, a strange light kindling his de Warlencourt blue eyes. 'We are so glad you could join us.' He was wearing a tweed suit just like Cass's – the de Warlencourts must buy them in bulk – and looked more like his twin than ever. 'You worked out who sent you the invitation then.'

'I had help,' I said lightly but didn't fess up, obviously, that the help came from his 'dead' cousin Henry.

'Let me introduce my father, Lord Peregrine de Warlencourt, and my mother, Lady Fiona MacLeod de Warlencourt.'

I studied the king and queen of the castle. Lord Peregrine wore a country shirt with a discreet green check, custard-coloured corduroy trousers and one of those army-green upper-class padded waistcoats. His wife was a strawberry blonde, with a lot more red in her hair than in her children's locks. Hers was cut in a neat bob and held to one side by one of those kirby grips you wear in primary school. She had a florid complexion, as if she'd been in a lot of wind and rain, and a clean, well-scrubbed face without a scrap of make-up. She had blue eyes but they were more insipid and watery than the strong de Warlencourt blue. She wore a Fair Isle sweater and a tweed skirt, plus doughty woollen stockings the colour of sludge, and her hardy walking shoes were planted firmly on the ground, her knees apart like she was manspreading. I thought of Henry's mother, Lady Caroline, with her brittle, blonde bone-china beauty, and marvelled at the contrast between the sisters-in-law. Lady Fiona was much more bull than china shop.

'Good journey?' asked Peregrine. I'd noticed, at every great house I'd been to, that the upper classes always seemed obsessed by how you'd got to where you'd ended up, and how easy that process had been. 'We'd have sent a car for you, don't you know.'

'That's extremely kind of you,' I said, trying to remember how you talked to posh people. 'But I was visiting friends in Glasgow, so I was halfway here anyway.'

'Oh?' His bushy eyebrows shot up.

'The Rennies,' I said in a panic before I could stop myself. I just had to hope that Peregrine wouldn't remember that a certain Lorna Rennie happened to be a kitchen maid at Longcross in the nineties and had been terrorised by his older brother. But if he was quite a chunk younger than Rollo, maybe he'd have been too young to attend that particular beasting. As it turned out I needn't have worried. He wasn't thinking of anyone so low. 'Ah, perhaps the Loch Lomond Rennies, from Blair Castle,' he mused.

'I don't *think* so,' I said. 'I think they're just ordinary common or garden Rennies.' Quickly changing the subject, I got him back on to my itinerary. 'I stayed one night, then trained it up to Fort William. Then a ferry from Mallaig, and a taxi here,' I said, just as I'd rehearsed in my head.

'Is Ty with you?'

Louis's sudden question took me by surprise, and for a moment I felt that his searching blue eyes could see right past me, back to the Peel Tower, where Ty was hiding out with her fellow rebels.

'No, just little old me,' I lied lightly.

'Ah, was Ty the young lady you were mooning after at Longcross?' asked his father. 'The one that we –'

'Don't keep the poor gel standing about, Perry,' said Lady Fiona bossily. I got the feeling that she was deliberately interrupting whatever he'd been about to say. 'Sit down, Greer. Will you take tea?'

That, I knew, was the upper-class way of asking if I'd like a cup, so I nodded gratefully. I was suddenly starving and I eyed the plate of cakes and sandwiches. Lunch in Glencoe seemed a world away, but fortunately 'tea' in posh land was a meal as well as a drink. Here though, afternoon tea seemed to be a bit more substantial than it had been in Cumberland Place, or even in India. There were no teeny-tiny cucumber sandwiches, or macarons no bigger than coins, but doorsteps of brown bread with smoked salmon, knobbly scones and these kind of flat, round pancakes. Lady Fiona piled up my plate, and I accepted it and the bone-china teacup gratefully. The cup had a crinkled gold rim and fruit painted on the side that was so vivid and glowing it looked ready to be picked. It was a world away from the mismatched mugs Dad and I drank from.

'You were at Longcross on Boxing Day,' said Lord Peregrine. 'When my brother died.'

Small talk was obviously over – he got straight in there with the big stuff. He didn't seem particularly grief-stricken though, and I wondered how close the brothers had been. With a massive age difference, how close *could* they be? 'Yes,' I said. 'I'm extremely sorry,' I added, trying to find the right words. 'My sincerest condolences.'

'That's why it's always good to have a spare,' said Lady Fiona with a weird kind of relish. 'Then if one pops orf, you've got a back-up. We managed to churn both of ours out in one go.'

I looked from Louis to Cass. This was a very strange conversation to have in front of your kids, as you were basically speculating on the possibility that one of them might die. 'Good job your father passed a couple of years before Rollo,' Lady Fiona said to her husband. 'Monty would have been devastated at the loss of his favourite son.'

Jesus, the knives were really out. This was obviously a pretty toxic marriage – no wonder there had always been something slightly off about the twins with parents like this. I looked to Peregrine to see how he would react. I had thought he was the downtrodden, henpecked one of the relationship, but at this latest slight the worm turned. He straightened up and his blue eyes hardened.

'Perhaps you're right, my dear. My father did indeed favour Rollo, but I exceeded my brother in two fairly important regards: I held onto my life, and I held onto my heir.'

To begin with I thought he'd said 'hair'. And to be fair, he did have a very good crop of de Warlencourt hair, thick and the colour of winter wheat. But he'd obviously said heir, because he stroked Louis's head as if he was one of the fat Labradors. 'I'm the head of the family now, and Louis will become so after me. Dear *Rollo* is worm food.'

Wow. My instincts had been right. The brothers had clearly not been close at all. In fact, I would go so far as to say that Peregrine had hated Rollo. My suspect list in the murder mystery of Who Poisoned Rollo de Warlencourt had just grown by one name.

Everyone was quiet for a moment. The twins seemed unaffected by this poisonous exchange – they were obviously used to the family vintage of vitriol and happily munched their tea, no more invested than the drooling Labradors who were watching them hopefully for crumbs.

'Well, my dear,' said Lady Fiona, crashing into the awkward silence, 'you're very welcome to our home. Although there was a time when one of your clan would *not* have been welcome in this castle. The MacLeods and the MacDonalds were once at daggers drawn.'

'So I've been told,' I said. People seemed really comfortable about sharing this fact. Maybe it was some sort of justification for what they were planning to do to me. Lady Fiona dropped a couple of sugar lumps into her tea with a little splosh. Then she took up a silver spoon and began to stir. The rhythmic sound of the spoon on the bone china reminded me uncomfortably of *Get Out*. Just like the mum in that movie, she fixed me with a hungry stare as she spoke. 'In 1395 a force of MacDonald clansmen landed at Loch Eynort, and headed north along Glen Sligachan, intending to invade MacLeod land. They were met by a force of MacLeods.' Still the spoon revolved in the weak tea – round and round and round – and I did feel a bit like I was going to sink into the floor. 'The battle was a victory for the MacDonalds, who fought the entire day till not one MacLeod was left, and the bodies of the slain were piled round the base of a huge rock topped by a rowan tree. Hawks stooped to drink the blood of the MacLeods and the place is still called the "Bloody Stone". It's not far from here. You can still visit it today.'

I thought I'd pass. This was a lot to process. Obviously *my* clan had taken down *their* clan back in the day, but now the tables had most definitely turned. The watery blue eyes were still looking at me hungrily. For the first time it occurred to me that it was very likely that good ol' Perry and Fi had been part of that cowled circle at the Red Mass in the undercroft at Cumberland Place. My heart began to thump uncomfortably.

What if they didn't wait for Saturday but just killed me now and threw me in the sea?

But then I remembered Ratio's words – *they're all about the sport*. If they had guests coming, they needed me, or there'd be no prey to hunt.

Lady Fiona reached suddenly for a bell pull, almost making me jump. I knew from reading Aadhish's diary that somewhere in the bowels of the castle a bell would be clanging to call a servant. A silent maid appeared to clear the tea things, and I thought of Ratio's mum, Lorna Rennie, acting as prey to Rollo de Warlencourt back in the nineties. Then I thought of Aadhish's great friend, Ina the kitchen maid, even further back in the sixties. I hoped that after her rooftop encounter with Gideon she hadn't had to endure any more creepy nobles invoking their *droit de seigneur*. But Lady Fiona barely glanced at the maid. As usual there were no pleases or thank-yous, just orders. 'Tell Compston to come and take Miss MacDonald to the North Tower.'

I gulped – it sounded a bit like I was being arrested, so when Louis eased himself out of his chair and said, 'Don't bother, Mummy. We'll show Greer to her room,' I was almost relieved.

10

The twins led me through stone passageways lined with priceless antiques and art, then up spiral stairways into what was clearly one of the towers I'd seen from outside. When the stairs ran out Louis produced a key and opened an arched oaken door. 'Welcome to the North Tower,' he said.

I'd never been in a room like it before – it was completely round. There was a bed, a basin and a fireplace. A lovely tapestry hung on the wall, depicting a deer hunt. The design reminded me of Ratio's sleeve tattoo, and I was momentarily comforted.

As well as a unique look, the room had a sound too – the wind whistled up and down the tower like an organ pipe and I wondered how I'd sleep.

The most notable features of the room were the two windows opposite each other. Louis opened one and the wind blasted through. 'Look,' he said. 'You have the best views in the castle.' The twins leaned out over vertiginous rocks and the sea pounding against the foot of the tower. I thought, once again, how easy it would be for them just to shove me out and have done with me. My grip tightened on the windowsill until my knuckles turned white, and my head spun with Hitchcock levels of vertigo. The Hitchcock vibe was heightened by a sudden gathering of birds – seagulls were wheeling and diving above the spray, screaming a warning. I looked up and saw what had spooked them – the HAWK, hovering high above, silent in the cacophony of the waves, winking its little red power light. It might have frightened the birds, but to me the drone was massively reassuring. It meant that Ratio had kept his promise, and he and the other Peel Tower Rebels were keeping an eye on me.

Like an idiot, I waved before I could stop myself.

'Who are you waving at?' asked Cass, amused. 'I don't think any ships can see you from here.'

'Oh, just the gulls,' I said, pulling myself back into the room, red-faced. 'I'm just so happy to be here. What's the other way?'

Of course they had to follow me across the room to the other window – so the drone hovered on unseen. Louis opened the opposite casement wide. 'And this way,' he said, 'is the mainland and England.' I could see just how close the Peel Tower was and made a mental note of how to get back there. I reckoned it would take me no longer than a quarter of an hour.

'Have you been to Longcross lately?' I asked Louis, knowing he had.

'I've been down a couple of times,' he said, perching on the windowsill. 'The repairs seem to be on track. Soon the family seat will be back to its best. In time for me to settle there as earl.'

I didn't dare meet his eyes but made the mistake of glancing at Cass, who shot me a knowing look. Cass, of course, knew that Henry was alive – she had seen him at her and Louis's eighteenth. But she'd obviously kept that small detail from her twin. Why? And did she know what was to happen to me on the Red Hunt? Or had Louis kept that from her?

I looked back at the pewter-grey roofs, towers and crenellations, and slapped the sturdy wall of the North Tower. 'I would have thought that inheriting this pile would be enough.'

'That's not how it works,' said Louis. 'You need land below the oat line. *English* land.'

As a MacDonald of the Clan MacDonald, that stung me, which was ridiculous really as I'd literally found out I was a Scot about five minutes ago. But I kept my feelings to myself. Ever the gentleman, except for when he was in murder mode, Louis helped me down from the windowsill and placed the heavy key in my hand. 'We'll let you get ready. We eat at seven in the Great Hall.'

'And you'll see some familiar faces,' smiled Cass.

With this terrifying thought, the twins left me to dress. Just as I'd anticipated, an outfit had been left for me on the inevitable tartan bedspread. I held it up. It was a posh frock, the colour of old gold, with a close-fitting bodice and a standout skirt. I peeled off my travel clothes and put it on – it was that stiff silk that felt cold to the skin, but the age-speckled mirror told me the colour did wonders for me. I was sort of glowing, all pale skin, black bob, iridescent silk. I did a nice smoky eye with a shaking hand, and instead of a red lip I went for pale sixties mouth, letting the eyes do the heavy lifting. I'd brought black heels and an evening clutch that would just about fit a lipstick and a phone. *Hell* yes, I'd brought my phone, and I woke it up to check the time. This time I wasn't about to

travel without it – I'd made that mistake at the first huntin'
shootin' fishin' weekend at Longcross. Ratio might be looking
out for me, but even the HAWK's electronic eyes couldn't
see through six-foot-thick stone walls, so while I was inside
the phone was my only insurance policy, my only Savage link
with the outside world.

The phone said 7 p.m., and as I read the time I noticed
something else. There were no little connectivity bars at the top
right of the screen, no friendly Wi-Fi symbol, that reassuring
little pile of smiles. Instead, there were two stubborn words
at the top left:

No Signal

My stomach lurched a little as I read that, but I wasn't really
surprised. I was in the arse end of beyond, all silver sea and
glowering black mountains. *Of course* there was no signal.

I supposed I'd better go down, but I chucked the phone
on the bed. There was no point taking it; it afforded me no
protection.

It was basically a very expensive clock.

11

I got lost on the way down to the Great Hall, so I was a bit late to dinner. Eventually I had to ask this footman-type person the way and he showed me, opening these huge oak doors for me to walk through. I can tell you it was pretty scary walking into that room. As my mouth dried and my heart speeded I reflected that in both of the great houses I'd visited – Longcross, Cumberland Place and Longcross again – I'd never been on my own. I'd always had my fellow murderers with me. But here at Castle MacLeod, for one night only, it was me, myself and I.

I walked into the Great Hall, a huge baronial room with the bottom half panelled in wood and the top half painted blood red. The ceiling was a forest of criss-crossed oak beams, and six ornate candelabras hung from it on long ropes, illuminating the inevitable stags' antlers on the walls. Those same walls bristled with pikes and swords and shredded banners, which looked like they'd been well used over the centuries. At one end of the room there was a vast stone fireplace and a bonfire-sized blaze burning. Above the fireplace was a huge picture of a pretty lively battle between two angry-looking bunches of Scots wearing two different tartans. A shiny oak table was placed in the middle of the room, and the distance between me and the only place setting left empty seemed incredibly long. I suddenly seemed to have forgotten how to walk, and I could feel eyes on me as I stumbled to my place as if I was the worst catwalk model at Fashion Week.

Once I was seated I had the chance to look around. Lord Peregrine was seated at the fire end of the table, his face above his dinner jacket even more florid than usual from the heat. Lady Fiona sat at the other end looking much cooler in green taffeta, a diamond clip replacing the kirby grip in her hair. The twins sat either side of me, in matching tuxedos and black tie, their blond hair slicked back, identical except for their partings, which were on different sides, making them a mirror image of each other. The lovely, super-duper, happy-happy surprise though was the presence of the original Medievals from the year above me at STAGS: Cookson, Piers, Lara, Charlotte and Esme, all dressed up to the nines, all looking as comfortable as I felt uncomfortable.

Great.

There was one more person at the table. A tiny, shrivelled old lady wearing a lace blouse and a Celtic brooch set with garnets who was sitting next to Lady Fiona. She had white hair scraped back in a bun, and milky eyes of watery blue. She reminded me of the creepy old blind woman in *Don't Look Now.* As soon as I sat down the old crone set up a querulous cry. She pointed in my general direction with a forefinger that resembled a twig.

'I see somebody . . . I see somebody . . .' Her voice wavered, and her accent was pure Highland Scots, quite different to Ratio's Glaswegian drawl.

Lady Fiona laid a hand on the old lady's arm, lowering the accusing finger to the tablecloth. 'It's the MacDonald girl, Nanny.' She turned to me. 'This is Nanny. She was my nursemaid when I was a girl, and the twins' nanny too. She's a part of the family.' I looked at the shrivelled lady – she was definitely more Nanny McPhee than Mary Poppins.

'Nanny, this is Greer MacDonald,' said Lady Fiona loudly, as if to a child. 'She's come for Lammas.'

The unseeing eyes narrowed. 'I never thought to be breaking bread with a MacDonald.' Then, I'm not kidding, she spat neatly over her shoulder. 'Is she pretty?'

Louis said, 'Very,' with a smile in his voice.

'Does she have dark hair?'

'Black as a raven's wing,' supplied Cass poetically.

Nanny shuddered. 'Pretty maids with dark hair get into trouble. Just like that other one.'

Other one? Who could that have been? But before I could ask, Nanny looked right at me and said, in a sort of actor-y, important voice: 'Rowan-tree and red thread keep the devils frae their speed.'

I had no idea what this meant. The only red thread I'd seen recently was in Ratio's room in Glasgow, linking all his aerial photographs of Longcross and its residents through the years on his Crime Scene wall. But the rowan tree reference I suddenly got. Rowan was the tree in the legend that everyone seemed so keen to tell me about – the MacDonald victory over the MacLeods. Rowan was the tree that grew at the Bloody Stone. I lifted my eyes to the picture of the battle above the fire and, sure enough, at the centre of the mêlée, there was the Bloody Stone and the rowan tree. It seemed weird to me to have a huge painting in your castle of your greatest defeat, a bit like having a poster of a football team that had thrashed yours, but maybe the painting had kept the desire for revenge alive all those centuries, a revenge that could be taken, at last, this weekend.

Hooray.

The old woman's words, which sounded suspiciously like a curse, presumably meant that the MacDonalds, including me, were the devil. It was not the nicest greeting I'd ever had at a dinner table, and I wasn't at all sure how to respond to it. So instead I turned to the Medievals, who were watching me hungrily.

'How's Oxford?' I asked, just as I'd done at Longcross on Boxing Day.

'Divine,' said Lara, sounding bored.

'Only two years left though,' said Esme, pouting like a little girl.

'I hear *you're* coming up in the Michaelmas *term*,' said Charlotte, italicising as usual. '*Super* exciting that we'll be *overlapping* by a *year*. We'll be able to show you *around*.'

'Yes,' said Piers, his voice already blunted by drink. 'We can show you how we do things down there.'

'Absolutely,' said Cookson. 'I think you'll feel right at home.'

Christ. As I'd suspected when I'd met them all at Longcross, they clearly had their own little fun and games going on at the heart of that ancient university as well. The thought of that made me even more determined that they must be stopped.

'So what happens on Saturday?' I said chirpily, helping myself to soup. Actually, I was feeling anything but chirpy – tonight was Thursday, so technically I had two days before I became their prey. 'On the Red Hunt, I mean.'

'Well, you can relax for much of the day,' said Lady Fiona. 'Deer stalking takes place in the first or last two hours of daylight, and we take the view that many of our guests may be . . . tired – from The Gathering the night before.' This might have been a joke, but as she never seemed to smile it was difficult to tell. 'So we'll set off in the evening on Saturday. It will be just kitchen sups that night, as we'll be back fairly late.' I didn't know what 'kitchen sups' were, but the catering was the least of my worries. I needed to know what actually happened on the hunt, specifically where it went, so Ratio could program the correct flight path into the HAWK, and film whatever happened to me.

'We'll cover the terrain in small groups, usually two guests to one guide.'

So I'd be with Henry then – that was something.

'No bright colours, no perfume.'

I remembered Aadhish's diary – tigers could detect perfume and I supposed stags were the same. 'And what route will we take? Where is the actual hunt?'

'Well, in your honour, my dear,' Lady Fiona said, collecting the glances of the others, 'we will take the route of the battle between the MacDonalds and the MacLeods. We'll begin at Loch Eynort.'

'A beautiful spot,' mused Lord Peregrine, to nobody in particular.

'We'll surround our stag and close in until he's at bay,' said Lady Fiona, as if he hadn't spoken. 'Then whichever group is closest will take a clean shot. Then the deer is gutted, we bind him on a garron and bring him home.'

'A garron?' I asked.

'A Highland pony. We've been after the same Old Imperial for a number of seasons, so hopefully we'll bag him this time – but we haven't managed it yet.'

I thought I knew why – the Old Imperial was a decoy, an excuse to have a hunt. The real prey was whichever poor innocent they'd brought here from the mainland – in this case: me.

The mains came around – something meaty with vegetables swimming in a red wine sauce that resembled venous blood. 'And what about Lammas Eve itself?' I asked, as they all munched hungrily. 'What happens on the hillside?' I didn't want to even say the name of Ben Horneval – that mountain had a hoodoo on it as far as I was concerned.

'Oh, it's a rare old party,' began Lord Peregrine, managing to squeeze out a few words before his wife took over.

'There's traditional Highland folk music and dancing,' said Lady Fiona, railroading over him. 'Then we all share the Lammas loaf, which is special bread baked for the day.'

'And the young folk "Flit the Fire",' said Nanny, a strange light in her unseeing eyes.

'Oh, is that where you jump over the bonfire?' I'd seen stuff like that before in the South of England on Bonfire Night.

'Nay,' said Nanny in her quavering voice. 'They jump *under* it.'

Not for the first time that night I thought Nanny might be losing it a bit. Jumping *under* a bonfire didn't make any sense.

'Then we roast the prey in the needfire,' the old lady went on hungrily. 'All his finery and jewels must be laid aside, and he must be naked as a babe.'

'Ah, these romantic Highland figures of speech,' said Lady Fiona smoothly. 'She means the stag, don't you, Nanny? The stag must be stripped and skinned before we can roast the venison on the needfire.'

I went cold. Nanny had given them all away. Stags didn't have clothes or wear jewellery. Lady Fiona had shut her up, but it was pretty clear that I was to be the prey. If their plan went smoothly, I would be dead by then – killed by 'accident' at the Red Hunt the day before. Did that mean they would strip and burn my dead body? The thought was utterly barbaric. I pushed my plate away – appetite suddenly gone.

'Old Imperial will be the biggest red stag we've caught in a hundred years,' Peregrine bumbled in. 'Plenty of fine meat to go around.'

This seemed irrelevant, since they wouldn't be roasting *him*; they'd be roasting *me*. I swallowed, feeling suddenly sick. Everyone was looking at me, and all I wanted was to run out of the room and keep going. But I knew the whole weekend depended on me keeping my cool, and not letting on that I knew what I was in for. Desperately I cast around for something to say, and St Aidan himself came to my rescue. 'Are there any *white* stags?' I remembered the legend of the saint and his white stag, and the stained-glass window in the chapel at STAGS, depicting a hind as white as snow.

71

Nanny started as if I'd said something blasphemous, and her milky eyes almost popped out of her head. She crossed her ancient heart. 'Graveyard stags,' she said spookily.

'White stags are messengers from the otherworld,' said Cass, by way of explanation. 'They are often seen in graveyards or near burial grounds.'

'Or battle grounds,' put in Louis.

'The white stag is an ill omen,' wavered the old woman, her voice rising. 'When the white stag is seen, he comes from the underworld to claim the head of the family. The heir of the house will die.'

'Thanks, Nanny,' said Louis drily.

She turned in the direction of his voice and smiled. Her teeth resembled a graveyard. 'Never fret, my love, my precious. Nothing can befall you while Nanny has the Faerie Flag.'

The mains were cleared and a pudding appeared – not a fancy iced concoction but something solid and schooly, with custard.

'What's the Faerie Flag?' I asked, as everybody but me tucked in.

'It's a pennant of yellow silk, stitched with gold crosses and red rowan berries,' said Louis.

Rowan again, I thought. 'How old is it?'

'No one knows,' said Nanny. 'It was brought by the wee folk many centuries ago. The heir to the MacLeods had been born in this very castle, and his nursemaid left him alone, not knowing how to soothe him. The faeries heard his cries and flew in through the window, covering him with the flag against the biting cold, and singing him a soothing lullaby.' Her voice had a strange power to it, as if she was telling a bedtime story.

By some odd magic, I could almost see the scene playing out before me, like a film. 'When the nursemaid returned she was shocked and frightened to see the wee folk, but the faeries told her not to be afraid, and that the flag would rescue the MacLeods in times of great need. Ever since then it has been kept in a casket in the castle.'

'The flag is said to have kept us safe throughout the centuries,' said Cass, cutting up her meat. 'It extinguished a fire in the castle, and some MacLeod servicemen took it on bombing missions during the Second World War, and all returned safely.'

'And ever since the night the wee folk visited,' said Lady Fiona, 'no nanny has been employed at this castle who cannot sing the faeries' lullaby.'

'That's so, that's so,' said Nanny, nodding her ancient head sagely. 'I remember at my interview, for your mother and father, I had to sing it word for word. Then I sang it to you every night when you were a bairn, and to Master Louis and Miss Cassandra too.'

'Go on, Nanny,' said Louis. 'Give us a blast.'

It was clear that Nanny was Louis's slave, and as we all fell silent she set up a haunting tune in her wavering voice.

'Behold my child, limbed like the kid or fawn, smiting the horses, seizing the accoutrements of the shod horses, the spirited steeds. My little child.

'Oh, that I could see thy cattle fold, high up on the mountain side; a green, shaggy jacket about thy two white shoulders, with a linen shirt. My little child.

'Oh, that I could behold thy team of horses; men following them; serving women returning home and the Catanaich sowing the corn.

'Oh, tender hero whom my womb did bring forth, who did swallow from my breast, who on my knee wast reared.

'My child it is, my armful of yew, merry and plump, my bulrush, my flesh and eggs, that will soon be speaking. Last year thou wast beneath my girdle, plant of fertility! and this year fair and playful on my shoulder, thou wilt be going round the homestead.

'Oh, let me not hear of thy being wounded. Grey do thou become duly. May thy nose grow sharp ere the close of thy day.

'Oh! not of Clan Kenneth art thou! Oh! not of Clan Conn. Descendant of a race more esteemed; that of the Clan Leod of swords and armour, whose fathers' native land was Lochlann.'

I didn't really understand a word of the lullaby, but the haunting song seemed to cast a spell over the twins and their mother. When it was over Cass snapped to, laughing at herself. 'God, I nearly went to sleep! I really almost went to sleep! It still works, Nanny.'

'Of course it does, my poppet. It's worked for centuries. The old ways do not die.' The old lady smiled, her head drooping. The song had obviously tired her.

Lady Fiona got to her feet, and of course all the 'gentlemen' stood up too. 'Come on, Nanny. Let's get you to bed. Perry.' Lord Peregrine came to heel as obediently as the gang of fat Labradors and followed his wife from the room.

I watched them leave and thought about what Nanny had said. The old ways were damned well going to die this weekend, if I and my little army of rebels had anything to do with it.

Because either the old ways died, or I did.

12

Once the 'grown-ups' had left the room I thought I'd actually be able to go to bed. The evening had been plenty weird, but I'd not been in any direct danger, and I wanted to keep it that way. I just had to get through tonight, and tomorrow Henry would be with me. At least then I would have an ally.

But it didn't look like the evening was ending just yet. Louis called for more wine, and all the Medievals readily agreed. Back at Longcross on Boxing Day I thought they'd been hinting that they'd known Henry wasn't dead. Now I didn't think that. They were really butt-kissing Louis, the same Pick Me Tryhards they'd always been, but this time for a different heir. They'd swapped teams as seamlessly as the guys in *The Departed*. As far as they were concerned Louis was now head of the family and heir to the twin fortunes of the de Warlencourts south of the border and the MacLeods in the north. Only Cass, with a small and secret smile on her face, knew what I knew; that the real King in the North was alive, and biding his time. Louis, oblivious, and comfortable with his borrowed power, lined up the multiple bottles of red the compliant servants had brought. Then, to my dismay, he dismissed them for the night, and a feeling of foreboding settled over me.

When people of this class got rid of the servants, that meant things were about to get messy.

Louis opened the bottles himself and filled everyone's glasses. 'What shall we drink to?' He looked directly at me. 'Greer?'

Any casual observer might think he was politely deferring to a guest, but I knew this was more of a challenge than a courtesy. Luckily I had my answer ready. 'I like to drink to the Siege of Gibraltar.' *Screw you*, I thought, *trying to mess with me*. I knew the rules better than he thought I did. All the Medievals laughed – never a pleasant sound – raised their glasses and chinked. Apprehensively, I wondered what came next, but I was not kept in suspense for long. Louis uttered the chilling words: 'Let's have a game of STAGS.'

The Medievals all clapped and cheered, banging the table until the silver cutlery leaped about, but I didn't like the sound of that at all. I didn't know what 'a game of STAGS' was, but I definitely didn't want to be a part of it. I wondered if I could just excuse myself, but Louis sloshed more blood-red wine into my glass, right up to the brim. 'Who's going to be Mr Chairman?'

'I will,' said Piers.

'Seconded,' said Cookson.

'Then, Mr Chairman, please explain the rules to our guest.'

'Better concentrate, Greer,' warned Charlotte. 'It's *bloody* complicated, and if you lose you have to drink, so you can end up absolutely *battered* if you're not careful.'

'Right,' said Piers. 'The rules. We'll start easy, just to give you a fair crack of the whip, and introduce the more complex bits as we go.'

STAGS did begin as a fairly simple drinking game. When Piers – or Mr Chairman, as he must now be known – called out 'On the hover!' all of us had to extend both hands horizontally in front of us and waggle them from the wrist in a hovering motion. When 'Mr Chairman' dropped the hover he placed his thumbs on his temples and spread his fingers like a stag's antlers. This position was known as 'having the stag'.

The two players on either side of the player with the stag (in this case, Piers) had to 'mirror' the stag with the hand closest to the antlers, by placing the adjacent thumb on the temple next to the stag and waggling the hand. The object of the game seemed to be to fool or catch out the other players with the speed, complexity and cunning of the various different ways it was possible to 'pass the stag'. When the stag was passed another player must recognise that he was the recipient of the stag and then 'take' possession by putting his own thumbs to his temples and waggling his stag antlers. Then, of course, the players on either side of the new possessor of the stag must 'mirror' the stag. What made the game more difficult was that there seemed to be various ways of 'dummying' a pass, by nodding or staring at other players, whereas in fact the stag couldn't fully be passed unless both of the player's thumbs had left their forehead. Picking up the stag from a dummy pass resulted in having to take a drink. How much you had to drink was determined by 'Mr Weights and Measures', in this case Cookson. He would ascribe one, two or even three fingers of red wine as a penalty, depending on the stupidity of your mistake. Just to make things even more complicated, one of the players (Esme) was elected to be 'Mr Thumb'. Mr Thumb could at any time place his right thumb on the table. Every other player had to do likewise, and the last player to realise what was happening was also given a drinking penalty. Of course, the game was further complicated by the fact that everybody was getting progressively more drunk, and there was one more role – that of 'Mr Chief Sneak' – who would point out to Mr Chairman when someone had breached the rules or made a blunder. Lara was appointed Mr Chief Sneak, a role perfectly suited to her bitchy, snitchy personality.

It was extraordinary watching these young people, supposedly the future of our nation, sitting there pretending to have antlers. The stags' heads on the walls looked down with patent disapproval, and I remembered my old friend Jeffrey, the stag's head from Longcross. What would he have said? Watching them all glorying in their daft posh game with its daft posh rules, I could quite understand why people despised elites like them. No: elites like *us*.

Fortunately, I was a quick study. I hadn't eaten much during the meal, but I hadn't drunk much either. That meant that even though I was the newbie, I still managed to stay ahead of the game and didn't have to drink nearly as many penalties as the others. Louis was the worst – he had to drink the most, as he kept making silly mistakes. This was compounded when it moved into 'Olympic stags' mode, when it was played at double speed and you had to 'pass the stag' within three seconds. The penalty to be dreaded most was the 'Evie', which apparently stood for EV or empty vessel. If you'd had to drink so much that your glass was empty, you had to suffer the indignity of being asked a question to which you had to – absolutely *had* to – answer truthfully.

Luckily I avoided this penalty too at first, although the questions were pretty asinine:

Q: Who's hotter, Prince William or Prince Harry?
A: (Lara) Prince William.

Or:

Q: What's the weirdest place you've made out with someone?
A: (Piers) The stables at Windsor Castle.

But then, of course, the rules began to break down as people got progressively more smashed, and the questions got deeper and darker. The rest of the STAGS game was abandoned, and it all just became one massive game of Truth. And once that happened, perhaps inevitably, there was only one subject of discussion.

Henry.

Pretty much everyone there had a complex relationship with the 'deceased' head of the house.

Charlotte was some sort of cousin and liked him. Cass was his actual cousin and loved him. Louis was his actual cousin and hated him. Piers was his friend and liked him. Cookson was his friend and hated him. Lara used to be his girlfriend, until he abandoned her and started hitting on me. And as for me – well, I didn't know what I was, or how I felt. So when Louis (as Mr Chairman) asked the next question, we all had to face our personal truth.

'All right,' he slurred. 'I've got one for the whole table. Who was glad when Henry died?'

It was like some sick election. Louis raised his hand to his own question at once. Lara, a woman scorned, also held up her hand. Cookson, who'd been cuckoo-quick to step into Henry's shoes as the head of his cohort of Medievals, raised his hand too.

Cass's hands stayed determinedly in her lap, and she looked neither left nor right. Charlotte and Piers looked discomfited. And Louis laughed his head off. 'Don't worry,' he said, 'he can't see you!'

My stomach, already acid with food and folklore, lurched with sudden nausea. If this toxic, divided crowd of privileged darlings felt edgy now, that was nothing to how they would feel when the object of their discussion actually turned up tomorrow night, like Banquo's ghost.

Then Lara leaned in, all languid, sleepy beauty. 'My turn. And this one's for Greer.' My sick stomach flipped over like a pancake. She fixed her luminous grey eyes on me. 'Are you in love with Henry?'

Esme inaccurately sloshed wine into her glass. 'Henry's dead, dummy.'

Lara did not shift her gaze from mine. 'Were you in love with him before he died?'

'No,' I said, 'absolutely not.' It was true. I'd always thought he was drop-dead handsome, if you'll pardon the pun, but I'd only become drawn to him once he'd begun to change his ways. When Shafeen had once remarked it was harder to battle the ghost Henry than the real Henry, he'd been right. I'd only got to like him *after* he'd 'died'.

I stood abruptly, before anyone could refine the question. I knew what was coming next. *Do you love him now?* And that was the one question I couldn't face. 'I'm going to bed.'

'Good idea, Greer,' said Piers, relaxing back in his chair. 'You should conserve your energy.'

'You might need it this weekend,' added Cookson.

They all laughed like hyenas, but, oddly, both the twins just sat there with indefinable, identical, uncomfortable looks on their faces. Their expressions were twins too.

Navigating my way back to my room in the North Tower was even more spooky than finding my way down to dinner. The atmosphere wasn't helped by the fact that I could hear footsteps following me – sounding rapidly on the flagstones and climbing the spiral stairs in my wake.

As it turned out, I wasn't being pursued by some ghostly child or headless phantom but by Louis, who caught up with me just outside my door. On balance, I think that was worse – I'd have taken the child or the phantom. In a horrible imitation of one of the more romantic moments of my life, he posed like a pound-shop Henry, leaning back against the ancient stones, bow tie carelessly unknotted just as Henry's had been that night he'd waited for me outside my room in Longcross. That night Henry had taken me up to the roof and kissed me. I just hoped his cousin wasn't about to do the same.

That hope was in vain. It was very clear what Louis had

come for, and it wasn't conversation. He pushed himself off the wall, in an inelegant parody of Henry's grace, and lurched towards me until I could smell the wine on his breath.

'I could still save you, Greer,' he said thickly. 'There's one way you can survive.' His words chilled me as effectively as the old stones at my back. So it was confirmed. This was to be my final act.

'Become my consort,' he murmured. 'I'll call off the DOGS. I'm Grand Master now, as well as Earl of Longcross.'

I cast about for an excuse to reject this lovely offer. I couldn't reveal, of course, that I knew what was planned for me at the Red Hunt. Then inspiration struck. 'What about Ty?'

He waved a hand dismissively. 'Ty was just prey.'

'Like me.'

'You're different,' he said, attempting a seductive gaze. 'You've always been different. Ty's not the sort of gel who could be . . . you know . . .'

'No, I don't know,' I said. 'What?'

'You know,' he said, his gaze wavering. 'Lady of the manor. She's not the right . . . sort.'

This made me mad, and anger chased away the fear. 'What on *earth*,' I said frostily, 'do you mean by that?'

'Well –' he waved his hands around – 'not quite . . . *top drawer*.'

'She's out of exactly the same drawer as I am,' I pointed out.

'I know, but you . . . you, Greer, you're . . . *special*.' He leaned in towards my lips, eyes unfocused.

I turned my head. 'Louis,' I said patiently, 'I'm with someone.'

I meant Shafeen but he misunderstood. 'You're still hankering after *him*, aren't you? Henry's dead. I'm very much alive.'

I wasn't going to be the one to tell him. His face was very close to mine, as close as Henry's had once been, the one and only time he'd kissed me, on the silver roof of Longcross. But this time there was no fire, only disgust. Disgust and perhaps a little pity. 'Louis.'

'Yes?'

'Go to bed.'

I shut the door gently in his face, then placed my back against it, heart thudding. I turned the key he himself had given me, in case he tried to kick it in.

I'd been afraid ever since I came to Castle MacLeod, but now I was cold-sweatingly, bowel-shrinkingly terrified. Had I just thrown away my only chance to save myself from the Order?

Needless to say, I found it pretty hard getting to sleep that night. In that half-land between wakefulness and nightmare I saw myself, as if from a drone, on the slopes of Ben Horneval. I was slung across the back of a garron, bound to the pony's back by ropes, naked and pale as death. For some reason Henry was holding the leading rope, and behind us, in a procession, walked perhaps a hundred figures in red robes with cowled hoods drawn up. Imperial antlers were attached to my bleeding forehead like a crown of thorns, and at every bumping step the Highland pony took down the slopes of Ben Horneval, blood dripped from my antlers to the ground.

Bump, bump, bump.

Drip, drip, drip.

I slept.

13

At breakfast Louis didn't mention our late-night conversation. He looked a little bit green – not surprising really, considering the amount of booze he'd put away – and was busy medicating himself with a cooked breakfast. The sunny morning room had a breathtaking view of the sea, so once I'd filled my plate from the contents of a row of silver domes I went to sit next to Cass, facing the windows. The Medievals weren't up yet – also not surprising – and nor was the creepy nanny. It was just the nuclear family, and never had that description seemed more fitting. There was some weird undercurrent, fizzing away radioactively, as if at any moment something would explode.

'What will you do today, my dear?' asked Lady Fiona distractedly.

'Oh, I think I'll go for a walk,' I said vaguely. 'It's a beautiful day.'

It was. The summer sun buttered the black hills and made them look a little less foreboding, and the pewter sea was a flat calm. 'Do take care,' said Lady Fiona. 'The mist can descend like a guillotine, and before you realise it you don't know your up from your down.'

'That's true,' said Lord Peregrine, whose mission in life seemed to be to agree with his wife. 'The weather on Skye can change without warning.'

'And you don't have any of the proper gear,' said Cass. 'The black hills can be tricksy. Especially Ben Horneval.' Then she looked like she wished she hadn't said anything.

I was not fooled by their touching concern for my welfare. The only reason they cared is that they did not want to lose their prey for their little weekend of fun. And besides, I knew exactly where I was going. I was going back to the Peel Tower to share the intel I'd gleaned last night with the rebels. Of course I didn't *say* any of that – I was deliberately vague about my plans. 'Oh, I'm not going up any mountains,' I said. 'Just a nice wander. You know, enjoy the scenery.'

As I spoke I feared I'd made a mistake – presumably there would be a whole timetable of events for me to participate in. But the noble couple just nodded and sipped their tea. Seemingly there was nothing in the diary until the ball later on.

Finishing my breakfast as quickly as I could to avoid the sticky small talk, I escaped to my turret. As I climbed back up the North Tower I could see why they hadn't tried to manage me – long, sleek cars were already arriving, decanting expensive-looking guests. Clearly the family had enough to do, getting ready for The Gathering that night.

I didn't have any proper walking kit, but I had my trainers on and zipped myself into a hoodie; despite the family's scaremongering I was sure that would be fine. I took a last look from my window before setting out, just to double check the route, but it looked pretty easy. The Peel Tower, once more reminding me of a rook on a chessboard, could be clearly seen. Unless it had the power to move like the chess piece it resembled, all I had to do was walk towards it – and I set off from Castle MacLeod to do just that.

The sun was already warm, and I could see for miles around. I wasn't quite sure what the family had been wetting their knickers about – it was the easiest stroll I'd ever taken. I glanced up at Ben Horneval as I walked. There were people milling around again, still building that bonfire or whatever it was, the sticks propped together like a scaffold, climbing higher and higher. I guessed this was all part of the Lammas festivities the creepy nanny had talked about.

It took me less than a quarter of an hour to get to the Peel Tower, so close was it to the castle. As I approached a figure came out of the door, at a half-run. It was Shafeen. He enfolded me in the sort of embrace you see in the movies and gave me the most passionate, last-reel-of-the-film kiss. He literally swept me off my feet, and to be kissed like that, by a tall, handsome guy, in that saturnine landscape, left me weak at the knees. 'You must be psychic,' I stuttered, attempting to recover my composure. 'How did you know I was coming?'

He smiled. 'I had help.' I looked up and, sure enough, there was the HAWK, hovering almost silently, its sound a low, natural hum like a swarm of bees. And halfway up the tower, another observer at the window – Henry. He'd seen the kiss, but before I could meet his eyes he quickly turned away.

Shafeen threw an arm around me as we walked toward the Peel Tower. 'How's the castle?'

'Five stars on Tripadvisor,' I said. 'But that's just for the room. As for the people . . .' I left the statement hanging.

'I miss you.'

'It's just a few days.'

'Is it, Greer?' His dark eyes scanned the horizon. 'I'm afraid. I'm afraid I might not get you back.'

I shot him a look. Shafeen wasn't the type to get spooked, and *him* being spooked spooked *me*. 'You mean I'm going to die?'

'No, not that. I'd die myself before I let that happen,' he said heroically. 'No – that something is going to come between us.'

'Louis tried to kiss me, if that's what you mean,' I confessed.

'*Did* he now?' Shafeen looked amused. 'I hope you knocked him back.'

'Of course. You've got nothing to worry about.'

But he didn't mean Louis and we both knew it.

'How are you getting on with Ratio?' I changed the subject.

'Really well,' he said. 'I'm sharing a room with him.'

'I know. Is it OK?'

'Very. He's a real social-justice warrior – just the guy to bring the de Warlencourts down. He hates them, Greer, he really hates them.'

'How's he dealing with Henry then?'

'There's not much love lost between them, but they're united in a common cause. I tell you who *is* getting on with Ratio though.'

'Who?'

'Ty,' he said, his voice heavy with significance.

'*Really.*' I drew out the word.

'Yes. Let's just say that when Henry moves to the castle

tonight, I get the feeling I'll be taking the sofa, and Ty will be sharing with Ratio.'

'Ooh, plot twist!' I said deliciously. I was really pleased for Ty. I wasn't sure if she'd genuinely had feelings for Louis, but Louis had made it clear last night that he'd never had any genuine feelings for her. Of course, Ratio was heir to nothing but a nerdy bedroom in Glasgow, but Ty didn't care about stuff like that. 'And how's Nel?'

'Fine,' he said. 'Just counting the hours until Abbot Ridley turns up.'

'Do you think he will?'

'At some point,' he said. 'And hopefully he'll bring a whole pack of FOXES with him. When it comes to the STAGS, Nathaniel Ridley seems to have a gift for being in the right place at the right time.'

I thought of the Abbot rearing up to knock Montgomery de Warlencourt off his horse at the Tiger Club in Jaipur, and then again in Longwood on Boxing Day, to unseat Monty's son Rollo. 'You're right about that,' I said soberly.

We went inside, and the rebels were gathered in the living room. Ratio, green hair wild and ruffled like a meadow in a storm, stood at the front like a teacher, while the others sat draped over various sofas and easy chairs. I found myself on the receiving end of fervent hugs from Ty and Nel, while Henry, who had seen that Mills & Boon kiss outside, simply raised a lazy hand. Ratio sent a friendly grin my way. 'Still in one piece, I see.'

'For now,' I said. 'You've been busy.'

He had. The room, which had once resembled the lounge of a comfy Highland hotel, now looked like the incident room of a police station. Ratio had set up his laptop, printer and iPad, and the cabling spilled out across the carpet like black spaghetti. A whiteboard was propped against the wall with open-ended questions like *Response time?* and *Extraction plan?* scribbled on it in magic marker. The tapestry had been removed from the wall and replaced with multiple glossy photos of the terrain around Castle MacLeod. The sea cliffs, the castle itself, the black hills and heathered hillsides. An Ordnance Survey map of the area was pinned up below them. There were other photos too – of Lord Peregrine, Lady Fiona and the twins, and of various members of staff I recognised from the castle. And then there were scans of menus and guestlists – God knows where he got those – photos of other prospective guests and even of tradesmen's vans arriving at and leaving the castle, complete with enhanced shots of number plates. The photos were connected to each other with a spider's web of pushpins and red thread, to recreate the CSI wall Ratio had in his bedroom in Glasgow. I pointed at one of the shots. 'That's me!' There I was, leaning out of my window in the North Tower with the twins, goofily waving at the drone.

'Thanks for the shout-out,' said Ratio, smiling laconically. 'But probably better if you don't do that again.'

'I won't,' I said shamefacedly.

'All right,' said Ratio, calling this little meeting of rebels to order. 'Let's review where we are. Henry, you'll be making your comeback at The Gathering tonight.'

Henry nodded.

'We have to hope that your presence doesn't derail the

90

whole weekend,' said Shafeen. 'If the family suspect you're there to protect Greer . . .'

'They won't,' said Henry shortly. 'Remember, I'm the one who invited Greer to Longcross in the first place, for a spot of huntin' shootin' fishin'. She was *my* prey originally. They don't know about anything that happened on Boxing Day, or in India.' He obviously didn't want to say that he saved two lives – Ty's and Aadhish's. I didn't think it was modesty though – just a very British reluctance to boast. 'They'll just think I'm the same old Henry, and I'll make sure I behave accordingly.'

'But Cass knows you're alive,' Nel protested. 'You saw her at her birthday, remember?'

'Cass is sound,' said Henry. 'You don't need to worry about her. And even she doesn't know I'm in league with you lot, and by extension the FOXES.'

'OK,' said Ratio, calling us back to order. 'We've got a lot of exterior data from the HAWK. Now, supposing you tell us, Greer, what happened yesterday inside the lion's den.'

I slotted myself onto the sofa, symbolically, between Henry and Shafeen, and told the tale of the day before. I covered the tea, the story of the feud between Clan MacDonald and Clan MacLeod, the dinner and the game of STAGS. I tried to be as thorough as I could, but I did leave out three things. I didn't reveal what the Medievals had said about Henry, nor what they'd asked of me. And I left out the part where Louis had followed me to my room and tried to kiss me.

Everyone listened carefully, then Ty said, 'And did you find anything out about where they'll be stalking tomorrow? On the Red Hunt?'

91

'Yes,' I said. 'You'll love this. It's going to take the route of the battle between the MacDonalds and the MacLeods in 1395, ending up at the Bloody Stone where my clan left all the bodies of their clan under a rowan tree. I can't remember any of the other place names though. They all sounded like breaking glass.'

'I can,' said Henry, rising languidly from the sofa. He took the magic marker from Ratio's hand and began scribbling on the whiteboard. 'In 1395 the MacDonalds landed at Loch Eynort and headed north along Glen Sligachan. They were met by a force of MacLeods at Harta Corrie, below Sgùrr nan Gillean.'

We watched as he scribbled the complex place names down on the white board. 'That's quite the Scrabble score,' I remarked.

He smiled. 'They're easier to say than they are to spell,' he said. 'May I?' He pointed at the pushpins.

Ratio made a 'go ahead' gesture with his long hands.

Henry collected a little handful of pins and moved over to the Ordnance Survey map. He'd now taken over the role of teacher, or lead detective, from Ratio. 'So the Red Hunt will start at Loch Eynort, *here*, which is a sea loch.' He placed the first pin on a long finger of inlet from the ocean. 'They'll move along this glen, Glen Sligachan –' he pushed in another pin – 'and then reach Harta Corrie, *here*, which is on the slopes of Sgùrr nan Gillean, which is this mountain *here*. The Bloody Stone, which is their end point, is *here*, and it's at this spot that Greer might be in a sticky situation.' He added the last three pins and turned to Ratio. 'Program that route into your drone-hawk-thingy or whatever it is, and you'll always have eyes on her.'

Ratio took up his ball of yarn and wound it around the pushpins. I watched, mesmerised, as the red thread described what could be my last journey, and gave a little shudder.

Ratio saw it. 'Don't worry. They think *they're* hunting *you*, but we're hunting *them.*'

'*Either the hunter or the hunted be,*' quoted Ty, in her best Queen Cynthia voice.

'Exactly,' said Ratio, looking at her fondly. 'We've got a three-pronged attack. Henry's protecting you on the ground. We've got the HAWK watching from the air. And we'll all be on the hillside ready to spring into action if you're threatened.'

'Four-pronged,' said Nel. 'Don't forget, the Abbot's cooking something up. He said he'd be in Scotland before us.'

'I think that's just a song,' I said doubtfully.

'Well, I trust him,' said Nel doggedly. 'You'll see.'

'Easy to have faith when it's not your head on the block,' I grumbled. I caught sight of the red thread and picked up the ball of yarn, winding a length of it around my finger.

Red thread.

'Can I have some of this?'

'Knock yourself out,' said Ratio affably.

I snipped off a little thread and pushed it into my pocket. It wasn't for me, but I couldn't exactly give it to the person I intended it for at that moment.

'I better push off,' I said. 'There's probably a lunch or something.'

'The Gathering will be seven for seven thirty,' said Henry, using one of those incomprehensible posh timings – why couldn't an event be at one time or another? 'So I'll meet you at seven.'

'Where?'

He considered. 'What about the battlements? There's a secret way up, and I don't want to run into anyone else before I'm with you.'

'How will I get up there?'

'Where are you staying?'

'North Tower.' Of course – Henry would know the castle like the back of his hand, if he'd been staying with his cousins since he was a child.

'The steps to your room – there's another turn of the stair that leads to the roof. Just keep going up. You'll find me.'

Shafeen walked me out. Our goodbye was much less romantic and much more troubled than our hello had been. Shafeen held me like he didn't want to let me go. 'For God's sake, take care of yourself.'

'I was rather hoping,' I said into his cheek, 'that you lot would take care of me.'

'Always,' he said. 'The moment you step outside, we'll be watching you.'

14

It can't have been much later than noon when I set off from the Peel Tower.

The sun was shining and I could clearly see Castle MacLeod in the distance. I would easily be back for whatever lunch was, even though I wasn't really mega-hungry after my full English – or rather Scottish – breakfast.

Then the unexpected happened. Without warning a white fog descended, so dense that I literally couldn't see my hand in front of my face. The castle, the mountains, the Peel Tower, everything was gone in an instant. I'd been joking to myself about the tower being a rook on the chessboard, but it was as if the tower had literally slid away.

I wasn't worried to start with. The tower and the castle were no more than a mile apart. All I had to do was just keep walking straight.

The thing was, it was really difficult to know what 'straight' was. I thought I could just walk back the way I had come, over the flat, rough grassy terrain, but suddenly the ground started going up, and my trainers were stumbling over shards of scree, black as chips of jet and sharp as knives. I carried on walking, not really knowing what to do, hoping that the mist would clear so I could get my bearings. I stood still, panting, the mist even muffling my exhausted gasps. Then the mist shredded and cleared for a tantalising instant – only to show me the castle and the Peel Tower seemingly miles away – in totally the wrong direction. Another thing that that glimpse had shown me – I had climbed to quite an altitude. From my vantage point, I was high up, looking down on everything. Then of course I remembered, with a sinking feeling in my gut, what Lady Fiona had said at breakfast.

The mist can descend like a guillotine, and before you realise it you don't know your up from your down.

By my calculation I was on the foothills of Ben Horneval, the mountain that had always given me the heebie-jeebies, and the very place I didn't want to be. Somehow I'd got myself totally lost and had meandered onto higher ground. I turned my back on the mountain, braced myself and set off, determined to walk down. But it was no use. However hard I tried to descend, the dense mist disorientated me, and the stubborn terrain took me ever higher. I stood still again, panting, heart thumping, head spinning with panic. What if I never found my way back? I'd broken Lord Peregrine's golden rule of Highland hiking, which was that I'd not told anyone where I was going. The rebels knew I was walking back to the castle, but no more than that. I looked skyward, hoping to see the friendly red light of the HAWK, but I couldn't see more than a foot above me – and if I couldn't see the drone, it couldn't see me.

Then, as I stood, the mist suddenly cleared to reveal an awful sight. A shape loomed above me – not a man or a beast, but an enormous structure – a cathedral of sticks and branches. I thought I knew what this was – it was the bonfire I'd seen those shadowy figures building on Ben Horneval. But in those moments of clarity I could see that this was no ordinary bonfire. A definite shape resolved out of the mist. Four legs as big as an oil rig. A body the size of a bus. Then a tapered head, and huge branched antlers rising impossibly high into the dense white sky.

A *stag*.

At that moment I swear I was the most frightened I had ever been. To be alone on the bare mountain, in this eerie silence, with this enormous structure dwarfing me, was terrifying. I'd much rather some of the mysterious builders had still been around, because however weird those locals were, they were still human. This thing, so vast and powerful, seemed as cold and distant as all gods, but definitely malign. Evil emanated from every twisted stick and branch.

I ran.

I didn't know where I was going, I just had to get away from the wicker stag. I don't know how long I ran, or where I went. All sense of direction, of date and time and season, was gone as the thick fog descended once more. But even so, my panicked senses must have figured out the right direction somehow because eventually I found myself back at the castle. The mist was so thick that the first I knew about it was when I almost cannoned into the ancient stones of the exterior wall and nearly knocked myself out. I pulled up sharply and felt my way to the gatehouse by trailing my fingertips on the clammy stone, constantly keeping contact as a guide. I didn't want to get lost again. But it was all right – at the castle entrance a thoughtful someone had lit torches down the drive to guide travellers home.

I'd never been so glad to see people in my life. It didn't matter if they were privileged predators – right now they just looked enormously welcoming. Everything was in happy chaos: guests, flowers, food, wine – all were arriving at the same time, in cars and vans edging carefully forward through the gradually lifting mist in a sort of elite convoy. On the stone steps and inside the Keep there was a bustle of servants who were far too busy to bother about a scruffy, sweaty teenager slipping silently to her room. To my immense relief I managed to climb all the way to my tower without bumping into anyone I knew. I was no longer hungry and couldn't face the prospect of lunch. I threw open the south-facing casement and gulped the bracing air. The mist was thinning but I still couldn't see the horizon. Nor, to my relief, could I see the wicker stag.

I shut the window, and the curtains too, and flopped fully dressed onto my bed like a felled tree.

Exhausted by fear and exercise, I slept.

15

I woke with that vague sense of panic that you get when you don't know quite where you are or how long you've slept. Once I'd woken up properly I actually felt pretty great. I'd had a proper disco nap and was ready to face the evening. I opened the curtains, and by some weird weather witchcraft there was not a shred of mist to be seen. The air was as clear as crystal, the late-afternoon sun varnished the black hills, and now it seemed to me that the wicker deer on the slopes of the appropriately named Ben Horneval had been some sort of nightmare – or rather, daymare.

It took me a good few minutes to realise that there was something in the room that hadn't been there when I'd gone to sleep. Not a horse's head, or a *Blair Witch*-style twig doll, but a dress.

A cream lace dress.

It was hanging, innocently, from the door of the wardrobe like a redundant ghost. I took it down and held it against me. It was pressed, fragrant and – of course – exactly my size.

I assumed that some maid had knocked and entered while I was asleep, and although the thought of that was pretty unsettling, it was very far from being the creepiest thing that had happened to me that day. After all, I hadn't turned the key when I'd returned to the room, and for all I knew this was standard practice in great houses.

Now I locked the door all right and went to boil myself in a scented bath. When I was undressing, the red thread I'd taken from Ratio fell out of my jeans pocket. It hadn't helped me much that afternoon, since the wicker deer had successfully scared the shit out of me – but then I remembered Nanny had talked about graveyard stags and the head of the house – maybe rowan and red thread didn't protect plebs like me but were to protect the heir. Her beloved Louis. Or my – was he beloved? – Henry.

Unwilling to interrogate this thought, I scrubbed all the grime and sweat of panic off me, washed my hair and listened to some music I'd downloaded on my phone. Once I was clean I felt about a thousand per cent better. Back in my room I dried and put on the lace dress and examined myself in the mirror. The dress was fitted, with scalloped cap sleeves and a long skirt, which swept the floor – definitely a ballgown. It was perfectly nice but a bit bridal, and it reminded me of the aborted debutantes' ball that was supposed to be held at Longcross on the night of the fire, when all the women wore white like at Queen Charlotte's Ball. There were gloves to go with it, which came up to my elbow, but the dress definitely needed something else. I didn't have any jewellery with me to speak of, and definitely nothing that was posh enough to complement that dress. Hoop earrings and my *Mean Girls* necklace wouldn't really cut it, so I slicked on a wing of black eyeliner and a scarlet lip – that would have to do. Perhaps it was the red of the lipstick that reminded me; I took the red thread from my pocket and pushed it down my bra, beneath the bodice of the dress.

At seven o'clock by my signal-less phone I left the room – locking it this time. In the dimness of the stone stairs I looked for the way up that Henry had described. Sure enough, in the shadows, I could see that a dark doorway led to an even smaller stairway, leading upwards. I climbed it, holding my skirts clear of the stones, feeling as if I'd gone back a couple of centuries. At the top was another door, which led directly onto the roof. A strong sea breeze greeted me, snatching at the skirts of my lace dress and blasting my damp black bob completely dry. A tall blond figure was pacing the crenellations, looking out to sea.

Henry.

He reminded me of Kenneth Branagh wandering round on the battlements of Elsinore looking for the ghost of his dad. 'Are you doing a Hamlet?'

And since *Hamlet* was (so I've heard) a play before it was a film, he got the reference. He turned. 'Except I wasn't waiting for a dead old man so much as a living young woman. You look flawless, Greer.'

So did he. He always suited evening dress, but I'd never seen him like this. He was wearing a black jacket with gold buttons and a white lace cravat – so far so STAGS. But below the waist it all got interesting. He was wearing a full-on kilt and a sporran. And of course his legs were excellent – long but muscular, and surprisingly tanned. He had on these kind of thick, cream knee socks – one of them, I'm not kidding,

101

had a small silver dagger stuck in it – and black shoes with complicated lacings. I wondered, of course, if he was doing the proper *Braveheart* thing of wearing nothing under the kilt, but I couldn't exactly ask. It would seem a bit like flirting, and I didn't want to encourage him.

As it turned out, he didn't need any encouraging. He took my hand and I thought he was going to kiss it, but he pulled me towards him and kissed my cheek. He took his time, placing his lips on my skin slowly and tenderly, and I remembered the time he'd kissed me on the rooftop at Longcross. I could feel his warm breath and it seemed to kindle something within me. It would be so easy to turn my head and place my lips on his, and I felt for a moment as if it was inevitable, as if nothing could stop me doing just that. My blood heated and I felt as if I was going to fall down, and before the dangerous fire could consume me I wrenched myself away. 'How many times do I have to tell you that I'm with Shafeen?'

'Let's go for one more.'

'*I'm with Shafeen.*'

He smiled. 'We'll see. We've got a whole weekend together. That's a lot of time, and I intend to spend every second of it wooing you.'

'You just put it all out there, don't you?'

He looked beyond me, over the battlements to the silver horizon. 'Life's too short, Greer. I've already died once. There's nothing like dying to make you focus on what you want from your life. And I want you.'

Well, he was honest, you had to give him that.

'And just to get the wooing off on the right foot, I got you something.' He brought a folded cloth from behind his back and placed it in my hands. It was prickly and woolly.

'What's this?'

'At The Gathering the women wear white lace dresses, and the men full Highland dress, but if the women are members of a clan they wear a sash of their clan tartan. This is yours – the tartan of the MacDonald. Here, let me help you.'

He draped it across one shoulder, beauty-queen style, and secured it at my hip with a little Celtic brooch studded with nuggets of amber.

I looked down at the tartan. It was a striking plaid in blood red, overlaid with a stinging check of green. I liked it a lot, but I had my doubts about going downstairs draped in enemy colours. 'At a MacLeod ball? I might as well be wearing a suicide vest.'

He laughed lightly. 'That's all ancient history.'

'Well, it seemed pretty modern to your aunt.'

'The stuff about the Bloody Stone? She tell you that, did she?'

'Like it was yesterday.'

'Well,' Henry said comfortingly, 'even if they peeve about a MacDonald in their midst, there's going to be at least one guest who's less welcome than you.'

'Who's that?'

He grinned. 'Me.'

That reminded me. 'Actually, I've got something for *you*.' I took the red thread from my bodice and wound it round his wrist, tying it securely. He looked like one of those celebrities that suddenly decide they're into Kabbalah. Somewhere far below in the belly of the castle, someone started playing the bagpipes, scoring the moment with the most Scottish soundtrack ever. 'I have it on good authority that "Rowan-tree and red thread keep the devils frae their speed",' I explained.

He smiled. 'Ah, Nanny.'

'Yes. We really hit it off. I'm thinking of going as her for Halloween. But she certainly seemed to know her folklore.'

'She does indeed.' He adjusted the thread on his wrist. 'Thank you.'

I touched the scratchy tartan that crossed my heart. 'Well, it's hardly as nice as this.'

'Still, I'm touched.' He seemed genuine and it occurred to me then that perhaps Henry had not had many people to care for him – a smothering mother, a distant father, a girl cousin who liked him a little too much and a boy cousin who wanted him dead. Maybe to this golden boy who'd had every material thing given to him all his life, a bit of old string given with genuine concern did mean something.

'Let's go and do the big reveal, shall we?' He tucked the thread under his cuff and crooked his elbow into a right angle like you see in the movies. I curled my gloved hand around it, and together we went down to face the music.

16

We went down the stairs of the North Tower and Henry led me to a part of the castle I'd never been to before.

The drone of the piper got louder and louder until we were standing outside an immense oak door, set into a stone arch and studded with iron bolts. We were a bit late after that little scene on the battlements, so everybody else must've already been inside. The skirl of the pipe was incredibly loud now, and I could feel it in my ribs, in competition with my thudding heart. My mouth was dry, my breath quick, and if I felt like that, goodness knows how Henry must have felt. He was about to come back from the dead after eighteen months in hiding. I gripped his arm very tightly and he turned to smile at me. If he was nervous he showed no sign of it – the only tell was that the de Warlencourt eyes were very blue. 'Ready?' he asked.

'Ready,' I replied, although I felt anything but.

Then Henry rapped on the door with his fist, as if he was a marauding invader come to besiege the castle. Which, I suppose, he was.

The door opened to a wall of sound: the piper, and hundreds

of loud conversations as people screeched to make themselves heard.

We were at the top of a short flight of stone steps and there was a kind of announcer guy at the top of them – like you see in films such as *My Fair Lady* – whose job it was to call out the names of the guests. Henry spoke in his ear and I saw the guy's eyes flare in surprise as he looked at him. There could be no doubt, from this latecomer's appearance, that he was who he said he was, and this smooth servant was obviously thinking about how the hell he was going to announce that the long-lost heir of the de Warlencourts, presumed dead, was back from the grave.

Then there was this really awkward pause while we had to wait for the piper to finish his tune before we could be announced. I had one of those weird moments of clarity when you notice everything, in intimate detail, about your surroundings; like those life-flashing-before-your-eyes moments people say you have before you're about to die. I got the feeling that if you asked me years later I'd be able to tell you everything about that ballroom. I'd remember the long, oak-panelled room with a minstrels' gallery crowded with musicians at one end. I'd remember the high, pointed windows with the sun setting over the hills and heather. I'd remember the wooden dance floor, polished to such a high shine that it looked more like an ice rink. The summer flowers banked against the rostrum below the gallery; those same flowers wreathed into the antlers of the stags on the walls and arranged in the empty fireplace. The men in their Highland dress, the women with the tartans of their clans draped over their dresses, just as I wore mine. The vast silver cauldron of punch with little silver cups hanging off its lip by their curved handles. Each detail was burned into my brain – I'd remember all of it.

The piper finished his tune, and into the sudden silence the announcer guy said, loud as an actor:

'Lord *Henry* de Warlencourt and Miss Greer MacDonald of the Clan MacDonald.'

Two things about that. One: he definitely put a special stress on the name Henry, presumably to distinguish him from Louis, whom he'd obviously already announced. Two: he'd made a point of stating not just my name, but my clan – so that every single person at The Gathering knew that the enemy was in their midst.

'Thanks a lot,' I said ironically from the corner of my mouth, but the announcer dude merely bowed obligingly.

If I'd thought the walk last night to the dining table in the Great Hall was long, it was nothing to descending those four stone steps on the arm of Henry de Warlencourt and walking the miles and miles to the middle of that polished wooden dance floor. There was utter, utter silence as we passed, as everyone stared, open-mouthed. As we arrived at the centre of the room the orchestra in the minstrels' gallery struck up a lilting Highland waltz. 'What do we do now?' I hissed at Henry.

He turned to face me and raised both his arms. 'Dance, I suppose.'

This was unbelievable. My entire knowledge of dancing had been gleaned from *Strictly Ballroom*, and now here I was, in a ballroom of fleet-footed Highlanders, opening The Gathering with what was destined to be the most awkward exhibition dance ever. I kept my head up, kept my frame locked and moved when Henry moved. He led me admirably, and I managed not to fall over, stand on his feet or trip over my skirt. I couldn't look at anybody else, locking my gaze onto Henry's blue eyes. After that dreadful period of total silence, I heard the murmur of talk start up again. 'Is anybody watching?' I whispered.

'*Everybody's* watching,' he said, with a smile. I thought, *He's* enjoying *this*.

It seemed like the tune was going on for ever, and I felt, just like Lizzie Bennet in *Pride and Prejudice* when she's having her awks dance with Mr Darcy, that we had to have some conversation. We had to style it out, since every eye was on us, from the servants to the guests to the stags' heads on the walls. As we danced, their glassy gaze reminded me of something that only Henry de Warlencourt in full Highland dress could have jolted from my mind.

'I had quite a scare on the way home,' I said. 'There's a huge wicker stag on the side of Ben Horneval, woven out of branches and sticks. Frightened the life out of me.'

'Oh, you mean the Damh.'

It sounded like he'd said 'damn'. 'The what?'

'Damh. It's old Gaelic for stag. They burn the wooden stag at midnight on Lammas Eve.'

'They do *what*?' I almost forgot the entire ballroom of people watching.

'They set fire to it. The burning of the Damh. It happens every year.' He looked down at me. 'What? You look as if your flabber couldn't be more gasted.'

'It's just . . . just . . . so *Wicker Man*.'

He shrugged lightly. 'I don't know what that is.'

'It's a film from the 1970s. These weird villagers build this huge man out of wicker, and then burn it, as part of a creepy local ritual.'

'Oh. That does sound similar,' he said calmly. 'It's quite a sight to see.'

'I'll bet,' I said grimly. 'And that explains something Nanny said at dinner. She said that revellers jump *under* the bonfire. I just thought she was getting confused, but now I can see she was right.'

'Flitting the fire,' said Henry. 'Yes, they run under the belly as the stag burns. Of course, it's not without risk, because burning branches can fall, and eventually of course the whole thing collapses.'

'Jesus.' But as I uttered that sacred name, I realised how inappropriate it was. What I'd just heard had nothing to do with Christ. I reflected that when good ol' St Aidan the Great had travelled the North of Britain telling everybody about Christianity, there were some parts he clearly hadn't reached. This was about a much older religion than Christianity, something dark, and pagan, and primal. And I was right in the middle of it.

The tune eventually came to an end, and I wondered what would happen next. Would everyone ostracise Henry? Would he be asked to leave? Would we be politely ignored for the rest of the evening? Or would everyone break into a chorus of boos? But as it turned out, the reverse happened. Everyone converged on Henry, pushing and jostling like it was the Black Friday sales. No one could get ahead of Cass, who cannoned into Henry's arms. 'I *knew* you would come,' she said. He hugged her

back and kissed the top of her head fondly. 'Hello, little cuz.'
Watching Cass so blissful in that embrace, however brotherly
it was, I felt a little jag of jealousy. Then I gave myself a good
talking-to. Shafeen was the only one I wanted to snuggle up
to that way.

This cousin love-in was short-lived because Louis walked
through The Gathering as if in a dream, the guests parting for
him like the Red Sea. Henry watched him approach with a
sardonic eye, and the visual of him and Cass as a team versus
Louis was such a strong dynamic. Louis came right up to
Henry, ignoring his sister completely, ignoring all of us. For
that moment, by some weird alchemy, there was only Henry
and Louis in the room, eyeballing each other with that de
Warlencourt blue gaze. Their family resemblance was clear,
and even more marked in their identical Highland dress and
MacLeod tartan kilts. But their expressions were vastly different.
Henry looked all-powerful, confident, even a little amused.
Louis looked filled with hate – hate as black and ancient as
the hills.

'I thought you were dead.'

'Yes,' said Henry, raising one eyebrow like Roger Moore's
James Bond again. 'It was a widely held opinion. But, fortunately
for me, quite untrue.'

'How the hell,' hissed Louis, 'did you survive?'

Henry looked down at Cass, where she nestled in the crook
of his arm. Cass said, '*I* know.'

Her twin looked at her as if she was a stranger. '*What* do
you know?'

'Don't you remember all those summers we spent at

110

Longcross as kids? Skating up and down the long gallery in our socks, playing in Longwood, swimming in Longmere?'

'Yes, of course I do,' he said stiffly.

'And do you remember Henry and I jumping off the waterfall? Jumping off Conrad's Force?'

Dawn broke across Louis's face. I could see that, up until that moment, he'd all but forgotten.

'Do you remember,' repeated Cass, almost as if she was hypnotising him, 'what we did? Henry's special dive: the Dead Man's Drop? You always funked it, but he taught me how.'

As if in a trance, Louis said, 'Remind me.'

Cass said instructively, as if schooling a child, 'You take a deep breath before you go over the edge. You make sure you jump far out, clear of the rocks. You wrap your arms over your head and press your nose into your elbow to help seal it from the water. You tightly close your eyes and mouth, tense your muscles and press your feet together. Then, on impact, you swim away from the falls immediately, without breaking the surface.'

So I had my answer at last to the eternal question – how had Henry survived when his fingers slipped from my grasp at the top of Conrad's Force? I could see him now, like a scene from a film, grasping at air and tipping backwards, falling down into the torrent like Harrison Ford in *The Fugitive*. Now I knew he'd been practising that fall ever since he was a kid. Clearly the cousins' special jump, forgotten since childhood, suddenly sprang back, perfectly, into the forefront of Louis's mind. '*That's* how you did it?' he said, incredulous, transforming just as suddenly from a boy to an angry young man. 'That old kids' trick?'

'That's right,' said Henry gently. 'That old kids' trick.'

The moment was broken by Peregrine, who embraced Henry with an emotion that probably had a lot to do with the fact that Henry was the image of his dead brother Rollo. There were real tears on his florid cheeks. Lady Fiona's greeting was far less heartfelt. As she applied her thin lips coolly to each side of Henry's face in turn you could see the cogs turning behind her eyes. I could tell she'd already come to the realisation that Henry being alive meant her precious Louis would lose the inheritance of Longcross, the earldom and all that lovely fertile English land 'below the oat line'. Nanny was nowhere to be seen – perhaps it was past her bedtime, and I imagined she was far too ancient to dance. Either that or she burst into a thousand ravens at sunset. I noticed too that Henry's mum Caro wasn't here either. Maybe her fragile grip on sanity had fractured and she was banged up in some posh version of Arkham Asylum.

The Medievals were next. Instantly forgetting the allegiances they'd expressed only the night before, they fawned over Henry; they plied him with drinks, told old stories from STAGS and recounted those kinds of posh anecdotes of royal weddings and ski holidays and shooting weekends that only bound people of their kind more closely together. Then everyone else in the ballroom wanted to greet Henry, like some crazy reception line at a wedding. And with every cordial greeting – every double kiss on the cheek from the women, every wringing handshake from the men – Louis's expression got blacker and blacker. His blue eyes followed us around the room, like those paintings in Hogwarts, and he watched Henry like a hawk.

Cass, who was holding onto Henry as if she would never let him go, waggled the hand she was holding. 'Now *you* can give the toast!' she said. 'As the heir of the de Warlencourts, you can give the traditional Highland toast that begins The Gathering. It's always the oldest boy.'

Appalled, I looked to Louis. I never expected to feel sorry for him, but when Cass said this I very nearly did. It was so *completely* insensitive. His face had gone suddenly still, his mouth was pinched in a tight line, and you could see he was totally devastated, possibly fighting tears. Louis had lost his earldom and his sister in a heartbeat, and was now expected to give way to Henry as the MC of the feast.

Henry smiled at Cass and spoke so that all the guests could hear. 'Always the oldest *MacLeod* boy,' he said.

'But you're the heir to the earldom. And that outranks the heir to the clan,' Cass persisted, winning tactless person of the night.

'But we're in Scotland, not England,' said Henry, gently but firmly. 'The honour of opening The Gathering belongs to Louis. As long as he lives, he will be the heir of the MacLeods.'

I felt as proud as a school-gate mum. I liked Henry very much in that moment and thought about how much he'd changed. Louis, without thanking his cousin, without saying anything, turned on his heel and walked back down to the other end of the room. He mounted the rostrum, and a footman handed him a bottle of champagne and – I'm not kidding – a sword. It was not one of those foppish, French fencing swords, like in *Dangerous Liaisons*, but a proper, full-fat broadsword like in *Braveheart*. Louis held the bottle in one hand and swiped the sword down it with the other, making a ringing sound that echoed round the room. As the sword met the neck of the bottle, it sheared cleanly off, and the champagne spurted everywhere, as if Louis had just won something, not lost everything. He lifted the foaming bottle high and declaimed, as if he was once again on the stage of the playhouse at STAGS, acting in *The Isle of Dogs*:

> *'The land of peaks, of glens and heroes,*
> *Where thrives the fair hawk*
> *And where the red deer finds shelter*
> *As long as mist is seen on mountains*
> *Remembrance will be made on the deeds of the brave;*
> *Health and victory forever*
> *To the MacLeods of Dunvegan*
> *Deers' Antlers Forever!'*

Ignoring the glass that the footman held out to him, Louis lifted the (presumably sharp) bottleneck to his mouth and practically drained the bottle. Then he threw the vessel into the fireplace where it smashed satisfactorily, and the ballroom exploded too in a rousing cheer. The last few moments between the old heir and the new had been so awkward that the pent-up tension had to release itself somehow. The atmosphere felt suddenly euphoric, the musicians in the minstrels' gallery struck up a jaunty Highland tune and couples whirled onto the floor for the first proper dance of the ball.

I stood, watching on, an island of stillness among the jollity. Everyone in the place seemingly wanted to talk to Henry so that left me at a bit of a loose end. I thought that would leave me prey to Louis but actually he didn't come near me. In fact, I'd go so far as to say that he was actively avoiding me. Not so the rest of the Highlanders. Every man in the place wanted to dance with me, and I was, quite literally, swept off my feet.

Scottish dancing is actually *mad*. Very little of it is that traditional ballroom stuff where you dance with a single partner, like the sort-of-waltz Henry and I had done to open the ball. Most of it is danced in 'reels' – these crazy group dances where you take turns to skip up and down the ballroom, or revolve in huge circles, or thread in and out of other couples. Yes, you dance in pairs, but the pairs are all part of a big communal dance – it's fast, sweaty and fun. The music is really jaunty and catchy, mostly because a big part of it is played on an accordion, not some polite string quartet. Added to that there was lots of whooping and shrieking, not at all like the restrained revolving around the dance floor murmuring politely you see in films like *Royal Wedding*. If I hadn't had the dark shadow of tomorrow hanging over me, looming like the wicker deer on the hill, I would've had the time of my life. The reels were so fast I couldn't really talk to anyone – my partners could do no more than nod and smile and shout helpful instructions about which way to turn, so there was no time to be shy. During the slower dances – like your waltzes and one that was apparently called a strathspey – there was time to talk, and all my partners were extremely charming. All of them asked me about myself, about STAGS, about my journey to Skye, and every single one told me the MacDonald story. It was as if there was a script. And that's

115

when it stopped being charming – I knew they were all doing it for a dinner-party story: the moment they danced with the MacDonald girl the night before she was chased to her death and laid like a human sacrifice on the Bloody Stone beneath the rowan tree. I was already knackered and over it when, right on cue, Henry appeared. 'Want to get something to eat?'

'*Yes*,' I said fervently. I hadn't realised just how hungry I was. Since I'd got lost on the way back from the Peel Tower and then slept, I'd missed lunch completely, and now it was nearly midnight. Plus, I'd been swigging punch between dances on an empty stomach and was starting to feel a bit unsteady. I definitely needed some food, and fast.

17

Henry hauled me off to another long, panelled room, which had an enormous table groaning with food – cold cuts, salads, loaves, cheeses, pâtés and even a hot soup, which Henry told me was called, brilliantly, Cullen Skink. Then there were jellies, trifles, fruit cakes and cream cakes, and at the very end of the table, Scottish cheeses and crackers. I piled my plate high and so did Henry – then, as he saw friendly guests closing in on him, he said, 'Let's find somewhere quieter to eat, shall we?'

'Definitely.'

We reverse-ferreted out of the room and he led me down various passageways and through a pair of double doors into a room that was clearly a library. There were books floor to ceiling, a lovely fire burning in the grate and a pair of French doors with a view of the sea, blue and silver in the moonlight. The fat Labradors I'd met in the family room earlier had wisely relocated here for some peace and quiet, and we had to evict them from the overstuffed armchairs by the fire. They lumbered down grudgingly but sat by our feet drooling hopefully as we gobbled our food. The midnight feast was all delicious and it was some moments before I could speak, but as soon as my hunger was satisfied I asked, mouth still full, 'How did you get on?'

Henry sat back in his chair. 'Everyone was very pleased to see me. Most of them asked where I'd been for the last year. They swallowed the "year out in India" story. And they all gave me their condolences about Father.' It was the first time he had mentioned his dad since he had come back.

'And did they say anything about tomorrow?'

'They just said that I would see some good sport.'

'Anything specifically about me?'

'No, but they all seemed to imply that I was doing a sterling job for the Order by giving you a good evening tonight – lulling you into a false sense of security, giving you a fun time. It's all part of the playbook for the Order's victims. You don't spook the prey before the big day.' He looked at me. 'How about you? What did you learn?'

'Just the "Old MacDonald Had a Battle" story,' I said. 'Over and over again. The MacLeods and their buddies sure feel like they have a score to settle.'

'I'm afraid that's true.'

We fell silent for a moment, and the clock on the mantel struck midnight with a silvery chime. It was the day itself – the day of the Red Hunt, the day when I was to be pursued to my death. My apprehension must have shown in my expression, because Henry leaned forward and took my hand across the fire. His face was, for once, serious.

'Greer,' he said. 'There is no way in this world that I would let anything happen to you. Don't you see? You are –'

Just then the door opened and Cass came into the room. Henry dropped my hand as if *it* was on fire and we both sat back with our plates as if we were having a perfectly innocent snack.

Cass didn't seem to notice anything amiss. 'Ah, there you are,' she said, pulling up a little footstool to sit between us, holding her slim hands out to the fire. 'Good idea to get away from the madding crowd for a bit. Great minds think alike.' She smiled at her cousin. 'What's it like being back from the dead?'

'Exhausting,' said Henry. 'I've had to tell about a hundred people where I've been for the last year.'

Cass put her hand over Henry's where it lay on the arm of the chair. 'Care to make it 101?'

Henry sighed. 'Longcross when the family was at Cumberland Place. Cumberland Place when they were at Longcross. Then India. That's the short version. Then I saw you at your birthday. And on Boxing Day.'

She smiled. 'Louis didn't believe me.'

Henry smiled too. 'He will now.'

Cass looked into the flames. 'Did you ever come up here?'

Henry looked at her, his blue eyes candid. 'It never occurred to me. I know Castle MacLeod is big, but there would still have been the risk of running into dear old Uncle Perry and Aunty Fi.'

'I didn't mean here. I meant the Peel Tower. Our old haunt.'

I had a sharp intake of breath. Despite the firelight, Henry and I froze. He was the first to recover. '*God* no,' he said. 'I haven't been there for years.'

'Same here,' said Cass, to my infinite relief. She turned to me. 'The Peel Tower is that mini castle you can see on the horizon. Look.' She got up and dragged me to my feet, steering me to the window. In the moonlight I could just see the Peel Tower – fortunately with no lights at the windows; either all the rebels had gone to bed, or they were being super cautious. 'Henry and I did it up when we were kids as a little den.'

I disputed that description of a 'little den' – my den when I was a kid consisted of my dad putting a duvet over the dining table. But of course, I wasn't supposed to have seen the tower, so I kept my mouth shut and just nodded interestedly.

'We should go down there,' said Cass, turning back to Henry. 'For old time's sake.'

I held my breath and waited for Henry to put her off. But he was too clever for that. 'That would be fun,' he said. 'But it's going to be a bit busy this weekend. What if you and I make a date to do it after Lammas, once everyone's gone. Just the two of us. It must be pretty mouldy by now – it's been abandoned so long. We could do it up together. Then it really will be like old times.'

Cass looked shiningly happy at this, as if she was lit from the inside instead of by the fire. 'Oh, *do* let's. That would be lovely.'

In the short silence that followed, as I looked out at the moonlight and the silvery gardens, I reflected, as I often had before, that Cass seemed to love her cousin much more than she loved her twin.

Then a face appeared at the window, inches from my own. I cried out and jumped back. 'Jesus *Christ*.'

The face stared at me – ghostly white, raddled by age, milky, unseeing eyes staring straight into my soul.

It was Nanny.

Even stranger – she was totally *naked*. In the light from the library I could see her pendulous breasts hanging down like popped balloons, pale flesh sagging from ancient bones like the wax from a bar-room candle.

Henry was on his feet in an instant and was by my side just in time to see the ghostly shape recede into the darkness. 'What on *earth* . . . ?'

Cass came to my other side. Her reaction, as we watched the old lady glide over the lawn, twig-like hands outstretched, was a little more relaxed. She actually gave an affectionate chuckle. 'Nanny's gone for a wander again.'

'Is she . . . is she *all right*?'

'Perfectly,' said Cass. 'She's always doing this. We're used to it by now. She won't even remember in the morning. I'll ring for a servant to bring her a coat and guide her home.'

She walked to the fireplace and pulled an ornamental bell pull, just as her mother had done the afternoon before.

Still in shock, I watched the pale figure wander the gardens. The old lady was pretty creepy, and hadn't exactly given me the warmest of welcomes, but I still hoped the servant got to her before she wandered over the sea cliffs. 'What is she doing?'

'She wants to meet the wee folk.'

'Who?'

'The faeries.' Cass smiled, a little sadly. 'Do you remember the story of the Faerie Flag? The wee folk brought the baby a blanket when it was cold. She thinks it might happen again. Dunvegan is a thin place.'

'What does *that* mean?'

'It means the veil between this world and the next is as fine as gossamer,' she said poetically. 'The spirits bleed through to the everyday. Nanny thinks if she is out naked in the night, one day the wee folk will clothe her.'

Dear God. The old crone was *literally* away with the fairies. Once again I got the feeling that I was in a curiously godless place, where the normal rules just didn't apply. It didn't bode well for the next day. But before I could question Cass further, the library door opened and a footman appeared.

'My lady?'

'Ah, Campbell. Could you take a coat to Mrs MacPherson – she's out on the Long Lawn again.'

'Certainly, my lady.'

'Oh, and Campbell? Could you have a room made up for Lord Henry, please?'

'At once. Which room, my lady?'

'The Flag Room, of course.'

The footman hesitated for the first time. 'But . . . that's . . . I mean to say . . . isn't that . . . ?'

'Spit it out, man.'

The poor fellow let out a small sigh. 'Isn't that Lord Louis's room, my lady?'

'He won't mind,' said Cass airily.

'Cass,' said Henry warningly.

'*No*,' she said firmly. 'You are the heir of the de Warlencourts.'

'But not the heir of the MacLeods. That's Louis,' he argued.

'You're still the oldest male heir, so the Flag Room is yours by tradition. And I don't need to tell you how strong tradition is here. This honour is *due* to you.' Cass turned back to the footman. 'Put Lord Louis in the South Tower. He'll get over it.'

The footman bowed. 'My lady.'

Cass followed him to the door. 'I'd better go and make sure everything's in order.'

'There's really no need –' began Henry.

'Shhhh.' She placed her forefinger on his lips in a curiously intimate gesture. 'Let me do this for you.' She turned back in the doorway. 'And don't go to bed without talking to me. I've got something to tell you both.'

'About what?'

'About Greer and the Red Hunt.'

I jumped a little. I'd sort of tuned out for this intimate cousin-y moment, but now I was firmly back in the shot. Cass gave an almost imperceptible little nod to the hovering servant. 'Not now. Later. Promise to find me. It's really important.'

Henry looked at me. 'We promise.'

This latest development made me pretty jittery. What was so important that she had to tell me? Of course, I wanted to press her right there and then, but I knew there would be no point so long as the servant was there. I turned back to the window as the door closed behind him and after a few moments saw the footman reappear outside.

He ran to catch up with the old woman, huddled the coat around her and turned her gently round to bring her back to the house. I could see the elderly lady mouthing as she walked, no doubt an incessant babble of word salad. I wondered then if she thought it *was* the faeries who had clothed her, and that made her content.

I wasn't the one naked in the middle of the night, but I was the one who shivered. Henry put his hands on my shoulders and gave me a little shake.

'Come on. I think it's time we had one last dance. If everything goes as we've planned this weekend, we might not be seeing each other again.'

With this troubling thought, I let him lead me back to the dance floor.

18

Back in the ballroom the pace was slowing down somewhat.

The dancing was less frenetic, the music a bit more relaxed. People were still dancing, just in couples now, but the other remaining guests were in huddles, chatting in that subdued small-hours way that people do when they are a little bit tired and a little bit drunk.

Henry led me onto the dance floor and this time we sort of swayed to the music – there was no attempt to pretend that I knew the steps. He held me close and I let him. It had been such a troubling, scary evening that my nerves were in shreds, but uppermost in my mind, above all the background noise of dread and foreboding, was a strong feeling that this was some sort of goodbye. I lifted my head from his shoulder. 'What did you mean when you said one last dance?'

His mouth was very close to mine. He opened it to reply to me, but then someone tapped him sharply on the shoulder.

'Mind if I cut in?'

It was Louis, blond hair ruffled, blue eyes unfocused, kilt askew, bow tie undone. He looked like a much less well-put-together version of Henry. He drew his dark brows together and addressed me, ignoring his cousin.

'You've danced with every other man in this ballroom, Greer. Must be my turn now.'

I'd seen enough movies to know that this was acceptable ballroom etiquette. It was perfectly fine for a gentleman to cut in on another gentleman – even in mid-dance – and claim his partner. It wasn't the most BuzzFeed feminist thing in the world, but I wasn't about to make a scene.

Henry, however, showed a marked reluctance to let me go. 'Louis . . .' he began.

'*No*,' said Louis, his voice thick with drink. 'You've got everything. *Everything*. And you always have had. Could you just give me this One. Little. Thing.'

Henry looked at me once, then released me and stepped back. Louis grabbed hold of me and carted me off to another part of the dance floor.

There was no small talk. 'He's even got my bloody room,' he grumbled.

I sighed. 'I think – from what Cass said – the Flag Room is supposed to be for the heir, or something.'

It was the worst thing I could have said. To think that people were plotting behind his back only enflamed him further. 'He's not the heir to Castle MacLeod!' he almost shouted.

'No, of *course* not,' I said soothingly. 'I think she meant of the de Warlencourts. To the earldom.'

This was even worse – it only served to remind him of what he had lost. There was no danger of him standing on my foot now, as it was firmly in my mouth. His jaw tightened. 'For now.'

'What's that supposed to mean?'

'Things can happen to the line of succession,' he said nastily. 'Look at what happened to his dear papa. To Uncle Rollo. You eat the wrong thing, drink the wrong thing, and *pffft*.'

I looked at him sharply. 'What do you know about that?'

He presented a bland, innocent face to me. 'What is there to know?'

'You tell me,' I shot back. 'Officially he fell from his horse. Then his . . . body . . . was conveniently burned up by the fire. No post-mortem. But we have it on very good authority that he was poisoned.'

He looked completely caught out by that, and that's when I knew the answer to the Agatha Christie country-house mystery I'd pondered on Boxing Day: Who Poisoned Rollo de Warlencourt? Shafeen and I had been the only people who'd been told, by the family doctor, what had really happened to Rollo. The only other person who knew what had happened was the murderer, and I was certain that I was dancing with him now.

Even Louis seemed to abandon any pretence at innocence. 'I'm just saying, dear Henry should be careful.'

That scared me. I'd spent so much time worrying about what would happen to me, I hadn't really thought about Henry being in serious danger. But in the face of Louis's hatred, it might take a bit more than a bit of red thread and a rowan twig to save him. I looked around for him, ready to knock any food or drink out of his hand. Henry was nowhere to be seen – no doubt he was trapped in conversation with some guest.

But I did see someone else.

A silver-haired old man, in Highland dress, was standing in the middle of a malignant circle of Medievals. All his little acolytes were talking to him animatedly, like kids badgering Santa Claus for Christmas presents – except the Medievals would definitely be on the naughty list. Then, as if he felt me looking at him, the old man turned around.

It was the Abbot.

Not Abbot Ridley – the *Old* Abbot. The benign, bearded, lovely old headmaster who'd interviewed me for STAGS. The man who'd turned out to be anything but benign – all along he'd been the Grand Master of the Dark Order of the Grand Stag. He'd started life as the 'honourable' Gideon Foster, but if Aadhish Jadeja's diary was to be believed, Gideon was the least honourable person in the world. Gideon was the little toerag who'd relentlessly bullied Aadhish and all but raped Ina the kitchen maid on the rooftops of Longcross.

I stood frozen to the spot, in the middle of the dance floor, as the Abbot met my eyes for the second time in his life. I remembered the first time very well and could play the scene now in my mind as if I were watching a movie. I was sitting in the chapel in STAGS, just after that first fateful weekend at Longcross. I'd thought Henry was dead, and that the Order had died with him. But then, as the Abbot had been giving the memorial address for his fallen pupil, I'd met his eyes. I'd realised in that moment who he really was – that he was still running the cult and that the Order was very much alive. And then, of course, he'd disappeared. He'd faked his death, to be replaced by Abbot Ridley, and vanished as effectively as Keyser Söze.

I'd seen him twice since – or rather, heard him. He had presided over my trial in the de Warlencourt playhouse at STAGS, and had conducted the Red Mass in the ancient undercroft of Cumberland Place, cowled in his red hooded robe, with antlers crowning his forehead. And now here he was again, at Castle MacLeod, to witness the final act: my execution.

Now, as he met my eyes, he smiled and, unbelievably, raised his glass in my direction.

I felt dizzy with fear. I was whirling around the ballroom; the ballroom was whirling around me.

I had to get out.

There was a door open to the outside, to the cool night, to the blessed fresh air.

I broke from Louis's arms and ran.

19

I gulped the cool night air thankfully as I walked across the dark terrace, as far away from the castle as the balustrade would allow.

But somebody had beaten me to it and was standing looking out onto the dark ornamental gardens. I would know Henry's silhouette anywhere. He was peacefully enjoying a cigarette, the clouds of smoke catching at the moonlight, and a flute of champagne stood sparkling on the wall. He couldn't have been more Gatsby if he tried.

At the sound of my footsteps he turned, and at the sight of my face he stepped forward. 'Are you all right?'

'Not really,' I said. 'I've just been renewing an old acquaintance. The Dishonourable Gideon Villiers, aka the Old Abbot.'

'Ah.' He took a final drag on his dwindling cigarette. 'I thought he'd turn up. He is the boss of the whole damned shooting match, after all.'

I leaned on the balustrade next to him, grateful for the cold stone after the heat of the ballroom. 'Well, he scared the bejeezus out of me.'

He shrugged elegantly. 'It's actually good, if you think about it. When we catch them at it, we want to catch them all. We don't want the biggest fish getting away.'

'I suppose,' I agreed.

Unhurriedly he ground his cigarette out on the wall and put the stub neatly in his pocket. He really had changed.

'Time was you'd have chucked that onto the lawn.' I picked at a frill of lichen on the balustrade. 'Remember the grate in the Paulinus well? It used to be stuffed with fag ends from all you Medievals. It was rank.'

He smiled, almost to himself. 'Maybe I have a newfound respect for life.'

'If you had a newfound respect for life,' I pointed out, 'you'd quit smoking.'

'Done,' he said, swiping his palms across each other three times in a gesture of finality.

'What?'

'I just gave up.'

'Why?'

'Because you told me to,' he said simply.

'I'm not sure I'm comfortable with that level of power,' I said truthfully.

'Well, you're the only one who has it,' he said. 'I wouldn't change for anyone else.'

I thought hard, trying to articulate what I wanted to say. 'I don't want you to change just because you're trying to impress me,' I said. 'I want you to change because you're truly sorry, and that you . . . *repent*.' I hadn't meant to use such a religious word, but it was the one that fitted best.

'I *am* sorry,' he said. 'There's one girl in particular on my conscience.'

'Well, that's what I'm talking about,' I said. 'You hurt more than just me.'

'I don't mean you. I mean Gemma Delaney.'

I hadn't thought about Gemma for so long it took me a moment to realise who he was talking about. Gemma Delaney had been a few years above me at Bewley Park Comprehensive School in Manchester. She'd gone to STAGS on a scholarship three years before I went; in fact, she was how I knew there even was a scholarship to try for. Then, once I was a pupil at STAGS too, she'd warned me not to go to Longcross for the Justitium weekend of huntin' shootin' fishin'. She'd been the year before, and the experience had transformed her completely – from a happy, confident girl into a grey ghost.

Henry looked out over the dark gardens. 'Before Gemma I was a spectator. Guilty as hell, yes, but too young to be an instigator. Hers was the first weekend that I ran. We stopped short of killing her, but we damned near frightened her to death.'

'What happened?' I said warily, hardly wanting to know.

'We nearly chased her off the waterfall. *The* waterfall – Conrad's Force.'

'But you didn't.'

'No,' he said shortly.

'Who stopped it?' I persisted.

'I did.'

'You see!' I crowed. 'Even then you must have had some good in you.'

132

'No,' he countered. 'I thought her death would be difficult to cover up. It was cowardice, not compassion.' He shook his head. 'Still, the experience changed her. She wasn't the same girl once we got back to school.'

I wasn't about to let him off the hook. 'No,' I said. 'She wasn't.'

'For her, if not for all the others, I deserve what's coming to me. I don't know how else to atone. I've got to pay for what I've done. What else can I do?'

I turned my back on the balustrade. 'You could apologise.'

'If I ever get the chance, I will. But there will also be a reckoning for me. Has to be, doesn't there? You have to settle your account sometime.'

'Is that what you meant before? When you said you might not be seeing me again after this weekend?'

Henry turned too, looked at the brightly lit castle and sighed. 'We are about to let the world in on this thing. There will be outside agencies – the police, Scotland Yard. Not just the tame plods that are in the pay of the Order, but hard-eyed professionals. What do you think they will make of someone like me?'

'But you were so young,' I protested. I wasn't sure why I was defending him.

'No excuse. The age of criminal responsibility is sixteen. When Gemma came to Longcross I was already that age.'

'But now you're on our side. You're *assisting* us.'

'That may help my case. But whichever way you look at it, I'm still in fifty kinds of trouble.'

'You mean –' I could hardly say the word – 'prison?'

133

'Quite possibly. And for a very long time. Attempted murder is quite the rap sheet.'

I stared. The notion of Henry behind bars was quite, quite unbearable. 'Can't you run?'

'I've been running for a year, Greer. It's time to stop.' He touched my cheek. 'Cheer up,' he said. 'There are worse things.'

'Like what?' I said, desolate.

'This whole redemption thing,' he said precisely, 'is for one reason and one reason alone: to rehabilitate myself in *your* eyes. I'd rather go to prison than have you think badly of me.'

'Don't go to prison!' I blurted.

He smiled gently. 'How can I avoid it?'

'When this is all over, don't hand yourself in. Run away again.'

'Why?'

I couldn't speak.

'Give me a reason.'

Our faces were very close together again – as close as they'd been when we danced. I whispered into his mouth. 'You know the reason.'

'I want to hear you say it.' His breath was warm and sweet.

'Because . . .' The truth was surprisingly hard to say. 'Because . . . because I . . .' I couldn't say it. 'Because I care about what happens to you.'

'That will do for now.'

Then his mouth was on mine, his hands in my hair. For a moment I kissed him back, hard, overwhelmed by the rightness of it. This was nothing like the fairy-tale kiss we'd shared on the rooftops of Longcross more than a year ago. That was for schoolkids. This was the big league, dark, urgent, passionate. A kiss between adults.

Then there was the scrape of a footfall on the terrace and we sprang apart.

'*There* you are!'

It was Cass. She had an odd light in her blue eyes as she walked towards us. I wondered if she was drunk like her twin, but that didn't quite seem to fit. Despite the hour, she looked completely wired. 'Time to say goodnight, I think.'

It wasn't entirely clear whether she meant us, or her.

'Yes, it's terribly late,' said Henry smoothly, recovering his composure much faster than I did. 'Goodnight, little cousin.'

He kissed her on the cheek, and I marvelled that two kisses could be so different – the one he'd given me and the affectionate familial one he gave Cass. How could a pair of lips be so . . . versatile?

Cass gave me a tight smile. 'Goodnight.' And she turned to go.

Just as she was crossing the terrace Henry called her back. 'Cass.'

She turned.

'What did you want to tell us? About Greer, and the Red Hunt?'

Her blue gaze slid away. 'Nothing. It's not important.' Then a radiant smile. 'See you tomorrow. On the hunt!' And she disappeared into the noise and light of the ballroom.

Then I knew, clear as day.

I looked at Henry, appalled. 'She saw. She saw everything.'

'Yes,' he said.

But it was worse than that. *So* much worse.

Far above us, I heard that very faint but unmistakable whine, like an insect but mechanical instead of organic. I looked up and saw the single red eye of the drone.

The HAWK.

Shafeen's parting words came back to me.

The moment you step outside, we'll be watching you.

The HAWK had seen us.

And that meant Shafeen had too.

20

'Oh my God. Oh my *God.*' I was beside myself, flapping around the terrace like an injured bird. 'How do we fix this?'

'Not much we can do,' Henry said fatalistically, watching the HAWK bank and turn back to the Peel Tower. 'What's done is done.'

'What do we do now?'

'You could come up to my room and see the Faerie Flag,' he said flippantly.

'Are you kidding?' I brayed. I pointed to the HAWK, jabbing the night sky with my forefinger. 'They *saw.* They all *saw. Shafeen* saw. And you're hitting on me with the Medieval equivalent of "come up and see my etchings"?'

'Shhh.' He grabbed my pointing hand and forced it down to my side. 'Stop shrieking. You'll give the whole game away.'

'This is *your* fault,' I spat. Our faces were almost as close now as when we'd kissed, but the sentiments were miles apart.

'Yes. A hundred per cent.' He looked down at me and half smiled. 'Well – perhaps ninety per cent.'

He was right. I'd kissed him back; he knew it and I knew it. And I was the one already in a relationship, not him. He shouldn't have done what he did, but I *definitely* shouldn't have done what I did. I had to deflect from my guilt, had to find fault with him, so I picked on his smile. 'You think this is *funny?*'

'No,' he said evenly. 'For me this is deadly serious. You know I love you. You know I want you. I've made no secret of it. And if Shafeen has to find out this way, then I'm sorry, but that's just the way it is.'

'Find out about *what?*' I raged. '*This!*' I pointed to myself, to him and then back again. 'This isn't *anything*. There's *nothing* going on here. There's nothing for him to find out *about*.'

Henry calmly put his hands in his pockets. 'If you say so.'

I felt wretched and began to pace up and down the terrace. 'I have to go to the Peel Tower.'

'Don't be insane,' he said reasonably. 'It's two in the morning.'

He was right, but it was unbearable to hear. I wanted to run to Shafeen *now*, to explain, to feel his arms around me, and to be prevented from that was torture. I couldn't stand myself. I wanted to rip off the itchy tartan, the scratchy lace dress, my very skin itself. 'Then I'm going to bed.'

He perked up. 'Good idea.'

'*My* bed.'

'Oh. Let me escort you then.'

'No,' I said. 'No *way*. You just . . . stay there.'

I could barely look at him. In fact, it was more than that. I knew I *couldn't* look at him – if I saw him there, in that *Rob Roy* Highland gear, looking into my eyes, I would be lost. But as I turned and fled I could feel his eyes on me, and however many six-foot stone walls I put between him and me it would not be enough to keep that damned blue gaze out of my soul.

21

I woke to a dawn as grey as my grubby conscience.

I'd only had a few hours' rest, but it was hopeless trying to get back to sleep. I went to have a bath, as it was pretty cold in my organ pipe of a tower, wrapped myself in a robe and went to sit in the window seat. I looked at the Peel Tower in the light of the breaking day and thought of Shafeen inside it.

What was he doing?

What was he thinking?

I felt dreadful for him – in addition to dealing with my betrayal, he was most probably having to fold his long body onto the sofa while new lovers Ratio and Ty made full use of the bed in the boys' room. I imagined their budding love only made him feel worse.

I missed Nel very much too – usually in a crisis I would talk things over with her – but if I couldn't get to the Peel Tower I was cut off from my best friend too.

I took my phone off charge and carried it back to the window seat. There were still no bars at all, so I don't know why I'd even bothered charging it. But I wrote Shafeen a desperate, heartfelt text.

```
I know what you saw. I'm so sorry. I want to
explain.
```

But I didn't even know how I would begin to explain it. I knew what had prompted the kiss – I'd been devastated at the thought that Henry might go to prison, and I'd admitted that I cared for him. But I couldn't see how I'd justify all that to Shafeen – surely to admit I had feelings for Henry would make things even worse. It was true that I didn't instigate the kiss, but even the HAWK would've been able to see that I didn't exactly pull away either. For the thousandth time I relived the moment – Henry's body pressed against me, his lips on mine, his hands in my hair, my hands in his. That kiss had shattered me, blown me apart, and I had no idea how to put myself together again. And if I was absolutely honest with myself, almost as devastating as the thought that it had happened was the thought that it must never happen again. In order to push that uncomfortable thought away, I picked up the phone again and added a deliberate lie.

```
I want you and only you x
```

I pressed send, but the phone, as if it knew I was fibbing, just put that little clock icon in the bottom right of the text box, which meant it was waiting for a signal to send. It was almost as if the device itself was saying, Greer, I'm going to give you time to *think* about this.

There was a knock at my door, and when I opened it Henry stood outside. Of course. Who else would it be? My treacherous

140

heart sped up, and my treacherous hands reached to arrange my wet hair.

He didn't even have the grace to look sheepish. He looked well rested, happy and as handsome as ever in his country walking clothes. I supposed last night was as big a triumph for him as it was a disaster for me.

'You'd better come in,' I growled ungraciously.

He bounced into the room, all Tiggerish. 'I thought you'd be awake.'

'You try having a restful lie-in if you think it's the day of your death.'

He went straight to my wardrobe and started chucking clothes on the bed. 'I suspected you might be in a pessimistic mood,' he said. 'So we're going on a little trip to take your mind off things. In view of last night's events, I'll let you select the underwear.'

'Gee, thanks.' I fingered the garments on the bed. Tough twill trousers, checked shirt, padded green waistcoat, Barbour. Good country clothes, just like his. Where are we going?' I looked up hopefully 'The Peel Tower?'

'Too dangerous. We can't go there again, not after what Cass said. What if she sees us? Or even worse, comes and joins us?'

A lump rose to my throat. 'If something happens to me tonight, I will never get the chance to explain to Shafeen.'

He looked serious for the first time. 'Nothing's going to happen to you tonight. I'd rather die myself than let that happen.'

That reminded me. 'When I was dancing with Louis last

night, he all but admitted to poisoning your father on Boxing Day.'

For a moment Henry looked furiously angry. But then you could almost see him mentally parking this revelation to act on later. 'Did he indeed?' he said lightly.

'Yes,' I said. 'Be careful what you eat and drink while you're here. He's got rid of one obstacle; I wouldn't bet against him trying to get rid of another.'

'Well, he won't have been anywhere near this.' He shook two brown paper packets at me. 'I've packed us breakfast myself. Straight from the kitchen.'

'I didn't know you could cook,' I said, with some surprise.

'I don't know that I can,' he replied. 'I may have been born with a silver spoon in my mouth, but I do know how to make a sandwich.'

I detected another change in him. I couldn't imagine the old Henry making a snack for himself rather than getting a servant to do it. Was this to do with me too? I decided that after the events of last night I needed to see Henry as a project, not a person. I was an intervention, and he was my personal outreach programme. All those other, dangerous feelings had to be kept at bay. I was with Shafeen – if he'd still have me – and that was that.

'Come on,' said Henry. 'Day's wasting.'

'Come on where?'

'Get dressed and all will be revealed. I'll see you downstairs, under the pistols.'

When he'd gone I looked at the clothes he'd assembled. I didn't really feel like a jaunt, but what else was I going to do all day? Sit around and wait for sunset and the inevitable attempt on my life? I started, rapidly, to dress.

In less than five minutes I joined Henry under the crossed pistols in the entrance hall, the Judas and Jesus pair from Aadhish's diary. 'Where are we going?'

'We're going hawking. I thought it was better than you moping about all day. The Red Hunt doesn't start until this evening so that's quite a lot of moping,' he said, echoing exactly what I'd been thinking. And if I wasn't consumed with guilt about Shafeen and God-knows-what about Henry, I would have been madly interested. I loved the idea of hawking – had been fascinated by the working-class falconry of films like *Kes*, and the much posher falconry of films like *Elizabeth*. So even I perked up when we crossed the green inner courtyard of the castle and followed the curtain wall round to the falconers' mews. We walked through an attractive walled garden, which captured the early-morning sun, into a long, low building, which had clearly been here as long as the castle itself.

'Here we are,' said Henry. Beyond a studded, wooden door was an interior lit by arched windows. Hawks of various sizes turned their heads sharply as we entered, fixing us with their yellow eyes and shifting on their blocks.

There was a heavy-set middle-aged guy scattering fresh-smelling sawdust under each perch. To my surprise he was wearing a faded kilt – clearly that famous garment was not just for fancy ballrooms but for the working day too.

Henry hailed him. 'Hello, Murdo.'

The guy shoved his tweed cap to the back of his head and started chuckling. 'Well, Mr Henry. I heard you'd come back. Must be two years since I seen you. You're a sight for sore eyes.'

'So are you, Murdo.' Henry shook the man's hand warmly. I'd never seen him be so nice to a servant before. I noticed the two men shook with their left hands, and I remembered Shafeen telling me once that this was how swordsmen shook, as they had their swords in their right hands. In this case it was not because Murdo was holding a sword, but he did have a stiff leather glove on one hand, which went all the way up to his elbow. 'This is Greer.' I noticed, gratefully, that Henry didn't give my surname – or, as it was known here, my clan name. Murdo nodded cheerfully at me. 'Mistress.'

'Murdo is Castle MacLeod's Master Falconer,' Henry said, with some reverence. 'Can we take Regina out?' he asked, almost deferentially. I got the idea that when you were in the mews, the Master Falconer was king, and no one, not even the heir to the family, could just walk off with a bird whenever he wanted.

'That you can, Mr Henry. She's not fed yet, so she'll be nice and sharp. There's a couple o' gauntlets on the hooks there.' Henry took down two stiff leather gloves from the wall, and we walked along the perches, the birds shifting their feet and fluttering their wings at our presence.

'Don't look them in the eye,' warned Henry as we walked. 'They don't like it.'

'Divas,' I joked. 'Just like movie stars.'

We stopped in front of a particularly beautiful bird with petrol-blue feathers, a creamy white breast and gorgeous eyes like nuggets of amber. At the sight of Henry she began to whicker, making a bubbling, throaty little chuckle in her throat. Henry caressed her breast feathers with the back of his scarred fingers. 'Hello, Regina,' he said. 'She remembers me,' he called to Murdo.

'Aye, they've good memories, Mr Henry. Better'n men.'

Henry looked genuinely touched. 'I was there when she was made, you see. Murdo and I took her out her very first time.'

'Made?' I asked.

'Taught to kill.'

'Ha.' I nodded sagely. 'Just like gangsters.'

'What?'

'They use the same terminology in movies like *Goodfellas*. You're "made" once you've committed a murder.'

'Ah,' said Henry. 'Well, there you go. Normally young hawks are "made" by the older ones. But if a falconer trains an eyess – a hawk taken from the nest – he's got to show her how instead. Now,' he said, 'we need to hood her and put her in a basket.' He brought over something that looked like a cat basket but taller. I was slightly disappointed. 'I thought she'd ride on our wrists, like you see in films.'

Henry smiled and gave me one of the gloves. 'Well, let's have a go. If she comes to you, grab hold of the jesses – those are the leather straps attached to her feet, with the bells on.'

I pulled on the stiff gauntlet and Henry guided my arm until it was level with the block. I gathered the jesses, and the hawk, after considering me for a moment, hopped onto the glove. My wrist nearly hit the pavings, she was so heavy. Regina promptly lost her footing and dangled upside down, enormous wings spread and flapping, shrieking bloody murder. 'You're witnessing what we call a "bate",' shouted Henry above the row, 'which is a full-on hawk tantrum. Keep her steady. They don't like changing levels.'

'I'm trying,' I complained, regaining my balance as the hawk righted herself on my wrist, fluttering her feathers angrily. 'I don't mean to fat-shame your hawk, but she weighs a ton.'

'And that,' he said, 'is why the basket. It's all very well to carry them for a bit, but with anything bigger than a merlin, your arm would soon get tired.'

'A merlin?'

'The littlest hawk. Hold her steady – I'll hood her.'

He slipped a little leather hood, sewn with ornamental stiches and decorated with feathers, over Regina's head and transferred the hawk to the basket. The hood worked some sort of magic because despite that hissy fit on my wrist she went into the basket with no fuss at all. 'Do you trust us to take her out without you, Murdo?' Henry called across to the Master Falconer.

'Aye, that I do,' he said with a twinkle. 'Never seen such a natural with a hawk,' he said to me. 'Regina and Mr Henry are kindred spirits.'

Henry packed a leather satchel with various other bits and pieces I couldn't identify, and we took the basket out through the precincts of the castle. We walked to the craggy cliffs a little way along the coast. The day was sunny, but a strong sea breeze blew, whipping my hair around my face. 'Right,' said Henry. 'Let's get Regina out.'

He talked to her quietly as he handled her, low-voiced

all the time – his tone at an even pitch, his calm chatter soothing the hawk. 'If you hold her for a sec, we'll try to get her to stoop to the lure,' he said, a sentence that was incomprehensible to me. I took Regina on my glove, holding tight to the jesses, while he produced from the satchel a bizarre-looking object that looked a lot like a dead bird.

'What the hell is that?'

'This is the lure,' he said. 'It's a canvas bag half full of sand. These are a pair of chicken wings, attached to the sides, and I've wrapped some strips of mouse meat around it.'

'Lovely,' I said. 'Now what?'

'Now,' he said, attaching a leather leash to the bag, 'I'm going to go a little distance away. When I start swinging the lure you take Regina's hood off, and she's going to fly to me when I whistle.'

He walked away across the seagrass, and when he was probably a hundred metres away he turned to face me. I could see he had a small silver whistle dangling from his lips like a cigarette. He began to swing the lure in a wide vertical circle, and I suddenly remembered this strange ballet from the movie *Kes*. Slightly nervously, I took off Regina's little leather hood. The hawk looked about her, spotting her falconer at once. After a few revolutions of the lure Henry blew the whistle and Regina took off at pace, with an immense wingbeat that all but knocked me over. She flew like a bullet at the gross mock-bird Henry was swinging, but at the last moment, as her talons stretched, Henry swung the lure in a wide arc around his body and began to circle on the other side. The hawk checked, banked around and came back for another go, bells jingling, and Henry did the same again. After the third dummy strike he lowered the lure, and instinctively I held out my fist, just in time to let Regina land. She clutched my forearm, swung a little and settled, beak open and panting. We looked at each other with pride. Henry ran to us and fed her something unspeakable from the satchel. 'A chicken neck,' he said, laughing at my expression. 'They don't eat birdseed, you know.'

I laughed too, with sheer exhilaration. I was hooked. I loved hawking, and I loved having Regina on my wrist. I grinned at Henry. 'I feel so Medieval I could burst.'

'You look it too.' Henry grinned back. 'It's the bob, I think. You look like a young Joan of Arc.'

I breathed in the fresh air happily. It was ridiculous to be so content, what with the Order of the Stag gunning for me and the whole Shafeen situation, but, so far as living in the present went, it would be hard to find a more perfect moment. The loveliness of the day, the hawk on my wrist, the natural beauty of the sea and the cliffs, and the man-made beauty of the castle in the distance; whatever dark fate awaited me that night it was a hell of a last day to live, if that was what it was.

'Let's try her on some live prey, now she's got her eye in,' said Henry. He took Regina to his wrist and flew her at a passing gull. Hopped up by her adventures with the lure, Regina gave chase at once, mounting high above her prey far beyond the cliff edge and over the open sea. Henry bit his lip as he watched with far-seeing blue eyes. Regina and the gull were mere dots in the stinging blue, the hawk's bells growing fainter.

'Will she get him?' I asked anxiously.

'I think so,' he said. 'He's a black-headed gull, so quite small. Not one of those enormous white herring gulls you see. If she strikes over the water though, she might lose him. She needs to drive him back inland.'

As if Regina had heard her master she switched and drove the panicked gull back towards us. The hawk dropped like a stone, yellow feet splayed like stars, and struck hard and once. Falcon and gull hit the deck in a confusion of feathers. Henry ran to Regina and picked her up from the tough seagrass, carrying her back to me. The hawk sat proudly on his wrist, clutching her grisly trophy.

'Ugh,' I said, with a queasy glance at Regina's prey. 'Why did you chop the gull's head off?'

'That wasn't me,' said Henry. 'That was her. Hawks hunt with their feet – she would have taken its head off when she struck.'

Jeez. The hunt really was cruel in all its forms, and I couldn't help identifying with the poor gull. But at the same time, I had to admit there was something beautiful – and natural – about what I'd just witnessed.

'Let's peg her out and let her have her lunch,' said Henry. 'And we should have ours.' He threaded Regina's leash through a wooden peg, which he drove firmly into the grass, and she settled quite happily to strip what remained of her quarry.

I hadn't realised how starving I was, because of course lunch was breakfast too. We sat in the sun and devoured our sandwiches with the same gusto with which Regina devoured her gull. While we ate Henry talked to me about falconry and taught me 'hawk talk' – there was so much terminology to get your head around. Wings were called 'sails', talons 'petty

149

singles'. Female hawks were falcons, male hawks tiercels. There was even a falconer's knot, which you could tie with one hand, while your hawk sat on the other. He told me about the stages of the flight of a hawk – it would mount, circle, soar, 'wait on' the prey and then stoop in a sudden dive. And there was always a chance that a hawk would 'rake away' – just fly off and return to the wild. 'Then they become a passager again,' said Henry, a little sadly.

'Passenger?'

'Passager. A wild hawk.'

We sat in a friendly silence, windburned and happy, munching away. The sandwiches, doorsteps of soft bread stuffed with ham and cheese, were actually delicious. I looked approvingly at Henry, as the breeze ruffled his blond hair. 'I think you might have a talent for cookery,' I said. 'Maybe you should consider ditching the servants and doing a bit more for yourself.'

He smiled. 'Maybe I will.' He got up and brushed the crumbs off his country clothes. 'Come on. Let's try to fly her once more before we go back.'

This time Henry flew Regina from his wrist – the other way this time, inland in the direction of the Peel Tower. We watched the hawk mount, soar and circle, just as Henry had said, and scout the ground with her sharp eyes, looking for some unfortunate mouse or vole.

But then, a dark shadow overhead. I squinted into the sun. Had some other, bigger raptor come to hover even higher than Regina and take her down?

I was half right. It was not a hawk, but *the* HAWK. Sleek and forbidding, in a black cruciform, the single red eye shining and the rotors spinning like blades, the HAWK hovered, waiting. Regina was spooked and shrieked at the sight of the drone. She circled, flapping clumsily, and dropped out of the sky like a stone.

22

Regina landed on Henry's fist, shifting and muttering, unsettled by the strange predator in her skies.

The HAWK, just as it had done the night before, hovered nosily for a moment, then banked and whirred back in the direction of the Peel Tower.

I felt like the sun had gone in – the lovely day was now ruined. I couldn't help thinking about how our little outing must look to Shafeen. That after that kiss at the ball I was off in the beautiful Highlands with Henry, doing montage-y stuff and looking for all the world as if we were together. I wished I could hold up a bunch of cue cards to the sky, *Love Actually* style, and say:

I'm not really with Henry

We're not together

I'm yours

Henry soothed the hawk on his fist. 'I don't think she'll go up again today,' he said, hooding her and slipping the leather leash through the jesses. 'The drone frightened her. Plus she's full, and that loses them their edge. They hunt for food, not sport.'

'Unlike you.' My guilt over Shafeen made me lash out.

He grimaced. 'I suppose I deserve that.'

He carried Regina on his glove, I took the basket, and we began to walk back towards the castle.

Henry shot a sideways glance at me. 'Did you enjoy yourself?'

There was no hiding it. 'Yes.'

'Do you remember that day on Longmere, when we caught the brown trout?'

'I'm hardly likely to forget that. That was the day I thought you were trying to kill me.'

He didn't deny it. 'I still thought I would spare you, even on that day. D'you know why?'

'Because you liked me?'

He smiled. 'That, of course. But it was because I thought you liked the kill. I saw something in you that I recognised in myself. And I saw it again today. Was I wrong?'

'No,' I admitted. 'I did enjoy catching the fish. And I did enjoy it today when Regina stooped at the gull.' I struggled to articulate what I wanted to say and thought suddenly of the movie of *Lord of the Flies*. 'I think we all have that killer instinct under all our layers of civilisation. It's just about how deep it's buried. We are all Savages. Or rather, Medievals.' I shot a glance at him. 'Did your father teach you to kill?'

'Yes.'

I thought about that. 'Such an odd thing to do with your son.'

'It was one of the only times we bonded,' he said sadly.

153

'It's no excuse, but he was never happy when I knew him. The only thing that pleased him was hunting – outdoors and indoors too.'

'What do you mean?'

He sighed. 'You might as well know. No housemaid was safe from him.'

'You mean . . .'

'Yes.'

'But he was gay!'

'It was like he had something to prove. I guess he was trying so hard to be straight.'

'Tough on the girls,' I said, thinking of poor Ina, the kitchen maid.

'Oh, undoubtedly. My grandfather had to keep sacking them – because then, of course, they were girls with a "bad reputation", through no fault of their own.'

'*Droit de seigneur*,' I said.

'Indeed.'

'Gideon set him off down that path,' I said. 'In Aadhish's diary, it was the Abbot, when he was young, who was harassing Ina, the kitchen maid. I guess your father followed his example.'

'Still, that's no excuse. He took out his own unhappiness on others. He just wanted to hunt and destroy.'

I thought about that as we strode along in silence for a while. 'I wish . . .'

Both he and the hawk looked at me, their gaze oddly similar. 'What do you wish?'

'This is going to sound like an odd thing to say, but I wish you knew him as I did. I wish you'd known . . . Horatio.'

154

'Who the hell is Horatio?'

'Rollo used to call Aadhish Hardy, and Aadhish used to call Rollo Horatio. And Horatio was quite a different person to the Rollo you knew. Horatio was young and in love. Oh, he was the arrogant young lord of the manor, but he could be funny, tender, charming.' *Just like you*, I thought, but I didn't say anything out loud. *Distance*, I reminded myself. *Distance.* 'I could ask Shafeen if he would let you read the diary. If,' I said ruefully, 'he ever speaks to me again. I think . . . I think if Rollo and Aadhish had been allowed to be together, your father could have been really happy.'

'But I wouldn't have been born, and nor would Shafeen,' Henry pointed out. 'I suppose then you wouldn't have a problem,' he joked darkly.

'My point is,' I said sternly, 'that Rollo used to be a different person. And I wish you'd known that person.'

'So what you're really saying is that not getting to be with the person you love can blight not just your entire life, but your character too.'

'Yes, I suppose I am, really.' I thought about that. 'But what if Shafeen is the one I'm supposed to be with?'

'Well, obviously I would dispute that. But if you *are* meant to be together, he'd be a fool to let you go for a kiss. He should only let you go if . . .' He tailed off.

'If what?'

'If you had true feelings for another.'

Once again I wouldn't, *couldn't* look at him. He sighed, ruffling Regina's feathers, and the hawk chirruped and shifted on his glove. 'If you want, I can tell him that it was all me. The kiss, I mean. I'll take the blame and make it right with him. If that's really what you want.'

'It is.' I tried to sound as definite as possible.

'You're sure?' He sounded completely desolate.

I looked at the bird, not him. 'You and me,' I said desperately, 'how would it really work? We're from different worlds. I played with Hello Kitty as a kid. You played with hawks. The only working-class kid I know who's ever owned a hawk is the boy in *Kes*.'

'Who?'

'This film from the sixties. About a northern kid from a council flat who befriends a kestrel and trains it.'

'Ah, yes,' said Henry. 'Well, that used to be perfectly commonplace. A kestrel for a knave. You know that book I was reading on the way up to Scotland?'

'The one about St Albans?'

'It's not *about* St Albans. It was written *in* St Albans.'

'What's it about then?'

'Huntin' shootin' fishin',' he said. 'What else? There's a big bit on hawking. And one of the things it says is that hawks were for everyone. There were birds for everyone in society.' He looked at the bird on his fist and quoted, as if to her: '"An Eagle for an Emperor, a Gyrfalcon for a King; a Peregrine for a Prince, a Saker for a Knight, a Merlin for a Lady; a Goshawk for a Yeoman, a Sparrowhawk for a Priest, a Musket for a Holy Water Clerk, a Kestrel for a Knave." So, you see, your film was quite right.'

'And when was that written? The Book of St Albans, I mean?'

'1486.'

'So back when people were *actually* Medievals.' I looked at the hawk on his fist. 'And what's Regina?'

'A peregrine.'

'Like your uncle.'

He smiled somewhat bitterly. 'Yes, I suppose so.'

'And peregrines are for a prince, right?'

'Right.'

'See, you're making my point for me,' I said. 'There's always a hierarchy, isn't there? Even with hawks. That's why we could never work. I live in a council flat; you live in a castle.'

He thought about that. 'You just held up the example of my father and Aadhish. They were from very different worlds. Yet you say they were in love and should have been left alone to be together.'

'Yes, but they were at least the same *class*. What divided them was convention – the rules of society at the time. Attitudes have changed towards homosexuality, but if this whole STAGS thing has taught me anything it's that the dial hasn't shifted one bit on class. If we were to . . . be together, how would it work? Would we settle at Longcross, as Lord and Lady de Warlencourt?'

He laughed. 'I'm nineteen, you're eighteen. I think we're a bit young to be settling down. I'm not offering you my hand in marriage.'

'Then what are you offering me?'

'My heart,' he said simply.

These two words, so direct, so heartfelt, threw me, but I had to be strong. 'You know I'm going to Oxford.'

'Good. So you should. I'd wait.'

'Eventually I want to direct films.'

'Then do that.'

'*And* be the lady of the manor? We'd live in your ancestral home, amid the ghosts of all the children who were hunted over the years? I'd be a county wife, like your mum, sitting on all the village committees, opening the house once a year for garden parties, reading the lesson in church at Christmas? That's not me, Henry. It just wouldn't work.'

For the first time, he seemed to have no comeback. Then he said, almost hopelessly, 'Surely love should be enough?'

'Tell that to Rollo and Aadhish.'

We were almost back at the castle and fell silent as we crossed the courtyard to the mews. These were conversations that mustn't be overheard, but in the mews Murdo was nowhere to be seen, and there was only the company of raptors to hear us. Henry put Regina back on her block, cleaned off her beak and talons, spread her wings with gentle fingers to make sure no feathers were broken and secured her leash to the block, presumably with the falconers' knot he'd told me about. I'd never seen him take such care with anything before, except perhaps me. Henry stroked the falcon's feathery breast in farewell, with that new tenderness I detected in him. He met my eyes over the hawk's head. 'What if it's me?'

'What if what's you?'

'What if it's me you are meant to be with? And you who I am meant to be with? To deny that would blight both our lives.'

The thought was dreadful, and the most dreadful thing about it was that now he'd put the thought in my head. The notion of that – being forever infected with a kind of *what if?* – made me especially curt to him.

'Forget it, Henry. It's best if you do. I'll see you tonight.'

He and the hawk watched me go, their expressions alike once more: noble, remote and desolate.

23

I went straight back to my tower, as I wasn't hungry for lunch after those doorstep sandwiches.

I also didn't fancy getting changed and running the gauntlet of a posh lunch in the Great Hall, with all the sticky conversations with my would-be killers. There's nothing like your own impending murder to suppress your appetite.

As Henry had recommended, I forced myself to rest. I lay down in my clothes, but I knew instinctively that I wouldn't be able to nap. I went on my phone for a bit, and as there was no Wi-Fi I had to content myself with the films I'd already downloaded while in civilisation. But, as always, I found movies a bit too stimulating to get to sleep. I was conscious of that thing teachers always tell you, about the 'blue light' of screens keeping you awake. What I needed was something less Savage. Something boring and Medieval.

I needed a book.

In a moment I was up again. I trod quietly down my staircase, the stone cold beneath my bare feet, to the library where I'd eaten with Henry last night.

Luckily there was no one in the vast room, and I quickly

scanned the gold-tooled titles for something positive-sounding.
I didn't want any bad dreams. One title jumped out at me:

THE GOLDEN BOUGH
by
SIR JAMES GEORGE FRAZER

That sounded ideal: cheerful but dull. I grabbed the book and
raced back upstairs with it.

Back on my bed I began to read, to find it was some weird
old tome about comparative religions and spooky traditions. I
idly flicked through, bypassing stories of corn gods and ancient
rites. Then fragments of text jumped out at me – *'Highlands
of Scotland', 'ancient heathendom surviving in our own country',
'sacrifices were offered in the open air, frequently on the tops of
hills'.*

Now I was wide awake all right. I stopped, heart thudding,
then read on.

*When the time came the victims were sacrificed by the
druids or priests. Some they shot down with arrows,
some they impaled, and some they burned alive in the
following manner. Colossal images of wicker-work or of
wood and grass were constructed; these were filled with
live men, cattle and animals of other kinds; fire was then
applied to the images, and they were burned with their
living contents.*

I continued, with sick fascination. In Paris it was customary to burn a sack of live cats, in Russia a white cockerel. Even squirrels were sometimes burned in Easter fires. In the Pyrenees a wicker column was filled with live serpents, which would desperately slither to the top of it in a vain attempt to escape the flames and, to the delight of the crowd, would be seen lashing out like so many whips before being obliged to drop into the inferno.

I lowered the book abruptly. There were some pretty sick puppies in this world, and since quite a few of those deviants were now staying in this very castle, the book was no comfort, and certainly not the way to read myself to sleep, unless I wanted some fairly intense daymares.

I put the book on the bedside table, but somehow, even with my eyes closed, I still knew it was there, emanating weird malign vibes like an angry beehive. So I put it under the bed, which, as everybody knows, is where all horrors belong, and determinedly thought of marshmallows and rainbows and unicorns and bunny rabbits until sleep eventually came to me.

I woke at about five in the afternoon, with that groggy, rumpled feeling you get when you've slept in your clothes. I smoothed my hair down in front of the mirror but didn't see the point in getting washed or changed. That would kind of be like putting lipstick on to meet the hangman. I wondered what the others were doing. Were they getting ready too? Henry, I knew, was to be my wingman, but surely the others would be on the hill too, ready to intervene if things got sticky?

My nervousness about when, and how, and even if they'd be *able* to intervene made me wear out the carpet with my nervous pacing. I looked out of the window to see all the preparations – the gathering of guests and Land Rovers. I was reminded of the very first time I was at a hunt like this, at Longcross, Justitium weekend. Then, on the huntin' day of deer stalking in the hills, Nel was the intended victim, although I didn't know it at the time. Today it was my turn, and I knew it very well. My hand shook as I opened the window catch to watch the hunt servants load the guns into the back of the Land Rovers, with their pewter barrels and caramel stocks. I remembered that day at Longcross as the beginning of all this madness. Today would be the end.

I went down the stairs and met Henry in our accustomed place, under the duelling pistols. He was as grim-faced as I, and neither of us spoke as we climbed into the back of one of the Land Rovers. Even on this day that might be my last I was not immune to the beauty of Skye. The evening sun was dipping, and by some trick of the lowering light the heather of the rolling hills turned a deep and beautiful purple. But before long we pulled up on the foreshore of Loch Eynort, a glassy dropped-mirror of a lake, starting point for the Red Hunt. As my feet hit the shingle I imagined my long-dead ancestors landing here, tartan-clad and sharp of axe, ready to make mincemeat of the MacLeods. I raised my chin an inch. This MacDonald wouldn't go down without a fight.

But despite my sudden adrenaline rush, the hunt began surprisingly gently. I remembered this from my only other experience of deer stalking, that fateful Justitium weekend at Longcross. The hurry-up and wait. The holding of fingers up to the wind to guess at the direction of the stag. Luckily Henry and I were able to stay in a pair, and we followed the others at a distance. He carried a gun, cocked expertly over his arm. I didn't.

As we climbed the hill a nasty thought occurred to me. I hadn't seen the HAWK since I woke. We'd driven a long way – what if the drone didn't catch us up? But then I comforted myself. We'd discussed, in the Peel Tower briefing, the MacLeod's batshit plan to recreate the battle route of the MacDonalds. Henry had told Ratio exactly the route the hunt would take. Then another thought occurred. What if, after that kiss, and the romantic hawking trip with Henry, Shafeen had decided to wash his hands of me, to leave his unfaithful girlfriend to her fate? But in another moment I knew that couldn't be true. Shafeen was, above all, an honourable young man, and whatever his feelings about me, he wouldn't abandon me in my hour of need. Nor would he abandon the opportunity to take revenge for the wrongs done to his father, and all those other poor kids over the years. Ty also had a personal score to settle – the death of her great-uncle, Leon, child of the *Windrush* who'd sailed right into the jaws of the de Warlencourts. And Nel, that gorgeous soul, was my best friend and wouldn't let me down, even if she thought I'd been shitty to Shafeen. Ratio, with his strange obsession with the de Warlencourt family, would not miss a chance to bring about the family's destruction.

Another issue though: Ratio might be tracking my every move, but how would he and the other rebels intervene in time to save me? I'd seen the headings for 'intervention' and 'extraction' plans on his whiteboard, but no details on how he was planning to save me when things got nasty. How could any of those plans be faster than the fate that was meant for me? I supposed I just had to trust him, but it was hard to trust someone you'd only just met with your life. I looked around at the other hunters walking the hillside in their little groups of two and three. Were the Peel Tower Rebels among them? I thought not. Ratio was the only one who would not be recognised by the Medievals or the twins, and he was the one who was meant to be operating the drone. No, Henry was clearly the only inside man on the Red Hunt and I was very glad he was here – he was all that was standing between me and the Order.

Henry was being polite but distant. Of course, that was the way it had to be. I wondered what would happen to him now – how not getting the person he wanted would affect his life. But I couldn't worry about him this evening. I was too busy worrying about myself.

The stag, wherever he was, seemed to be more successfully keeping himself out of danger. Young and sprightly hinds took fright and bounced away from us through the heather, their white tails bobbing as they fled, but even I knew, to paraphrase Obi-Wan Kenobi, that these weren't the deers we were looking for. We walked down the breathtaking natural gorge known as Glen Sligachan, craggy mountains rising either side of us, crests in the clouds. We were following in the footsteps of the MacDonald ghost army, but the wily stag was nowhere to be seen, running from us like a MacLeod. 'He'll be near water,' said Henry. This, too, I remembered from that weekend at Longcross – the stag at bay, standing hock-deep in Longmere until the hounds tore him apart. There were no dogs today, but apparently the rules were the same. 'Stags seek out water to hide their scent. If he wasn't at the lake, he might be at the burn at Harta Corrie.'

We began to climb a sharp incline, where silver birch trees flanked an impossibly high cataract, white water blowing in the wind like a net curtain. Ahead of us I could see Lady Fiona trudging doughtily up the hill, two steps ahead of Lord Peregrine, as always. Louis and Cass climbed together, indistinguishable in tweed caps and Barbours. Even their guns were identical. And, behind us, princes and politicians, in twos and threes, all armed to the teeth. I felt, just as I had at The Gathering, that I was inside the pages of some society magazine. It was so weird being surrounded by people I normally saw online or on TV, in celebrity magazines or in photos of parliaments or palaces, and yet being somehow the most important person on the hillside. I felt like I had a target painted on me – and my back, under my own Barbour, began to itch.

At the top of the hill, a bubbling burn raced along to the lip of the waterfall, and there, at last, we caught sight of the stag.

He was magnificent.

He was bigger than I ever would have imagined, and for the first time I began to appreciate what it meant to be an Old Imperial. I'd only seen a stag head of that size and nobility before, and that was at Longcross, in Lowther, the room where I'd twice stayed. I realised then that Jeffrey, my disembodied companion, must have been an Imperial too. I'd felt him to be a kindred spirit, and he'd listened patiently, like Wilson in *Cast Away*, when I'd had no other friend in the world. From that moment, mentally, I began to call this Old Imperial Jeffrey too, as if the two stags were one. Now, as then, I felt we had much in common.

The walk had been long, but Jeffrey was cornered, and as last stands went, it couldn't have been more cinematic. He was standing at the very lip of the waterfall, above that vertiginous drop, looking back at us. He looked incredibly noble, and by contrast we were insects for attempting to capture him. His russet-red flanks shone in the late-evening sun, his head was majestic, his antlers massive as the branches of an oak. His eyes, large and liquid as a cow's, regarded us, unafraid. As we trod carefully through the burn, water breaching our wellies, he did something remarkable.

With one last look to his pursuers, Jeffrey stepped backwards off the lip of the fall.

I think I cried out. I looked at Henry, and he looked back at me, wide-eyed. It was so exactly what he had done himself at Conrad's Force, back at Longcross, falling backwards into space rather than being caught. The similarity was eerie.

Louis slapped the water with the flat of his hand in frustration. 'Damn it!' he exclaimed. 'Blasted animal committed hara-kiri!'

Beside him, Cass, by contrast, was utterly calm. She raised her head, as if she was a seeker hound sniffing the evening air. 'No,' she said, looking at Henry as I had done and putting two and two together. 'He's alive. Come on.'

Grabbing her twin, she almost pulled him back down the hillside, with Henry and me in close pursuit. Suddenly it became crucially, massively important that we got to Jeffrey first. I thought it unlikely that the stag could have survived a fall like that, but I knew better than to count him out. I'd made that mistake with Henry.

We were among the first to reach the bottom of the glen, where the burn raged and boiled over the ragged rocks. We waded unsteadily to the centre of the torrent, scanning the turbulent water. Sure enough, a dark shape surged from the deep, a leviathan, which resolved into the shape of a deer. Jeffrey stumbled out of the burn, his pelt black with water, his antlers laden with crystal drops like a chandelier. Once on dry land he limped to a nearby tree and, exhausted, collapsed at the foot of it, waterlogged and heavy, his body at one with the stone below, his branches as one with the branches above.

'Well, he's got a sense of theatre, I'll give him that,' said Henry, low-voiced, pulling me down to the ground.

'What do you mean?' I whispered, lying belly-down on the rough heather.

'That's *the* rowan tree. And that slab below it is the Bloody Stone.'

At that moment my fears transferred from Jeffrey to myself. This was *my* destiny. This was the place where the MacDonalds had slaughtered the MacLeods and left that very slab running with blood. I looked back over my shoulder. The cream of Britain's aristocracy crossed the burn in ones and twos and crouched low to surround the stag, a privileged firing squad. The barrels of their guns glinted evilly, and every one of them was pointed at Jeffrey.

And at me.

'Will they shoot now?' My voice cracked in Henry's ear. I was kind of hoping, even now, that the hunters would put up their guns and spare him, like Robert de Niro in *The Deer Hunter*.

'Not yet,' Henry replied. 'They need him to get up, so they can shoot at his liver. It's the biggest organ, the most effective kill shot.'

'I didn't mean at him,' I said.

'They need to startle him, so he'll rise,' said Henry, still not getting my meaning.

Just then, a barely perceptible whirring sounded from somewhere far above. I'm pretty sure none of the other guns heard it because of the roar of the cataract, or perhaps the pulse of bloodlust beating in their ears. But I heard it. And Jeffrey did too.

As the drone hovered above him, red eye shining, the stag had to weigh up the relative dangers presented by earth and sky.

He chose wrong.

Jeffrey lumbered to his feet, and three things happened almost simultaneously.

The stag took a hesitant step away from the tree – now there was a clean shot.

From behind us, Louis shouted, '*Mine!*' and fired a single, deafening shot like the crack of a whip.

And Henry de Warlencourt threw himself on top of me, shielding my body with his.

For one horrible moment, feeling Henry's dead weight, I thought the bullet meant for me had killed him. But then I saw the huge Old Imperial crumple and collapse to the ground, huge antlers crashing like timber.

All the prone guns rose out of the heather and ran to the

body. Henry rolled off me and in an instant we were on our feet too. I scrambled to the rowan tree and saw that Louis's shot had been true. The mighty stag was felled at last. Jeffrey was dead, I was alive. I was standing in something – something sweet and sticky. I looked down and realised that, once again, after an interval of centuries, the Bloody Stone was running with gore.

24

Jeffrey's medieval torture was not yet over.

One of the servants took a hunting knife and slit the stag from throat to genitals. Then he dumped the deer's guts on the grass, a steaming mass of red and blue snakes. 'Gralloching,' said Henry. 'They leave the guts here for the kites. No point in the poor pony having to lump all that weight home.'

It was like the end of *Braveheart*. I stood frozen during the whole process, watching the stag being tied to the garron hill pony, numb with the terror of a close call, ears ringing with the kill shot. Sure enough, the hill hawks fluttered down to feast on the blood and guts, just as they'd made a meal of the MacLeods centuries ago. One of my hands involuntarily grasped a branch of the rowan tree for support and, when it was time to go, Henry had to physically prise my hand free. My fingers had snapped off a little branch laden with red berries, and as we walked down the hill I gave the twig to him. 'Thanks for protecting me.' My voice didn't seem to work properly. 'This is to protect *you*.'

He took the twig and smiled, somewhat shakily. 'A twig. Amazing. I didn't get you anything.' He was doing a Greer MacDonald, making a joke when things were too serious.

'*Rowan-tree and red thread keep the devils frae their speed*,' I said, quoting Nanny. I hadn't seen her among the murderers today. Hopefully a house had fallen on her by now.

We followed the garron along the glen just as in my dream, watching the freshly dead stag's head lolling with each step, his antlers running with blood like a crown of thorns. And as we walked I developed a new and quite different worry. They hadn't been shooting at me after all. Louis could easily have picked me off on our way down from the waterfall and written it off as a misfire. So what if *nothing* happened to me now? What if the Order decided that the presence of Henry was a game changer and altered their plans? They'd had a 'normal' deer hunt, now they could have their weird Jeffrey bonfire tomorrow and just go home. Were they not going to reveal their hand after all?

I must have fallen silent, because Henry, who always seemed to be able to read my moods like no one else, said, 'What's up?'

'I don't suppose you're a fan of *Breaking Bad*?' I said. 'Or the *El Camino* film?'

'It won't surprise you to hear that I've no idea what you're talking about.'

'It was a big TV show, then film, and the central character was called Heisenberg. The Savages in the online community reckoned that he was called that because of the twentieth-century physicist Werner Heisenberg. Anyway, Heisenberg – the physicist one, I mean, not the TV character – came up with this theory called the Observation Principle, which stated that the very observation of an experiment affected the outcome, preventing a full analysis.'

He thought for a moment. 'You're saying that, just by being here and observing, I altered what happened to you.'

'Yes. I wonder if your presence made them hold back.'

'I wouldn't have thought so,' he said. 'If anything, I think that would make them go harder. Everyone I spoke to last night seemed to think I was here to make sure you were having a good time, didn't get spooked and were at the right place at the right time for the Red Hunt. I think they just changed their plan about what to do with you. Remember, I am one of the DOGS, the Dark Order of the Grand Stag, the top level of the Order, which comprises all the Grand Masters. They don't suspect that I am a turncoat.'

'What the hell's a turncoat?'

'There's another Highland reference for you,' he said. 'When the English soldiers lost a Highland battle they turned their distinctive red coats inside out. That way they could join the other side.'

'I don't suppose they'd notice with a Barbour,' I quipped weakly. 'If they changed their plan, why didn't they tell you?'

'Well,' he considered, 'we both skipped breakfast; we were out all morning hawking; I didn't go to lunch, as I was still full of sandwich.'

'But they could have found time to brief you,' I said. 'Why didn't they?'

He thought about that. 'I think it's likely that Louis is freezing me out. He can be a poisonous little beast – literally, according to you – so he's perhaps convinced them to grab onto his branch of the family tree. But that's just speculation,' he admitted. 'I don't actually know.'

That was not exactly reassuring. It just meant I was much more likely to be hurt on another day. This weekend wasn't over yet.

Back at the castle everybody had 'hot toddies' in the Great Hall, in front of a roaring fire. A hot toddy, I quickly learned, was a steaming-hot whisky, honey and lemon juice, and it ripped through my innards from my throat to my stomach like a gralloching knife. There was a roar of chatter to rival that of the fire, and with a drink in my hand and Henry by my side, even I began to relax a bit. I got the feeling that the immediate danger was over. People began to go up to change for a late dinner, and Henry and I were about to go too when Cass came up to us. She had a parcel in her hands, wrapped in brown paper, which, to my surprise, she gave to me.

I looked at the direction. The parcel was marked with my name and the castle's address. I didn't recognise the writing. 'Who's sending me presents?'

'No idea.' But her eyes flickered, and when I turned the package over I could see why.

It had been opened and stuck back together rather clumsily.

'Who delivered this?'

'*I* don't know, Greer. It was delivered by hand to the castle this morning. But in all the craziness I forgot to give it to you. Not important, is it?'

'No,' I said. 'Not at all. Thanks.'

For one crazy moment I thought it might be a bomb, but it didn't feel like a device. It was soft and heavy, like clothes. Telling myself I'd seen too many films, I arranged to meet Henry in half an hour and went alone to my tower. Locking the door behind me, I opened the package and tipped it out on the bed.

It looked like a body warmer. It was made of tough black canvas and was incredibly heavy.

I'd seen enough films to know what this was.

A bulletproof vest.

A note fell out of the folds:

Just in case . . .
Ratio and the Peel Tower Rebels x

As it had turned out, it was Jeffrey who had needed it, not me.

25

I did some serious thinking while I bathed and dressed for the late supper, putting on a clinging wine-coloured dress I'd found in my wardrobe.

I came down to meet a suited and booted Henry in our usual spot. He looked at me appreciatively, but I had no time for flirtation. I got straight to the point.

'I think I know why they left me alone today,' I said in a frantic whisper.

'Why?' he hissed back.

'Because Cass saw us last night. She saw us kiss.'

'Well, that was patently obvious.'

'Yes.' I relived the moment for a second and felt my cheeks heat until they were probably the colour of my dress. 'I think she hates me now, because she thinks you and I are together. And because of that she's even given up on you. She's been in love with you for years, but after last night she thinks you're in love with me.'

'I *am* in love with you,' he said simply.

'But that's making her hate you too. Hell hath no fury like a woman scorned and all that.'

A Renaissance drama reference was something Henry did understand. 'You're making a lot of assumptions there.'

'But you have to admit it makes sense. You said yourself you weren't informed about the change of plan, even though you're the heir of the family.'

'But don't we think that might have more to do with Louis than with anyone else?' he reminded me.

'Yes, but *no one* clued you in,' I protested. 'Not your cousins, your uncle or aunt, or the Medievals. Did *any* of those people, or *any* of the guests, speak to you explicitly today about what was going to happen to me?'

'No,' he said thoughtfully.

'Then I think they *do* know you're a turncoat. I think it's now them versus me *and* you.' He seemed to absorb that fact, so I pressed on. 'I think you're in as much danger from Louis as I am from Cass. Remember, last night at the ball he as good as admitted that he poisoned your father, and was quite ready to do the same to you.'

He snorted. 'I might have known Louis wouldn't do it in a gentlemanly way.'

'What would be a gentlemanly way? To slap you in the face with a single glove and challenge you to a duel?'

He smiled bitterly. 'Something like that.'

'Then there was all that Nanny stuff about graveyard stags and the death of the heir of the house. They've been pretty explicit.'

'All right,' said Henry. 'Suppose we are *both* marked targets. What do we do now?'

'Well, we skip dinner for a start,' I said sadly, because I was in fact starving. 'Unless you fancy a strychnine starter and arsenic for afters.'

He nodded slowly, then grabbed me by the hand. 'Come on. I've got an idea that I think you'll like. We'll go somewhere we'll find friends. People of your tribe. Or rather, your clan.'

Henry borrowed a Land Rover from the stable block and we took off down the drive in a spray of gravel, giggling like kids. In the back was a hamper containing a picnic dinner. We'd gone down to raid the kitchen, and the harassed cook, busy enough with getting the evening meal out to hundreds of guests, just told us politely but distractedly to help ourselves from the pantry. Well, she was hardly going to say no to Henry, was she? Mindful of Louis's threats, we'd been careful to take foodstuffs that had not been opened yet or tampered with, and had swiped fresh loaves, unopened cheeses, cans of pâté and even a mini bottle of whisky. I felt like we were Bonnie and Clyde in a getaway car, loot in the boot, liberated from another deadly dinner with deadly guests.

With every mile we travelled away from the castle I felt safer. I knew the drone couldn't follow us tonight – it would lose acquisition as soon as I got in the car, but that was quite nice too. If Shafeen hated me, I didn't want his eyes on me wherever I went, particularly not if it looked like I was going on a moonlit date with Henry.

Skye at night, pardon the pun, was beautiful. We drove right across the island to the southern coast, until we reached another castle, a square and hollow ruin with empty windows and crumbling ramparts silhouetted against the starry sky.

Henry parked the Land Rover and led me inside. 'This,' he said, with a special significance in his voice, 'is Armadale Castle.' We wandered through the lovely ruins until we stood framed in a stone arch, which was overgrown with rock roses, looking out to the silver sea.

'That's the mainland,' said Henry, pointing. 'That's Inverie, there, and that's Mallaig, where we took the ferry over.'

'Oh yes!' It was good to recognise bits of Scotland, since it was, as I'd discovered, my heritage country. Until two days ago I'd pretty much only heard of Glasgow and Edinburgh.

'Let's eat, shall we?' Henry said. 'I'm starving.'

We sat where we could see the lights of the mainland across the narrow sea, curving around the neck of the channel like a diamond necklace. It was the oddest dinner I'd ever had, us sitting there together like we were in some movie scene, Henry in his tuxedo and me in my venison evening dress, with a luxury hamper between us and its innards spilled out on the tartan rug. It reminded me of something.

'Did you know,' I said through a mouthful of Stilton, 'that when you "died" you became an internet sensation? People used to do this in your honour – dress up to the nines and have midnight picnics by water.'

'What kind of people?'

'Oxbridge students, Americans, you name it.'

Henry looked amused. 'How *completely* bizarre.'

'I'll show you sometime when my phone actually decides to work.'

'I believe you. But I hope they had better fare than this. It was just what we could grab in a hurry.'

Actually, it all tasted amazing, as things do when you're outdoors and hungry. 'Whisky and cheese isn't so bad.'

'In point of fact it's very fitting. Your clan, the MacDonalds, used to feast on these very things while they settled their feuds.'

'What are you talking about?'

'There's a place in Loch Leven, just over there –' he pointed to the lights of the mainland – 'called the Isle of Discussion. They'd be marooned there, with just whisky to drink and cheese to eat, and they wouldn't be allowed off the island until they'd resolved their issues.'

I looked at him. It felt like he wasn't just recounting a legend but had some other message for me. 'Have you and I had a disagreement?'

'I think so,' he said. 'It felt like it earlier.'

'I think so too.'

We were silent for a time. There didn't need to be any more talking. That distance, that strained civility that had settled over us on the Red Hunt, was quite, quite gone. We munched in silence, the cheese and bread satisfying our hunger, the whisky filling our bellies with fire. I began to feel pleasantly tipsy, and weirdly at peace.

'Henry,' I asked at length, 'why did you bring me here? I mean, to this place specifically.'

'Didn't I say? This place used to be yours.'

'Mine?'

'Armadale was the MacDonald castle.'

I got to my feet. I touched the cold stone with my warm fingertips, wondering. These were my birthstones. This was where I was from.

'This was all ours?'

'Not just the castle, but the island as far as the eye can see.' He got up too. 'You said this morning that we could never be together because you were from a council house and I was from a castle. Well, I wanted you to know that, once, you were from a castle too. We're not that different, you and I.'

There was that Bond-villain cliché again, but this time it was true. I touched the stones once more. 'I never realised.'

'Did your father never tell you about his Scottish ancestry?'

'How did you know I'm Scottish on my dad's side?' I asked suspiciously.

'Because of your name, MacDonald, clot,' he said affectionately. 'Your mother would have been called something different.'

'Oh.' I laughed at myself. 'Well, my grandad used to talk about Scotland a bit. Skye especially, now I come to think about it. But he died before I was old enough to have proper chats with him. And Dad never really talked about here at all. He was too busy raising me after Mum pissed off.'

He was quiet for a moment. Then he said: 'You never talk about your mother.'

'She never wanted to be around,' I said bluntly. 'So she forfeited the right to be talked about.'

Henry grimaced. 'Mine wanted to be around *too* much. She smothered me with love. Compensating for my father's distance, I suppose.'

'That's what my dad does.'

'So we both had one parent to love us, while the other kept us at arm's length. I told you we were not that different,' he said, once again using that classic archvillain line. But it was hard to see him as a villain now. Besides, here in this hollow ruin I felt safer than I'd ever felt in the populated light and warmth of Castle MacLeod. I felt surrounded by friendly ghosts. We were on MacDonald land. 'You were right,' I said to Henry. 'I've found my tribe.'

Just then a sound pierced the night, and we both jumped a mile. It had been so long since I'd heard it that it took me a moment to recognise. It was Savage, and electronic, and deeply intrusive in this medieval setting. It was my text alert.

I took my sleek silver phone out of my evening bag and looked at it. There were three strong bars of signal.

'What's up?' asked Henry.

'My phone's woken up. Must be because we're so near the mainland.'

A notification flashed up from the night before – Shafeen. My heart began to thump. I tapped it open.

A text.

Three words that changed my life.

It's over, Greer.

My thumping heart plummeted. It had been expected, of course, but that made it no less of a shock. I showed the text to Henry, wordlessly. Unused to reading from a screen, he squinted at the text, then sat back. After a moment he said, 'I'm sorry.'

'Sure,' I said sardonically.

'No, I really am.' He sounded sincere. 'This is all my fault.'

'You bet it is.' I felt like crying but I was damned if I was going to do it in front of Henry.

'It will be all right,' he said, and tried to put a comforting arm around me.

'Are you *kidding* me?' I exclaimed. I meant the arm, but also the statement.

He retracted the arm. 'Look, I said I'd explain to Shafeen and I will.'

'How can you when we can't even go to the Peel Tower?' I said, my voice suspiciously wobbly.

He thought about this. 'I think we can now, so long as we're careful. The Red Hunt is over. We need to work out what we're going to do next.'

I turned to him. 'Really?'

'If that's what you want, yes.'

'When?'

'Tomorrow morning, first thing?'

I could have hugged him, but in the circumstances I thought I'd better not.

I shivered, suddenly cold. I'd worn Shafeen's love like a coat. A coat that I could put on whenever I liked. I'd taken him for granted, and now he was not there I felt exposed.

Henry looked at me with concern. 'D'you want to go?'

I shook my head. 'Not yet. I just need to process this.'

He packed all the food detritus back into the hamper, lifted it off the picnic rug and wrapped the rug like a blanket around me. It was thick, and tartan (of course), and warm. 'What do you do when you're feeling low?' he asked. 'I mean, what normally cheers you up?'

I considered. 'Films,' I said. 'It's always been films.' My whole childhood, after Mum had gone, I'd been alone a lot while Dad was on shoots. If I ever felt sad or lonely, my solution had always been the same. I'd stick on a movie.

'Well then. Don't you have any on that . . . phone thingy?'

'Loads.' I had a whole library downloaded.

'Then why don't we watch something now?'

'I've got a better idea,' I said, perking up a bit. 'The Saros 9s has projection capability. I can show you on the castle wall.'

'Then let's do that. Educate me. I'd like to learn.'

He was just being kind – I knew he didn't care about all this Savage stuff, but it was sweet of him to try to take me out of myself.

I let him get under the rug – it couldn't matter now – and we sat there, turned away from the view, concentrating our attention on the dark wall of the keep. I activated projection mode, sending a silent prayer of thanks to Nel's tech-genius dad, and the dark wall was illuminated with what was for me the holy rectangle – that golden ratio of cinematic aspects, Academy 16:9 – projected onto the stones like *Cinema Paradiso*.

I showed him everything – my greatest hits of the cinema. To begin with I toyed with the idea of screening one film, but it was late and there were so many I wanted to show him – he'd seen nothing, so a lifetime of wonder was ahead of him; Henry was a blank sheet, a dream pupil, an ideal Padawan who could one day become a Jedi. So in the end, instead of going to my downloads, I just went to YouTube and found my top-ten favourite scenes ever.

I showed him the first scene of *Saving Private Ryan*. I showed him the last scene of *The Usual Suspects*. I showed him the 'left-handed' swordfight between Inigo Montoya and Westley from *The Princess Bride*. I showed him the courtroom scene between Jack Nicholson and Tom Cruise in *A Few Good Men*. I showed him the bit where the Joker dances manically on the Highbridge steps in the Bronx. I showed him the part where Indiana Jones gets chased by a giant boulder in *Raiders of the Lost Ark*. It was an unforgettable experience, a beautiful synergy of the Medieval and the Savage. A digital film showing on the ancient wall of a ruined castle. Henry was a willing student and he asked me constant questions. I actually had to shush him to listen to bits of dialogue, explain where they fitted into the wider plot, make him understand why they were so great. He loved Bond. He hated *Star Wars*. I told him why he was right, and why he was wrong. I showed him the first scene I'd ever talked to him about, that night on the roof at Longcross when he'd first kissed me – the bit in *The Shooting Party* when the faithful retainer gets shot instead of the birds, and of course he identified the hell with that. It wasn't until we both laughed aloud at the ballgame scene in *When Harry Met Sally* . . . when Harry and Jess are trying to have a serious conversation in the middle of a Mexican wave, that I realised how well his plan had worked. I hadn't forgotten Shafeen's text – I still wore it like a painful little tattoo just under my heart – but I'd been distracted for a good hour.

Eventually, reluctantly, we packed up our things and got

back in the Land Rover. My head lolled against the window as we drove back to Dunvegan, and Henry let me doze, his eyes on the road, taking care of me still.

26

The following morning I headed down the stone stairs of the North Tower with renewed optimism.

After the night at Armadale Castle I felt that Henry was a friend for life, and this morning he was going to help me get my boyfriend back. I wouldn't think about the kiss again, or the midnight screening on the wall of my ancestral castle. That had made me feel even closer to him than the kiss.

It was a shock, therefore, to realise that the blond young man waiting under the crossed pistols was not Henry.

The surprise must have shown on my face as Louis wished me a good morning. 'Were you expecting someone else?'

'No,' I blustered. 'No, not at all. I was just –' I smelled the unrivalled smell of frying bacon and improvised – 'going to breakfast.'

'Ah, yes,' he said pleasantly. 'Yes, I imagine you must be rather hungry, since you missed dinner. And my cousin did too, did you know?'

'Really?' I said innocently. 'Well, I was pretty knackered after the Red Hunt. Maybe Henry was too.'

Louis's eyes flickered. 'Quite so. I say, if I could persuade you to postpone your breakfast for a few moments, there's something I'd like to show you.'

I was torn. On the one hand, I didn't want to go anywhere – I'd agreed to meet Henry at 7 a.m. and if I wasn't there he would think I'd stood him up. Then I'd miss the chance to go to the Peel Tower bright and early and talk to Shafeen. But on the other hand, I couldn't exactly refuse Louis's request. He was, technically, my host. I just had to hope that whatever he wanted to show me was pretty quick and I could get back here before Henry gave up on me.

'Sure,' I said, smiling brightly. I followed Louis out of the castle and around the Great Court. I thought for a moment we might be heading for the mews and that he was going to show me the hawks, but we went in the opposite direction, into a cold stone outhouse. 'This is the hanging room,' he said.

I breathed the smell of death even before I saw the grisly sight that was hanging from the ceiling.

It was the huge stag, partially skinned so the pelt hung down around his majestic head like a cloak – a superhero's cape, which had failed to provide any protection or salvation. The white fatty tissues and red muscle were revealed, the dead eyes stared and the black lips rolled back from yellow teeth in a grimace of death. Jeffrey had been such a big beast that his antlers nearly scraped the stone floor, and the lake of black blood beneath him. The whole carcass was suspended by the hind feet from a wicked iron hook. And it resembled nothing so much as a scene of medieval torture.

'Why are you showing me this?' I said, horrified. It was like something from *Hostel*.

Louis shrugged, a weirdly brutal gesture in this context. He had a complete indifference to life and death, and I wondered if that was what had made it possible for him to kill his own uncle. He walked all around the dreadful thing, his shoes making a sticky sucking sound in the blood. 'I thought you might like to see what happened to him. He's my greatest trophy.'

So far, I thought. I felt disgusted by his triumph over Jeffrey, but I had to save some contempt for myself. It had been the HAWK that had killed Jeffrey, had made him get up from his safe haven, and as I was complicit in the drone's presence I'd been a part of this murder too. 'Why is his skin draped around him like that?'

'Because we're not just hanging this one for meat. We're caping it. So we can mount it on the wall.'

Just like the first Jeffrey in Longcross. 'Well, thanks for the TED Talk, Louis,' I said lightly, trying to leave, but he pushed the carcass with a single finger and it began to gently swing and pivot, blocking my way.

'There's something curiously beautiful about death, isn't there?' said Louis dreamily. He then put his finger in his mouth and, to my horror, sucked it. He was really scaring me now, so I had to make a joke of it.

'Honestly, Louis, could you be any more supervillain? *No*, there's nothing beautiful about death. Jeffrey . . . I mean . . . this stag . . . was much more beautiful when he was skipping around in the heather.'

'Oh, I don't know,' he said, looking pointedly at me. 'When something lovely dies, there's a certain poetry to it.'

At that moment there was the scrape of a boot in the doorway and Henry stood there, a strangely blank look on his face. '*There* you are.'

As the cousins faced each other across the carcass, I wondered, as I always did when they were together, how I could have ever thought them similar. Both the boys were in country tweeds, but Henry was Hollywood-actor, Burberry-model beautiful, and Louis was smaller, lesser, duller.

'Were you looking for Greer?' Louis asked suspiciously.

'No,' lied Henry smoothly. 'You. Aunt Fi wants you. Something about the Lammas Feast tonight.'

Louis could barely contain his hatred for his cousin. 'Couldn't you handle it?' he sneered.

'I could,' said Henry evenly. 'But it seems to be a job for the head of the house.'

That did it. 'Oh, well, in that case.' Louis made for the door, but as he passed the revolving carcass he paused.

'Doesn't look so powerful now, does he?' He looked at his cousin. 'Just goes to show, even the most powerful one, the alpha male and the head of the herd, can be brought low.'

Henry raised his chin a fraction. 'I was just thinking the self-same thing.'

Louis regarded Henry for another beat, then pushed past him out of the room.

I breathed a sigh of relief once he'd gone. 'Was his mum really looking for him?'

'No,' he said. 'I was looking for you, but I reckoned it was better he didn't know that.'

'I reckon you reckoned right,' I said. 'Phew. It's a good job you came back from the dead. Louis shouldn't be in charge of anything, particularly not your earldom.'

Henry put his hands in his pockets and leaned against the stone wall, with that curiously graceful gesture he had. 'Yes, that's the thing about the heir dying. You have to worry about who comes next. Pa was a monster, but he was a good custodian of the land. Uncle Peregrine doesn't quite cut the mustard.'

'What's wrong with dear Uncle Perry?'

'Nothing's wrong with him as such,' said Henry. 'He's just a bit useless. Tell me, honestly, have you ever heard my uncle say anything that you remember for more than five minutes?'

I couldn't. It was harsh but true.

'And he's weak. You've seen how Aunt Fi browbeats him. Papa was born to rule, and Peregrine is a poor imitation.'

That was almost exactly what I'd been thinking about their sons. 'Just like you and Louis.'

'I would give everything up,' he said, a catch in his voice, 'if it meant I could have you.'

He looked me dead in the eye, with complete honesty. Stripped bare, as raw and skinned as the stag. It was so intense I had to break the tension, and as always, I made a joke. 'And give everything to Louis? He should be in Arkham Asylum, not Longcross Hall.'

Now he blinked; it was clear I'd lost him. 'Explain, please.'

'You remember last night, I showed you a clip from *Joker*.'

'The chap who had green hair a bit like Ratio's, dancing on the steps?'

'That's it. The Joker was Batman's arch-nemesis. Actually, he

191

was also his half-brother – Batman's dad, Thomas Wayne, got the Joker's mother pregnant when she was a maid at Wayne Manor, but that's not the point of the story.' I was babbling so I made an attempt at clarity. 'The point is that the Joker was banged up in Arkham Asylum, the mental hospital in Gotham, because he was crazy. Genuinely loop-the-loop, cuckoo-farm crazy. And I think Louis might be too.'

Henry's face had taken on that odd, glazed look that people get when they've tuned out.

'Henry? Are you even listening?'

'Yes,' he said dazedly. 'Yes, I most *certainly* am.' Then he seemed to wake up. 'Come on. We have to get to the Peel Tower. I've got to talk to someone.'

'Yes,' I reminded him. 'Shafeen.'

'Well, yes, him too,' said Henry confusingly, and he practically dragged me out of the outhouse, leaving the caped stag swinging.

27

As we approached, a figure burst out of the Peel Tower and strode towards us, as fast as that gardener guy in *Get Out*. Shafeen barely paused but drew back his fist and punched Henry squarely in the face.

Henry staggered backwards, holding his jaw. 'I guess I deserved that.'

'Yes, you did, you bastard,' said Shafeen, and he hit him again.

Henry held up both hands. 'I don't want to fight you.'

'Well, you're bloody well going to.' Shafeen was like a whirlwind, raining down blows on a passive Henry so hard and fast I genuinely thought he was going to kill him.

Henry was on the ground now, and still Shafeen hit him, while Henry, doll-like, was just letting him, as if this was all part of what he had been saying to me the other night, that he deserved to pay for his sins, and this was all a piece of his punishment. A nasty-looking cut had sprung through his eyebrow and was bleeding profusely. 'Get up, damn you!' shouted Shafeen, now on top of Henry.

I grabbed Shafeen's arm. 'Stop it!' I screamed. 'He's had enough.'

He shrugged me off so violently that I fell to the ground too. Henry was blinded by blood now and I had a last, desperate thought. 'Remember he saved your dad!' I yelled. 'Remember Hardy and Horatio!'

At this Shafeen, panting, stopped and sat back. He looked down at Henry, and at that moment they could have been their fathers, but engaged in war, not love.

'I came to apologise,' sputtered Henry, through the blood. 'And to tell you that it was all my fault. *I* kissed Greer. She had nothing to do with it. And I promise you,' he gasped, 'I will never kiss her again.'

I'm sure you won't think very well of me when I tell you that my heart lurched at this. But the fire went out of Shafeen. He got up and he held out a hand.

He hauled Henry to his feet and together they lurched inside, Henry leaning on Shafeen, and Shafeen helping him, for all the world as if they were comrades after a battle. Men are very confusing.

I followed them into the little sitting room. Ty and Nel were there on the couch and jumped up at the sight of us. 'Jesus Christ!' exclaimed Nel. 'What the hell happened?'

Shafeen didn't reply but eased Henry down into an armchair and poured him a whisky. 'You'd better put something on that cut,' he said gruffly.

'On it,' said Nel, who'd brought some loo roll and a glass of water. She sat on the arm of Henry's chair and dabbed at the mess. Thankfully, once the blood was cleaned off, it wasn't as bad as it looked, but the eye below it was beginning to swell and close. Ty got some ice cubes and wrapped them in a tea towel. 'Hold this to your eye,' she said.

Henry complied, wincing just like they do in films.

'In movies they put whisky on the cut,' I observed from the sofa.

'Not everything is a movie, Greer,' said Henry, and I remembered when he'd said that once before, at the top of Conrad's Force, just before he'd plunged off the waterfall. I wondered at how far we'd come. 'I think the whisky will do more good in me than on me.'

He eased his aching back into the chair, so he was more upright. Then, suddenly, he said, 'Where's Ratio?'

'When I woke up this morning, he'd gone,' said Ty, before she realised what she'd said. 'I mean, I haven't seen him.' We all smiled at her and she sighed. 'OK, OK. He said last night he was going for a recce this morning. He's plotting the course for tonight so we can film the Lammas Eve celebrations.' I looked at the HAWK where it squatted, black and sleek, on the coffee table, then back at Ty. 'You two are pretty hot and heavy then.'

'Lucky,' grumbled Nel. 'Everyone's getting some but me.'

'Let's leave aside everyone's love life,' said Shafeen sharply, 'and get to the business of the day. Let's go over the plan of campaign.' In Ratio's absence, he took over the briefing. 'Right, tonight the Lammas Eve celebrations take place on the slopes of Ben Horneval. They will centre on this massive effigy of a stag.' He went over to the CSI board of photographs and red thread and pointed to a large aerial photo right in the middle. Even in print the wicker stag looked scary.

'It's called the Damh,' said Henry, slightly indistinctly

through swollen lips. 'Every year they build and burn one.'

'So any remaining danger you face, Greer, is likely to do with the Damh and some ritual.'

'The revellers jump under the fire,' said Henry. 'Through the legs of the stag. That might be one element of what they want you to do.'

'In which case the Kevlar vest will be no good to you,' said Shafeen.

'Besides, there won't be guns at Lammas,' said Henry. 'It's a feast, not a hunt. So that means the HAWK won't be in danger of being shot down.'

'So that's two big differences,' said Shafeen. 'No guns, and this time we'll be there.'

I leaned forward at this. 'I'm sorry, but how can you be there? Asian guy, black girl, green-haired super-nerd . . . I mean, you won't exactly fit in with the gammons.'

'This is how,' said Nel. She went to the sideboard, where a tartan throw was covering a number of objects, making a bumpy, chequered landscape. Nel lifted the covering to reveal four objects that made my stomach flip.

They were masks, each in the shape of an animal's head. Beautifully designed and deeply stylised, I nonetheless recognised a badger, a stoat, a hedgehog and a boar. They were slightly different colours of gold and bronze and copper, and all had summer flowers entwined about them. Even on their own they looked scary – part *Eyes Wide Shut*, part *Midsommar*.

'Ah,' I said. 'In that case, it might just work.'

'Yes,' said Shafeen. 'Actually, it was Henry who gave us

that piece of intel – that the Lammas revellers always wear animal masks.'

It was very odd. Ten minutes ago they'd been re-enacting *Raging Bull* and now they were strategising like allies.

'We'll all be somewhere in the crowd tonight,' said Ty. 'If something happens to you – and in a way, sorry, Greer, but we have to hope it does – we'll be on the spot.'

'Nathaniel . . . the Abbot –' Nel swiftly corrected herself, 'promised to come with reinforcements, but there's been no word as yet. So for the moment it's just us.'

That was both reassuring and terrifying. We'd all be on our way home tomorrow, so tonight was our last chance to nail the Order, but it was good to know that my friends would be around me, and I included Henry in that group.

I looked at Shafeen – would he still care about my fate? – but he nodded reassuringly at me too. 'The drone will be following you at all times. We have your facial-recognition matrix, but that will have a limited use after dark. So we'll use the heat signature. The HAWK will "box" you as before, and it will only lose acquisition if you go indoors.'

'Sounds like you know a lot about it,' I said.

'Ratio's been teaching me to fly it. I was really interested in the technology, so I've been assisting him. He thought it best that someone else knew how to do it, just in case, so I've been doing a lot of the recce flights.' He looked at me pointedly. 'Quite the Savage I've become, Greer.'

God. I was now facing the possibility that he had actually been the one flying the HAWK when it had spotted me and Henry kissing.

'We should be getting back,' said Henry, as if he sensed the awkwardness. His eyebrow had stopped bleeding, but his face would take some explaining.

'Just a minute.' I couldn't leave without talking to Shafeen in private. There was something I just had to say. I got to my feet and dragged Shafeen outside. Once we were a good distance from the door I turned to him. 'I owe you an apology too,' I said. 'For the kiss.'

He eyed me. 'I thought it was all Henry's fault, according to him,' he said sardonically.

'Well,' I said. I had to be honest. 'He might have felt . . . encouraged, because we've . . . we've become friends.' I tried to explain. 'Henry was a monster, and no one is more aware of that than him. But he's changed, and he's sacrificing a lot to help us. He went from chasing Gemma Delaney (and us) around Longcross to saving Ty's life, saving your dad's life, and now he's risking everything to bring the Order of the Stag down. Do you realise that if our trap works he'll probably go to jail?'

This gave Shafeen pause – I could see that the thought hadn't occurred to him before.

'I think Henry began to change when he shared that story of his childhood with me – you know, the "fox in a box" story about the time his father trapped him in the boot room with Reynard and wouldn't let him out? After that he took me to the Red Mass. That was like the moment in *The Wizard of Oz* – I got to see behind the curtain and see all the workings inside.' I took a breath. 'Because I sort of *created* this new Henry, I do feel attached to him.'

He snorted. 'Are you actually giving me the *Frankenstein* defence? That you start to love your creation?'

'No, not that,' I said quickly. 'But he's turned against his family, left everything behind, and I'm kind of all he's got.'

He looked at me coldly. 'Your hands were in his hair,' he said.

So he had seen everything. 'I know.'

Suddenly I felt incredibly sorry for him. Shafeen must have really suffered over the last two days. In his tower bedroom, deserted by Ratio who was now snuggling up with Ty, he must have suffered lonely agonies thinking about his faithless girlfriend and what she might be up to at the castle.

'I just don't know if I can trust you again.'

'I don't blame you,' I said. 'But I want you to try.'

'It'll take time.'

'As long as you need.'

Just then Henry emerged, somewhat sheepishly, from the door of the Peel Tower. 'Sorry, but we'd better go.'

Shafeen stood back without looking at either of us, but as we walked away I could feel his eyes following us.

'What now?' I said to Henry, a question that could mean many things.

He took it literally. 'Let's go and see Regina on the way back. She's going to be my alibi for this injury.'

We walked into the walled garden but didn't have to go into the mews proper because all the hawks were pegged outside on bow perches, fluttering and preening in the sun.

'Hello, old girl,' said Henry, using that warm and tender voice that seemed to be reserved for Regina and me. 'We'll say she bated, and caught my brow with her beak. They don't know her as I do. They don't know she'd never do that.' He stroked her breast feathers with the back of his scarred fingers; I could see the red thread I'd given him tied around his wrist. I wondered if he carried the rowan twig with him too.

Regina whickered and trilled, making happy little noises in her throat. I smiled, oddly moved. 'She *loves* you.'

'No. She doesn't love anyone. Every time you release a hawk for a hunt, there's a chance you'll never see her again. You spend time crafting something beautiful, and then you let it go.'

I thought about what Shafeen had said about the *Frankenstein* defence. What I'd said to Shafeen was true – I'd become attached to something I'd helped create. But just like Henry when he flew Regina, I had to be ready to lose him one day.

And that day could be any time now.

28

The mask lay on my bedspread when I got back to my room.

It stared up at me, malign and hollow-eyed, suddenly more frightening than anything I had yet seen.

It was beautifully crafted, like those Venetian masks you see in films like *The Wings of the Dove*, and in the form of a hare's face. I feared there was a significance to the disguise they had chosen for me. Hares were chased. Hares were prey. *Was* my hunt still to come?

I picked the thing up in my hands. The eyeholes were almond-shaped, the fur was rendered with incredibly delicate brushstrokes, and there were no ties, but rather the whole thing was part of a soft brown hood, so not a hair on my head would be seen (no pun intended). The ears were woven with garlands of summer flowers, twined by careful, skilful hands. Why? The ritual nature of it all chilled me. A little note, which looked as if it was written with a quill on parchment, fell out of the mask.

Please don your mask, hood and gloves before leaving your room.

We wish you a joyful Lammas!

The rest of the outfit was draped over my chair. There was a floor-length floral dress in all shades of brown – copper, cinnamon and umber – and a fur jacket the colour of caramel – I hoped not hare fur. There was a pair of chunky hill boots, glossy as conkers, and as a finishing touch a pair of pliant brown gloves. Clearly no skin was to be seen, and actually I found this reassuring. Ty and Shafeen, as the only people of colour on the island, would be able to mix with the guests undetected, and Ratio's grass-green hair would be hidden by his hood.

I got ready. On any other day I would have loved that dress, but that evening my hands shook as I buttoned it. I noticed there were no zips or hooks on the outfit – everything about the costume was natural. But there was nothing natural about my reflection. I couldn't look at the strange hare/girl hybrid in the glass – I turned away and headed downstairs.

A hawk waited for me below the duelling pistols. He was wearing a tweed suit in the same natural browns as my own outfit, and his mask was the face of a peregrine falcon, with petrol-blue feathers and a sharp raptor's beak. Henry crooked his arm for me as he'd done on the night of The Gathering.

I took it without speaking.

We knew we were in the endgame.

We walked outside in the company of other pairs of

woodland animals, like some kind of reverse Noah's Ark. Other creatures were milling around, and I could see wolves conversing with rabbits, squirrels chatting with hedgehogs. All the ladies were in flowing florals, and the gentlemen in suits of earth colours – greens, browns and ambers. They reminded me of Beatrix Potter characters, only much, much scarier, with their human clothes and animal faces. I looked at all those gathered, wondering which among these strange hybrids was Lord Peregrine, Lady Fiona and the twins. Which of these beast masks covered the Medieval faces of Piers, Cookson, Lara, Charlotte and Esme? Then I considered the fact that I'd probably seen *all* of these people before. Not just at The Gathering, but at the STAGS Club, at Longcross, in the crypt of Cumberland Place, in the House of Lords. This cult ran like a cancer right through Britain's high society. And maybe tonight was the night we could cut that cancer out.

In the time we'd been standing there, twilight had thickened to darkness. and masked footmen lit torches as big as clubs, which they held high, passing the fire from hand to hand. Then, almost as one, the company turned to face the castle.

'What's going on?' I whispered to Henry.

'It's called the Dousing,' he said. 'Watch.'

I did. One by one, every light in the castle went dark. Every tower, every battlement, every floodlight, every arrow slit, every light was extinguished. I looked at the landscape around me. In the little farms and crofts that were dotted about the hills, every light went out too. If it wasn't for our torches, Skye would be in utter blackness. I clutched Henry's arm more tightly. There was something incredibly creepy about the removal of light. Such a primal thing for humans, the need to see what is going on.

'It's part of the festival,' said Henry. 'The locals put out all the lights in their houses and douse their fires. It's all about death and rebirth. The fire that we light at the Damh symbolises a new day. In medieval times it was all about asking the sun to shine to give a good harvest and plentiful crops, to see the island through the darkness of winter. The revellers would take the fire home from the Damh and light their lamps again from that.'

The torchbearers, in their animal masks, began to process down the drive, and all us guests followed. As we reached the slopes of Ben Horneval other revellers joined us from the farms and crofts, and I fervently hoped that the Peel Tower Rebels were among their number. I looked hard, I can tell you, for the badger, the stoat, the hedgehog and the boar – the masks I'd seen earlier at the tower – because they would indicate the presence of my friends – but I couldn't see them.

In the foothills of the black mountain we came to a flatter place, which I realised must have been where I'd got lost in the mists two days ago. The lightbearers thrust their torches into the ground and I could see the wicker stag – the Damh – rising into the darkness, huge and looming. In front of it was a long trestle table, covered with food and drink and garlanded with summer flowers. A folk quartet, all masked, played jolly Highland tunes on an accordion, guitar, drum and flute, and a girl in a magpie mask sang beautiful lilting folk songs in – I assume – Gaelic.

I wasn't particularly hungry, but I took a plate and picked at all the delicacies – pies and pastries and stews and scones and cakes and cheeses. There was wine too – something strong and sweet – and whisky. I made sure that everything I took was from a communal jug or plate and Henry did the same.

As the revellers began to drink more and eat more and laugh more, the music changed subtly – it was no longer beautiful vocal folk that made you think of Highland streams and heather, but upbeat instrumental music that invited your fingers to drum and your foot to tap; music that made it almost impossible to stand still. At this point the folk band organised everyone into a dance on the hillside – a formation that was a little like a dance we'd all done at The Gathering – the one called, appropriately, Strip the Willow. We made two lines across the grass, and as the music began each couple would go down the centre, breaking off to link arms with other partners, spinning back down the lines. As Henry and I waited our turn, clapping along to the music as was obviously customary, I looked again for the masks of the Peel Tower Rebels. I identified the stoat and the boar, but I couldn't see the badger or the hedgehog anywhere. As I looked about me I was struck by another thought – no one in the company was wearing a deer mask. Which I found quite weird, considering why we were all here.

Then it was mine and Henry's turn. Holding both his hands, wondering how this looked to Shafeen if he was watching from somewhere in the crowd, we polka'd down the centre of the clapping lines. Then, as we divided at the end of the lines, I happened to link arms with the stoat. I knew from the body shape that this was either Nel or Ty, but of course they wouldn't know that the hare was me. I took a shot. 'Ty?'

'Greer? Thank Christ it's you.' She clutched my arm with relief, as if she might fall over without it.

'Keep dancing,' I said. 'What's up?'

She held my gaze as we whirled around – her dark eyes burning through the mask with fear. 'Ratio's gone. He's disappeared.'

29

'Disappeared?' I repeated, probably a little too loudly.

'Shh,' she said. 'He never came back from the recce this morning. I'm freaking *out*, Greer.'

'Wait,' I said, as we exchanged arms and spun round the other way. 'Who's flying the drone?'

'Shafeen,' Ty said. 'He's hiding out somewhere nearby, controlling it with Ratio's phone.'

'Wait. Ratio left his *phone*?' I'd only known Ratio a short time, but he struck me as the kind of guy who'd sooner leave his right hand at home than his phone.

'That's what I mean. Something's not right.'

Then we were obliged to swap partners again, and I whirled around with a rabbit and then a robin, until at last the music stopped, so of course we all did too. My head was spinning with the wine and the whirling and the worry that Ratio hadn't come back from his recce. I told Henry, low-voiced, what Ty had told me, but before he could react, one of the musicians, the one with the accordion and the head of an otter, began speaking again in his booming islander's accent. 'Before we light the needfire, we will make the Lammas Circle.'

I expected this to be the part where we all linked arms and danced together, *Mamma Mia!* style – but actually what happened was much stranger. People started scrabbling in their pockets and fumbling at their wrists, ears and throats. 'What's happening now?' I asked Henry.

'We make the Lammas Circle by removing any metal from our persons,' he said, his voice a little altered by the hawk mask. 'You have to take off any jewellery, take any coins out of your pockets, belt buckles, etcetera.'

It was pretty strange seeing everyone acting like they were at an airport about to go through that metal-detector thing, but such a Medieval version of that Savage process. With a jingle and a clink, everyone laid their stuff in little piles, in this huge circle around the wicker stag. Henry said, 'The circle of finery is supposed to make what happens inside the circle sacred.'

'OK then,' I said sceptically. Luckily I only had on a pair of cheap little hoop earrings, and I laid them down in the grass next to Henry's coins and signet ring with the little antlers stamped on them. Henry said something like, *The trick is to remember where you put your stuff*, so I took especial notice of the little piles either side of mine. On one side, obviously, was Henry's signet ring with the little stag's antlers. On the other was a little heap of metal that had been put there by an unseen hand. A shining shape sprang out at me in the torchlight. An antler earring – not a spangly dangly one, but one of those butch ones that goes through the earlobe through an extra-big hole. I had seen it before in Glasgow, in the most techie bedroom I'd ever known, worn in the ear of the room's owner. It gave me a warm feeling to know that Ratio must be here after all. I looked around to tell Ty and reassure her, but just then an owl and a dormouse came forward bearing a huge wooden board between them. On the board was some sort of cake in the shape of a deer – not one of those fancy birthday-type cakes, but a rough, bready construction, plaited and baked to a uniform golden brown. Two pieces of the cake were different to the rest. There was a round white bread bun for a tail, just like those little bobbing tails I'd seen on the fleeing deer at the Red Hunt. Then, at the other end, the antlers were baked a darker black-brown. The revellers applauded this creation, then the owl and the mouse set the thing down on the table and began tearing it into pieces in a swift, practised way. They put each hunk, including the antlers and the tail as separate pieces, into a canvas sack held wide by a goat-headed fellow. The goat then went around everyone, and each guest reached into the bag and took out a piece.

I looked at hawk-headed Henry through the holes in my hare mask, hoping he could see the question in my eyes.

He could. 'It's just bread,' he said. 'It's the Lammas loaf – glazed with a custard of eggs and milk. Don't worry. It's nice.'

When it was my turn I reached into the bag and brought out a hunk – it was still warm. I fed it under my mask and it was indeed delicious, and as I ate a kerfuffle broke out on the other side of the circle. A mountain cat was shrieking and jumping up and down. 'What's her deal?' I whispered to Henry.

'She got the antlers,' said Henry. 'That means she's the Queen of Lammas.'

I watched as the delighted cat was crowned with a flower garland, wrapped in a gilded cloak and carried shoulder-high around the circle.

'What happens if you get the tail?' I shouted above the cheers.

'Watch,' said Henry.

The person who had drawn the tail was a very tall man in a fox mask. He was ushered to the centre of the circle by the goat, who said in loud, ringing tones: 'I declare the fox the Lammas Fool!' The crowd jeered good-naturedly while the owl and the mouse went round the circle in opposite directions, handing out eggs and cups of milk. The goat took to his heels, leaving the fox alone in the circle, and the whole company threw their eggs at the fox, and their milk too, so in a very short time he was covered in a hideous custardy mess.

Then, almost imperceptibly, the atmosphere turned. I looked around at all the beastly animal faces. Of course they hadn't changed at all, but they seemed to be wearing warped, bestial expressions as they pelted the poor fox with increasing force. Soon the Lammas Fool was staggering backwards, gloved hands held up, shielding his face. 'Someone should stop this,' I said to Henry. 'He'll get really hurt in a minute.'

'Wait,' he said.

The cat, lowered to the ground, raised a gloved hand and the pelting stopped. 'Now as the Lammas Queen, she'll speak the Bidding,' said Henry in my ear. The cat read from a page of parchment, clearly and distinctly, in a voice that was like a chime.

'I call upon the warriors of the past,
those who would stand up and fight,

210

those who would do what is needed,
those who would make sacrifices on behalf of others,
those who would die that others may live.
I call upon them this night,
to give me strength of heart, soul and spirit.'

There was an expectant silence. The poor fox, panting through his mask, sat soaked and stained on the grass. Then the otter from the folk band struck up a beat on his drum – a slow, dour tempo like you might hear on a march to the gallows. Below us in the valley, a glow of torchlight, which split and lightened into separate brands, carried by a procession of figures.

Antlered figures.

The DOGS.

The Dark Order of the Grand Stag approached to the beat of the drum, marching up hill in time. They were wearing red floor-length monastic robes, with red hoods drawn up over their heads. And here, at last, were the deer masks. Every one of the red-clad figures wore the face of a deer, with antlers rising above, and they gathered in a circle in front of the wicker stag. As before, one of the DOGS had antlers that were larger than the rest, with the crowning branches I now knew to be called surroyals. This, I knew, was the Grand Master – presumably Gideon Villiers, the Old Abbot. The DOGS were, by far, the creepiest figures of all the creepy figures I'd seen that night, and my body had a visceral reaction to their arrival. I'd last seen them like this, in their ceremonial robes, at the Red Mass in the subterranean chapel of Cumberland Place. The time before that, they'd circled me onstage at the De Warlencourt

Playhouse at STAGS and branded me on the thumb for the murder of Henry de Warlencourt, the young man who stood next to me now. I began to shake, and my legs suddenly felt totally unequal to the task of keeping me upright.

Henry gripped my arm. 'Steady,' he said. 'Look up.'

I did as he asked. And there, high above us, far beyond the reach of the torchlight, was a tiny red dot – a little glowing eye in the sky looking down on me. The HAWK was there. 'The Peel Tower Rebels won't let anything happen to you,' said Henry. 'And neither will I.'

Now there was more activity around the Damh – four young girls, by the look of their dresses, all with the heads of songbirds, were arranging a frothy green plant around each foot of the stag. Then four DOGS stepped out of their malign circle and touched their torches to the piles. The plant, whatever it was, caught immediately, and long tongues of flame began to lick and rise around the wicker legs of the stag, like serpents of fire. 'That's the *tein-éigin*,' said Henry. 'The needfire. It's kindled with an ancient herb called agaric. The branches of the Damh represent the tree spirit of fertility and vegetation, and the fire is purification – it burns up and destroys all harms.'

I shot a look at him but of course it was impossible to read his expression behind the hawk mask. Was there an ironic tone to his voice? It was so hard to tell.

As we watched, the needfire leaped up each leg and the body of the stag began to burn. The surreal scene before us was now as bright as day – and if we could see everything, the drone could too.

Something else was happening – the whole company was

forming some kind of line, with the DOGS at the very front. 'Now what?' I said to Henry, with the weariness of dread.

'Now the company process under the belly of the Damh three times. It's supposed to bring luck for the following year.'

'Luck?' I bleated. 'Are you crazy?'

'Come on,' he said. 'We don't want to be at the back. The longer the stag burns, the more unstable the whole structure gets.'

'No shit,' I said. So we joined the queue and followed the revellers as they danced under the bonfire, just as the creepy nanny had said at our first-night dinner. Even on our first go it was incredibly hot and bright, like actually being inside a fire, and I emerged on the other side with relief, even euphoria. The revellers were getting wild again, and I began to understand the heady rush of cheating death. This was why successive generations of de Warlencourts, even Henry himself, had tried to explain to me that the fox enjoys the hunt.

'You think this is strange?' bellowed Henry, as we passed beneath the burning belly a second time. 'In olden days they used to drive all the Highland cattle under the legs too. You can imagine how much they liked that.'

'Why?' I yelled back over the crackling of burning willow.

'They used to think that if they didn't the cows would be attacked by giddiness and convulsions and dance in their stalls.'

'Okaaaaaayyyy. Any more lovely surprises?'

'Well, there's a fertility element to the proceedings,' he said, more softly now as we emerged on the other side of the fire.

I didn't like the sound of that. 'What kind of element?'

'Well . . .' He actually sounded quite shy for once. 'Later

in the night couples used to . . . fornicate – on the ashes, around the glowing stag. They believed it would make the men fertile and the women fruitful.'

I looked at him sharply through the holes in my mask. 'Used to? Or still do?'

He didn't quite meet my eyes.

'Got it,' I said. 'Well, hopefully we can go home before the orgy stuff starts.'

Our third revolution under the stag was by far the scariest – burning brands were already beginning to fall from the belly of the structure. The stag was really roaring now, the flames almost reaching the neck. We emerged safely, as did all the other revellers, but there was still someone left to go. The Lammas Fool, alone, had been held back to run last of all. The fox-faced man stood, psyching himself up, alone on the one side, while the crowd stood, baying, on the other. On a signal from the goat he ran, shielding his head from what was now an inferno. I said: 'They do this so he has more chance of being burned.' It was a statement, not a question.

'Correct,' said Henry, watching too.

I was afraid for the tall foxy man, as even by his second revolution fire was positively raining down. 'Henry,' I said, 'does anyone ever get hurt?'

'Singed a little maybe,' he said. 'But the violence to the "special guest" usually happens at the Red Hunt. I've no idea why it didn't this year. But I've never known a death at Lammas, if that's what you're asking.'

That was what I was asking. I was a little reassured, but I still fixed my eyes on the tall, slim man anxiously, willing him to get round unscathed. As I watched, I was struck by a sudden notion. I couldn't see the fox's hair, but I was absolutely convinced it was Ratio. No one else I knew was that tall, plus I'd seen his antler earring in the Lammas Circle. I saw him emerge from the conflagration untouched following his third and final pass, and the crowd, won over after jeering their fool, cheered instead.

I breathed a sigh of relief. I had high hopes that after all the fun and games everything would start winding down. Surely in the next few minutes the Damh would be completely burned up, the hillside would be dark again and we could all go home? I no longer cared if nothing happened that we could pin on the Order. Things had got weird enough and my only concern was to leave the place alive. I was already jumpy as a jackrabbit so when someone clutched at my elbow I nearly skipped out of my skin.

'We've got a problem.'

It was Shafeen.

Alone among the company he wasn't wearing a mask. Luckily everyone else was intent on the burning stag, because he didn't look at all like the rest of the revellers. He was dressed head to toe in black and clutching Ratio's phone, the one he was clearly using to pilot the drone. He looked like James Bond, but now wasn't the time to swoon over him. He was saying something that put all other thoughts right out of my head.

'*Someone's in the stag.*'

30

'*What?*' In my shock I turned to face him.

'Keep looking forward,' he hissed fiercely. 'I can't be seen.'

Henry, who had now detected Shafeen's presence, came to stand on the other side of me, to hide the interloper from sight. 'What's up?'

'There's a person *in* the stag,' whispered Shafeen. 'I was flying the drone, and I couldn't see a thing before the fire was lit. So I switched to infrared like Ratio taught me. And it picked up all the heat signatures of the people on the ground of course. But it also picked up a signature of someone *in the deer*. In the head, just under the antlers.'

Suddenly Ty and Nel were with us, and we stood in a tight circle about Shafeen as he rapidly explained the situation once again.

'Jesus,' I breathed. All those times I had jokingly referenced *The Wicker Man*. Well, now we were living it. 'We have to do something. And *fast*.' The fire was now burning along the body towards the neck of the stag. 'It's so lucky Ratio taught you the infrared thing.'

'He's still not back?' asked Henry urgently.

216

'No,' said Ty, her voice strangled with tears.

'I think he is here though,' I said. 'I saw his antler earring in the Lammas Circle.'

Then I realised.

The words I'd read in *The Golden Bough* wreathed around my head like glowing embers.

Colossal images of wicker-work were constructed . . . these were filled with live men . . . fire was then applied to the images . . . they were burned with their living contents . . .

'Oh God. Oh God. Oh God,' I breathed. 'It's *him*. It's *Ratio* in the stag.'

Now the flames had mounted higher I could see a figure, lying prone, obviously bound and gagged, writhing like the serpents in the book. 'We got this all wrong. *He's* the sacrifice. It was him they wanted, not me. They stripped him of his metals, ready for the ritual.'

Ty ripped off her mask, her face a picture of agony. 'We have to save him!'

'I don't *think* so.'

For a moment I didn't recognise the voice – because I had heard it so seldom. It sounded like a younger Rollo, an older Louis.

It was Lord Peregrine.

We were surrounded by a circle of the Dark Order of the Grand Stag, cloaked and antlered and absolutely impassable. 'Nice to see you again, my dear,' said Lord Peregrine, nodding his antlered head towards Ty. 'Although it is customary to wait to be invited.'

'Ah, sir,' said Henry, 'I'm so glad you're here. I'm afraid we have some uninvited guests. If you'll allow me, I'll find the servants and have them removed.'

I turned on him quickly, feeling the sting of betrayal. Had he been stringing me along all this time? Had he been on the Order's side all along? But his blue eyes in the hawk mask held mine steadily.

Trust me.

Then I knew what he was up to – he was trying to break free so he could help Ratio. Admiring his quick thinking, I held my tongue and looked back at Lord Peregrine. He was silent beneath the mask, as if thinking, but this wasn't his call. He looked to the figure with the largest surroyal antlers. And then I clicked. It wasn't a question of whether Henry's uncle would buy it. It was a question of whether the Old Abbot would buy it.

He didn't.

'I'm sorry, my boy,' said Gideon Villiers. 'More sorry than I can say, because of the great esteem in which I held your father Rollo. But I'm afraid you have proved to be a cuckoo in the nest, and your loyalties to the Order have, however understandably –' he inclined his great antlers gallantly at me – 'been compromised. No. You will stay and observe the ritual. *All* of you. And then you yourselves shall be tried by the needfire.'

This was the stuff of nightmares, and I willed myself to wake up. I, Henry and all the Peel Tower Rebels were imprisoned in a tight circle of red-robed figures bearing antlers on their heads and torches in their hands. Of course we struggled desperately and tried to break out of the circle, but even Shafeen and Henry, by far the strongest of us, were silently and firmly repelled by the dreadful, silent figures in the deer masks. Meanwhile, the fire crept slowly but surely up the neck of the wicker stag, to the desperate figure trapped in its head. Ty started to hurl abuse at the DOGS, dredging up every curse she'd ever learned on the Limehouse Estate, while Nel, softly and hopelessly, began to cry. It was horrible to see Ratio twisting and turning in the cage of wicker that was the stag's head, knowing there was nothing we could do but watch him fry, knowing that we ourselves faced a similar fate.

Quickly, silently, Shafeen slipped Ratio's phone up his sleeve. The HAWK, unobserved, presumably still whirred and watched above us, but that was no consolation. We'd never wanted it to witness *this* – the dreadful sight of its inventor being burned alive.

But the drone was destined to capture another narrative entirely. As we watched, the Lammas Fool, the man in the fox's mask, ran towards the burning stag and began, incredibly, to climb up one of the fiery front legs. At every instant it seemed that his clothes would catch fire, but doggedly, determinedly, he climbed above the fire to the stag's neck, where the flames were only just beginning to lick. A crowd of revellers converged below him, screaming and throwing whatever they could, but no one else was man enough to climb the burning effigy. Meanwhile the fox, having reached the stag's head, was pulling its face apart, wrenching aside the pliant wicker until he could gain entry. Then there were two figures silhouetted in the head, as the fox fumbled at Ratio's gag and untied his hands. Then, only seconds ahead of the flame that roared upwards and consumed the head entirely, they jumped down onto the soft grass, as the fire finally reached the antlers and the entire stag burned in a beautiful, terrible blaze.

For a moment I lost sight of the pair who had fallen to the ground. But the revellers, in their demonic animal masks, converged on them, arms outstretched like zombies, claw-like hands grabbing – but foxy-face held on to Ratio with one hand, drew a gun with the other, and fired it into the air.

Instantly the revellers drew back and froze in place, as if they were playing a parlour game.

'Everyone stay where you are!'

I heard a little gasp from Nel a split second before I recognised the voice.

Then Abbot Ridley took off his fox mask.

31

There was a breathless silence – the crackling and roaring of the grim golden fire-stag was the only sound.

Ratio was sitting on the grass, coughing up smoke, green head in hands. His features were blurred with soot, eyes and mouth red – never had he resembled the Joker more. He seemed weak but otherwise fine. His clothes were black with smoke but, by some miracle, not even scorched. Abbot Ridley, eyes streaming from the smoke, panting like the fox he'd pretended to be, held the gun high. I didn't exactly know what type it was, but I thought it was some kind of revolver. I'd seen enough movies to know that there were six bullets in the cylinder, and he'd used up one of them already. But there were far, far more than five people here, and if the crowd rushed him, he'd probably only be able to loose one shot before he was overwhelmed. The stakes were so high now – an interloper had witnessed what the DOGS had done, and surely they couldn't let Nathaniel Ridley leave this mountain alive?

The beasts began to creep forward, and Abbot Ridley turned around and around, pointing his gun at one animal then the next. There were far too many of them for him to cover. But just before any of the beasts could leap for him there was the sound of a whistle, and the roving beam of a powerful torch scanning the hillside. Then another whistle, and another beam. Then another, and another. A man in uniform ran forward to stand with the Abbot, to be joined by five, ten, twenty more.

Thank God.

The police.

The revellers tried to run but were prevented – there were policemen coming from all directions. The first officer produced a megaphone. 'Stay where you are,' he said in a commanding Scots voice. 'You are surrounded by officers. Remain in place and take off your masks.'

The beasts looked at each other.

'I repeat: Take. Off. Your. Masks.'

Now the hapless creatures looked to their Grand Master. Very, very slowly the Old Abbot lifted his gloved hands to his antlers and took off his mask. His white hair dishevelled, his face crumpled and sweaty, his power and command had gone. He just looked like a sad old man. One by one, all the DOGS followed his lead. The faces of Peregrine de Warlencourt and his son Louis were revealed, followed by the rest of the Dark Order – famous people, politicians, minor royals. Then every other creature removed their animal head, and I saw once again all those characters from The Gathering, the STAGS Club, the Boxing Day hunt, Cumberland Place and Longcross. Some I knew, like the Medievals and Cass. Some I didn't. But all were guilty as hell.

'Shafeen!' Abbot Ridley yelled across to him. 'The drone.' Shafeen, understanding at once, slid Ratio's phone from his sleeve and began to tap the HAWK's controls. The drone obediently flew down to head height and hovered around the company, recording every naked face, before returning to the skies when bidden by Shafeen.

The burly man with the megaphone (an inspector?) began to speak again. 'You must all consider yourselves under arrest. You must not attempt to leave Skye. I repeat, *you cannot leave Skye*. The bridge is guarded, the ferry suspended, and the coast will be policed in case you attempt to leave in private boats. Return to your accommodation where you will each be questioned over the coming days. I repeat, you will not be permitted to leave the island until you have given a statement as to your part in tonight's proceedings.'

The crowd began to disperse, escorted down the hillside by the uniformed officers. In the background, the wicker stag was a glowing red skeleton. Once the DOGS left our side we ran over to Abbot Ridley, who was talking to the police inspector. Now he wasn't using the megaphone the officer seemed much less scary – a big but twinkly Scotsman with laughter lines around his eyes. 'Mr Ridley,' he was saying, 'thank you for the leads you gave us. You were certainly right about the atrocity we witnessed tonight. But I sincerely hope you have a licence for that gun.'

Abbot Ridley grinned. 'I do.' Obviously the Abbot had all sorts of hidden depths we didn't know about. He really *was* James Bond, and I could see his glamour points increase about a thousandfold in Nel's eyes.

The inspector smiled too. 'Very well then, I'll take your word for it. But you too will please stay at the address you gave us. We'll be round in the morning.'

When the inspector had gone, Nel threw herself into Abbot Ridley's arms and they kissed passionately.

As soon as she could speak Nel said, 'Are you all right?'

'Yes,' said the Abbot. 'It was actually lucky that I got pelted with the eggs and milk – my costume and gloves were so saturated they protected me from the flames. Being the Lammas Fool might just have saved my life.'

'And mine,' Ratio croaked from the grass.

'Good,' said Henry to the Abbot. 'I thought you might have ended up with hands like mine.' And I remembered then when someone else had been saved from a different fire. Ty. The object of Henry's salvation now sat with Ratio, her arms wrapped around him.

'Has that ever happened before?' Nel asked Henry. 'The stag sacrifice, I mean.'

'No,' he said, shaking his head vehemently. 'I swear not. Huntin' shootin' fishin' is one thing – it's indefensible and I admit I was a part of it – but to burn someone alive? In cold blood? As a human sacrifice? No. Not in my time.'

'It must be because they didn't kill you on the Red Hunt,' said Shafeen to me. 'They needed a sacrifice, and they found one in Ratio.'

'Did they grab you when you were out on the recce?' asked Ty of Ratio.

'No,' he gasped, wincing. 'They took me directly from the Peel Tower.' He looked up at Henry, eyes still bloodshot with smoke. 'Looks like someone gave me away,' he said pointedly.

'Yes,' I said, suddenly seeing how it had been. '*You* did.'

Now Ratio looked at me. 'What do you mean?'

'The bulletproof vest you sent me,' I said. 'Cass opened it. She saw your note. From *Ratio and the Peel Tower Rebels*.'

'Ah,' he said ruefully. 'Yes, that would do it.'

'She gave it to me too late as well,' I said. '*After* the Red Hunt. I bet that was no accident.'

Just then there was a creak and a crash as the fiery stag structure finally gave up the ghost and fell into ashes. We watched the glowing embers for a moment. It seemed so symbolic – the destruction of the Order and the end of STAGS. We looked at each other. 'What do we do now?' I said.

'Go home, I suppose,' said Shafeen. 'House arrest until they talk to us. But it's over.'

We walked down the hill together, Ty and Shafeen supporting a sooty, limping Ratio. I felt an overwhelming sense of relief, followed by a wave of tiredness. Dread is very draining – and when it lifts, you have nothing much left.

'Where will you go?' Nel said to Abbot Ridley.

'I told them I'd be at the Peel Tower,' he replied. 'If there's a space for me.'

'I'll make you comfortable,' said Nel, and he smiled down at her. It took a bit of getting used to, the idea of the Abbot and Nel together, because it was hard to get it out of my head that he was our headteacher, even though I knew now that he was an agent of the FOXES and hadn't really ever been our teacher at all. It wasn't *that* weird that they were together, since he was late twenties and she was nearly nineteen, and older men and younger women were, as Mrs Potts might say, 'a tale as old as time'. But it still took a bit of mental adjusting to accept it – maybe calling him Nathaniel instead of 'the Abbot' might help, so I resolved to do that in future.

'I might have to sleep with the HAWK under my pillow and this gun in my hand,' said Nathaniel as we walked. 'That drone contains solid evidence against the Order.' He looked at Ratio. 'They clearly attempted your murder tonight.'

'No shit.' Ratio grimaced.

'Unless they claim he was in the stag by accident?' said Ty. 'You know, was helping to build it and got trapped? I wouldn't put it past them.'

'Might have been better not to bind and gag him if they wanted to use that defence,' said Nathaniel. 'No – we've got them this time.'

I shivered. Away from the fire, I was finally cold. 'I wish we could leave tonight,' I said. 'I don't want anything else to go wrong.'

'Like what?' said Henry.

'I don't know.' I couldn't articulate what I was feeling. 'Like they try to harm one of us.'

'I've made sure we'll all be properly guarded,' said Nathaniel reassuringly. 'But be ready to leave in the morning.'

'What about all that house arrest and statements stuff?'

'Don't worry about that,' said Nathaniel, not quite meeting my eyes. 'As soon as those ferries are running, we're away.'

'And what if the Order steal the drone, like you said?' Worrying had become such a habit I couldn't quite stop.

'It wouldn't do any good,' croaked Ratio. 'The footage has already uploaded to the Saros Orbit.'

I stole a glance at Henry. We'd done exactly the same thing

with the footage of his confession at the top of Conrad's Force. I wondered what would happen to that now – I supposed in the trial that would follow that would all come out too, and I felt a little stone of unhappiness settle just below my heart.

It was decided that Henry and I would spend one more night in the castle as there wasn't exactly room in the Peel Tower, especially now that Nathaniel was there too. If I went back with them I'd have to share the living room with Shafeen, and neither of us were ready for that yet. He did, however, hang back at the entrance to Castle MacLeod to say goodnight to me. 'You'll be all right?' he asked.

'Yes,' I said, not at all sure I would be. 'They know the police are on to them. It's just one more night. Shafeen . . .'

'No,' he said, but kindly. 'Not tonight. Tomorrow.'

He didn't kiss me, but he hugged me tightly, and I felt in the strength of that hug that maybe there *was* a way back for us.

In the atrium Henry and Louis were talking to each other at the bottom of the staircase underneath the duelling pistols, furious and low-voiced. Neither one of them was wearing their mask, and Louis only had one glove on. I almost went to them but Henry looked up and gave his head a tiny shake. It was obviously some private matter, so I went into reverse and mounted the stairs to the North Tower instead.

I didn't know whether I desired or dreaded Henry coming to say goodnight once he had finished speaking with Louis. I knew I wanted to get back together with Shafeen, but I did want to talk over the dramatic events of the evening with Henry. As it turned out, I was bathed, in my nightclothes and in bed before the knock came.

He closed the door gently behind him but didn't come all the way into the room.

'I came to say goodbye.' He seemed unusually hesitant and wouldn't look at me. 'I . . . I made a deal with someone. If I go now, you won't be touched.'

'But there are police everywhere,' I protested. 'They won't harm me now.'

'If you think that,' he said ruefully, 'you really don't know the Order. No. It has to be this way.'

God. He was going to do it. He was going to give himself up. 'Will . . . will I see you again?'

'No.' He gave a small, sad smile. 'It's the only thing to do, Greer. I have to make things right.'

He held out his fire-scarred hand – the one that usually bore the signet ring with the little antlers stamped on it. I looked at the hand. Was that how this ended, the culmination of everything we'd been through together? A handshake?

'This can't be it.' My voice clotted with tears.

'What else can there be?' he said. 'I made a promise to Shafeen that I would never kiss you again.'

I got up. 'But I . . . *I* didn't promise.'

As if in a dream I walked towards him. And now I knew I *had* dreamed of that moment, over and over again; had to admit to myself how much I'd wanted it, even though I'd fought so hard against it.

I took Henry de Warlencourt's face in my hands, and for the first, and last, time, I kissed *him*. The kiss went on and on; our hands were in each other's hair, our bodies pressed together hard. The fire that had been threatening to engulf me all weekend burned me right up like the stag on the hillside. We fell back on the bed, and I knew it was no good fighting it any more.

I knew exactly how we were going to say goodbye.

32

I woke the next morning with a brief feeling of complete happiness.

All the complications and worries and doubts of the future would come later – the loss of Henry to the authorities, the complicated situation with Shafeen, the trial and hopefully punishment of the Order – but for now I was where I was, and there was only one thought in my mind. I'd slept with Henry de Warlencourt, and in a moment I would turn to find him naked in my bed next to me, and would snuggle back into his arms, where I'd spent the night.

I turned over.

There was no Henry, just a note on the pillow, just like in the movies.

I love you, Greer.
Goodbye.
H x

And right by the note was a rowan twig, scarlet berries shrivelled on the bough, and a circle of red thread.

I'd never dressed so quickly in my life. I ran downstairs so fast I almost tripped over myself. I couldn't let Henry give himself up. I didn't know where he'd gone, so the first place I went was the duelling pistols, where we'd met every morning of that fateful weekend, hoping against foolish hope that somehow, magically, he would be waiting for me.

He wasn't there.

Neither were the pistols.

Then pieces of memory began to slot together in my mind:

Louis had killed Rollo in order to be Earl of Longcross.

Henry's resurrection stood between Louis and the earldom.

Louis wanted Henry dead.

Louis and Henry talking, furious and low-voiced, underneath the pistols last night.

Louis wearing just one glove.

Henry saying: 'I might have known Louis wouldn't do it in a gentlemanly way.'

Me saying: 'What would be a gentlemanly way? To slap you in the face with a single glove and challenge you to a duel?'

A *duel*.

'No,' I said aloud. 'No, no, no, no, no.'

Suddenly every movie I'd ever seen about duels flashed into my head. *Barry Lyndon. The Duellists. Hamilton.* Always at dawn. Always in a misty meadow. Always with the duellists back to back, taking ten paces, turning and firing. Two men enter, one man leaves. But where would Henry go to fight a deadly duel with his cousin? He could be anywhere on Skye and I only had one chance to get this right. It wasn't light yet, but it soon would be. There was only one person who could find him – or rather, one thing.

231

The HAWK.

I ran to the Peel Tower as fast as I could. No one prevented me, but actually I'm not sure any policeman in the world could have stopped me that morning.

It took me perhaps ten minutes to get to the tower, and I hammered on the door until someone answered. That someone was Shafeen, hair everywhere and eyes half closed. He was dressed in tracksuit bottoms and a hoodie and I knew he'd been first to the door because he was sleeping alone in the downstairs sitting room. That didn't make me feel better about my betrayal, but I didn't have time to flagellate myself right now. A life was at stake.

'Henry,' I gasped, almost doubled over. 'He's gone to fight a duel with Louis.'

Shafeen went from being half asleep to fully awake in about a second. 'How do you know?'

'I saw them talking last night, underneath those duelling pistols. Louis only had one glove on, as if he'd issued a challenge, you know?'

'I do know.'

'And last night, when he came to say goodnight –' I swallowed guiltily – 'Henry said he'd done a deal with someone. That if he gave himself up I would not be touched. I assumed he meant the police. But now I know he meant Louis. And when I went downstairs this morning the duelling pistols had gone.'

'Come in.' Shafeen dragged me inside. The little sitting room was warm, since the fire was still glowing, and Shafeen's sheets and blankets were all over the sofa. He swept them away. 'Sit down,' he said. 'I'll make you some coffee.'

'No time,' I said agitatedly, and stayed standing.

The others filtered into the room in ones and twos, wearing variously T-shirts, pyjama bottoms and tartan blankets.

'What's going on?' asked Nel.

'Henry's gone to fight a duel with Louis,' I repeated. 'And I don't know where.'

Ratio, bless him, got the point straight away. 'We'll send the HAWK up,' he said. He grabbed the drone and phone from the console and we all headed outside. Ratio activated the drone from the palm of his hand in the Savage version of what Henry did with Regina, when he'd flown the falcon from his wrist. The HAWK mounted into the sky, high, high over the Peel Tower. It banked as he sent it over the castle and towards the cliffs. We all huddled round the phone, which Ratio held landscape-wise in his hands. He had it on infrared, the mode which had saved his own life the night before. Desperately I squinted at the screen, willing the heat signature of a figure to appear, a body I now felt I knew as well as my own. After a few roundish blobs of warm oranges and reds made my heart leap – 'Deer or sheep,' said Ratio – we saw two similar-sized figures striding towards open ground. One was taller than the other. 'That's them!' I exclaimed. 'Where are they?'

Ratio studied the picture-in-picture of a real-time map of Skye in the corner of the screen. 'They're going north along the cliff walk, past the castle. It looks like they're heading to Dunvegan Viewpoint. Quickest route would be to go through the castle – past the walled garden and then the round garden.'

'Right,' said Shafeen, cramming his feet into his trainers. 'Let's get moving. Remember, this isn't a fair fight.'

'What?' said Ratio.

'It isn't a fair fight,' Shafeen repeated. 'It's rigged. Both those pistols are designed to kill the same person.' Shafeen turned to me. 'Don't you remember? In my father's diary, when he was at Longcross in 1969. Rollo de Warlencourt and his own bunch of Medievals did this kind of haunted-house thing where they put out all the lights and scared my father half to death. He was so freaked that he took a duelling pistol from the wall and shot at Rollo in the Long Gallery.'

'You're absolutely right,' I said. 'The pistol backfired, and Aadhish nearly shot his own ear off.'

'That's it. And do you remember what Rollo said? He said Aadhish *used the Judas pistol*. And then Gideon (who grew up to be the Old Abbot) said, *If he'd used the Jesus one you wouldn't be standing here*.'

'I'm not following,' said Nel.

'The de Warlencourts own a pair of antique duelling pistols,' said Shafeen. 'They used to hang on the wall at Longcross.'

'Then they were moved to Castle MacLeod after the fire,' I continued. 'Cass told me.'

'One of them, the Jesus pistol, fires true,' said Shafeen, explaining as rapidly as he could. 'The other one, the Judas pistol, is designed to backfire and kill anyone who shoots it.'

'How do you tell the difference?' asked Ty.

'The Jesus one has a little cross on the handle, right way up,' I said. 'The Judas one has the same cross, but upside down.' The details were ingrained in my memory.

'And do the duellists know about this difference?' Nathaniel asked the crucial question. 'Louis and Henry, do they know?'

'We don't know.' I looked at Shafeen, eyes wide. 'We've got to go. *Now*.'

'Yes,' said Ratio. 'Go. I've got you covered. The HAWK will be watching.'

'And we'll be right behind you,' said Nathaniel, 'with the police.'

Shafeen and I ran.

33

The short distance to the castle now seemed like an incredibly long way.

We just had to hope there were some formalities to get through before you fought a duel – maybe some trash talking between the two combatants like they did before boxing matches, or maybe measuring out the ten paces or something. Because if they got straight to it, we'd already be too late. As we ran, too breathless to speak, I thought, out of nowhere, about Ben Jonson. The playwright had fought a duel in Hoxton Fields with Henry's ancestor and killed him. Jonson was thrown in Newgate Prison and branded on his thumb with an M for Manslayer, the same brand that I bore on my own thumb. But Henry had no such brand. He wasn't a manslayer – yet. And Henry had never, despite the dark games of the Order, killed anyone. Jonson had saved himself from the noose by reciting the 'neck verse', but if Henry got the Jesus pistol and killed Louis, there would be no release on a technicality for him. He would *definitely* be going to jail for the rest of his life. I was pretty sure that outside the rarefied little world of London's STAGS Club (where I remembered they'd built an underground passage expressly for the purpose), duels were illegal. This was a lose/lose for Henry. If he got the Jesus pistol he would surely shoot Louis dead, as he was such a crack shot. But if he got the Judas pistol, he would shoot himself. As I ran I clenched my own left thumb in my fist, hard enough to hurt. I wasn't a manslayer either. I'd been tried for the murder of a person who was still alive – for the moment. But if Henry died today, had I killed him after all? I'd been the one to set him on the path to goodness, and that had led to his downfall.

And crucially, did they *know* about the Jesus and Judas pair? The pistols had hung on the walls of Longcross Hall for centuries, until it burned down in the Boxing Day fire and the guns were moved to Castle MacLeod. Had the boys played with them as children? Had they been told by concerned parents of the pistols' secrets? Did Louis realise he could rig the duel so that he would win either way, or was he, in his crazed and misplaced notion of honour, convinced that the righteousness of his cause would win the day?

As the sun lightened the eastern skies, we raced north as fast as we could. Past the walled garden, past the round garden, past the castle itself. We ran towards the cliff and the viewing point that Ratio had identified.

On the horizon, and in the dim of the dawn and the mist of the meadow, I could see the outline of a bulky figure – then, in the next instant, I realised it was two figures back to back. The figure cleaved in two and I thought I could identify Henry, but in the fog the two figures were so close in appearance that it was impossible at this distance. They began to pace away from each other and Shafeen and I began to yell and gesture wildly. I had no idea what I was shouting. My thudding heart and running feet outpaced their slow march, but we were still too far away to be heard. While my mouth screamed at them, another part of my brain – some cold, mathematical lobe – counted, inexorably, their steps.

One.

Two.

Three. The almost identical figures in tweeds walked in lockstep.

Four.

Five.

Six. Pistols held at their shoulders, pointing skywards.

Seven.

Eight.

Nine. Blond heads looking straight ahead, away from each other.

Ten.

The figures stopped and turned and time splintered and slowed. One of the figures raised his gun straight above his head, like a starting pistol, and, instead of pointing it at his opponent, pointed it harmlessly at the sky.

Alexander Hamilton, I thought.

It was Henry. Henry who had pointed his flintlock into infinity. Then I understood. He was attempting suicide by duel. He wouldn't kill Louis, but he would allow Louis to kill him. I might have realised the terrible truth if I'd just stopped to think about it for one second. He'd had one first and last night with me and now he would rather die than go to jail. But it almost didn't matter – if he had the Judas pistol, it didn't matter where he pointed it. So long as he held it in his hand it would backfire the same way, the bullet travelling backwards along the line of his arm and into his brain.

'*No!*' I screamed.

But it was too late. As I shouted, the deafening report of two guns going off sounded almost simultaneously, and twin flashes burst from the flintlock of each pistol, twenty paces apart. One blond young man fell to the ground, the other still stood, and for one dreadful, heart-stopping moment I could no longer be sure which was which.

Then, at last, we were upon them and we could see the truth.

Henry's bullet had discharged harmlessly into the infinite blue of the sky.

Louis's bullet had backfired, travelling along the line of his firing arm, through his right eye and into his brain.

34

I cannoned into Henry, enfolding him in a bone-crushing hug, face buried in his shoulder. 'I thought I'd lost you.'

I felt my way down his arm and took hold of the hand that held the still-smoking gun and had to prise the frozen fingers apart to see the handle. There, on the silver scroll, was the design of a cross – right way up.

The Jesus pistol.

The flintlock fell to the grass and Henry closed strong arms around me, but I could feel him shaking. 'It's all right,' he said, over and over, stroking my hair. As if he was soothing a hawk. As if I was Regina.

But it was not all right for Louis. Soberly, we walked together to where Shafeen was kneeling over him. There was no chance for him. His right eye was a horrible void; his left eye, blue as the sky, stared at the matching heavens. His pistol had fallen from his hand too. 'Don't touch it,' said Shafeen, closing the single eye. 'It's evidence.' But I didn't need to. I could see from where I was standing the decorative scroll on the stock of the pistol. It featured an upside-down cross.

Louis had chosen the Judas pistol.

As we stood, heads bowed, the Peel Tower Rebels caught us up, panting.

Ratio said, 'Should we get a doctor?'

Shafeen shook his head. 'Too late for that,' he said. 'But someone should go for the inspector.'

'I'll go,' said Nathaniel. 'I know him best.'

'I'll come with you,' said Nel.

As they ran Ratio landed the drone. There was an unspoken agreement that this was not something we should be filming. As the HAWK landed on his palm, Ty said, 'Shouldn't we cover Louis up?'

I shot a glance at her. I couldn't imagine what she must be feeling. For a while she and Louis had been together, and even though she'd claimed later that she'd got together with him to infiltrate the family and bring them down, they'd still been close. And now her old boyfriend was lying at her feet, while her new boyfriend comforted her.

Ratio, to his great credit, began to remove his jacket to use as a shroud, but just then a commotion sounded in the direction of the castle.

There was a terrible, keening singing. A wavering, otherwordly voice sang an ancient air I'd heard once before. Nanny emerged from the mist, carrying a length of golden silk in both hands, walking in a strangely ceremonial way, singing as she came.

Unerringly, as if she suddenly had some supernatural ability to see, she walked forward with the Faerie Flag, sank to her knees and, without once pausing her eerie song, laid it gently and precisely over Louis's dead face. Then she picked up his lolling head and cradled it in her lap, as she must have done so often when he was a baby, but this time the dark blood soaked and spread along the fibres of the golden silk, to meld and merge with the MacLeod blood of his ancestors.

As I averted my eyes from this deeply personal scene I saw an unmistakable silhouette resolve in the mist to the north of us. Four finely muscled legs, elegant as those of a racehorse, a noble head and magnificent antlers curving skywards.

A stag.

For a moment I thought it was Jeffrey, the venerable Imperial we had killed at the Red Hunt, come to gloat at the demise of his killer. But as the creature trod precisely forward I saw that, instead of a red pelt, his fur was completely white.

This, then, was a graveyard stag – the fabled creature who would visit at the death of the heir of the family. I watched him, slack-jawed, as he returned my gaze with wise and liquid eyes. Slowly I reached out both hands to tap Henry and Shafeen and point, but before I could alert them something spooked the pale stag and he turned to run, becoming one with the white mist as he disappeared, as if he had never even existed.

Then, in the other direction, we could see what had startled him: a group of people approaching from the castle. In the early-morning mist they resolved into Nathaniel, Nel and the Inspector of Police, followed by Cass, Lord Peregrine and Lady Fiona. They were doing that half-walk, half-run thing people do in a genuine emergency.

As the party approached, Henry and Ratio helped Nanny to her feet, and as she rose she took the bloodstained Faerie Flag off Louis's face. 'Here,' she said. 'It's yours now.' But instead of giving it to Henry, she gave it to Ratio.

I could understand the mistake – she was blind, she was old, she had two tall young men helping her up, she'd heard Henry's voice and had obviously meant to give it to the new heir of the family, but she gave it to the wrong tall young man. I saw Henry's and Ratio's gaze meet over her head, blue eyes meeting blue eyes. Ratio gave the bloodstained banner to Henry. 'This was meant for you.' As their eyes met, their hands did too, joined for an instant by the Faerie Flag.

What I'd just seen seemed somehow hugely significant, but I had no idea why.

And then the party from the castle was upon us, and Lady Fiona saw Louis and began to scream and scream as if she would never stop.

35

We gathered in the library, like suspects in an Agatha Christie film, anxiously arranged around the room on various armchairs and sofas. And, just as in one of those movies, we'd been asked to wait there by the inspector, to be questioned in turn.

There were a few notable absences. Cass was nowhere to be seen. Lady Fiona was being treated by a local doctor for shock, and the coroner had been called from the mainland. Lord Peregrine was standing where I'd first seen him, warming his mustard cords by the fire, a glass of whisky in his hand and the open bottle before him on the mantel. His very presence, of course, meant that the rest of us maintained a sober silence.

The continuity of the scene, the lord of the manor by his fireside, meant things might have been normal. But they weren't. The hands that he held out to the flame quivered, and his lip quivered too. He spoke, low and rapidly, as if to himself, a constant stream of self-recrimination. *Should have secured the guns . . . Should have made sure they weren't loaded . . . Fiona was right . . . Fiona will kill me . . . And the police : . . And the stag . . . and the Order . . . Storm coming. Should have secured the guns . . .*

Henry looked at me and got to his feet. 'Sir,' he said gently, 'wouldn't you like to sit down?'

Peregrine looked at him distractedly, almost as if he didn't recognise his nephew. Then he seemed to come to himself a little. He patted Henry on the shoulder and smiled, an almost childish smile. 'No, my boy,' he said. 'For the first time in my life, I'm going to do the honourable thing.' He took the bottle, left the glass and stumbled out of the room.

We all watched him go.

'Where's he off to?' wondered Nel.

'Sounds like he's going to confess,' I said.

'To what?' said Shafeen. 'Having unsecured firearms?'

'No,' said Henry. 'To the burning stag, the sacrifice. Everything.'

'Well,' said Nathaniel with an odd look on his face, 'that would certainly make things easier.'

'But we have the footage,' protested Ratio.

'Testimony in person will always give greater weight,' said Henry.

If things weren't so dire I might have thought this was funny. Ratio and Henry sitting in adjacent leather armchairs like mirror images. One Savage, one Medieval. One extolling the virtues of technology, one of the spoken word. One was all green hair, tattoos and the 'OH, FOR FOX SAKE' T-shirt, the other all tweeds and waistcoat and country colours. I noticed for the first time that as well as having the same blue eyes, they had the same catlike grace. If it wasn't for the Joker hair they could have been brothers. I wondered, idly, what colour Ratio's hair was under the green.

Then my mind did that odd fitting-stained-glass-pieces-together thing that it sometimes did, to make a full window. It had done it at the end-of-term Mass in my first year at STAGS, when I'd realised the Old Abbot was, in fact, the Grand Master. It had done it at the foot of the stairs to the North Tower when I'd realised the pistols were missing and that Henry and Louis were going to fight a duel. And it did it now – to fit together the pieces of what was perhaps the most significant discovery of all.

Suddenly I was back in Ratio's techie bedroom in Glasgow. There, clear as day, was the Joker POP! figure on the console, oversized head sporting green hair, white face, red slash for a mouth. Then I heard Ratio's soft Scottish voice:

Ratio is my given name . . .

Rollo pursued my mother . . .

Rollo paid for me to go to STAGS . . .

I gawped at him, eyes and mouth wide.

He looked at me quizzically, with those blue, blue eyes. 'What?'

'Louis wasn't the Joker,' I choked. '*You* are. *You're* Arthur Fleck, aren't you?'

He understood me at once. He would, wouldn't he? But he was the only one in the room who did.

'Care to explain?' said Nel.

'Arthur Fleck,' I said, eyes never leaving Ratio's face, 'was Batman's half-brother. He was the product of Bruce Wayne's dalliance with a kitchen maid at Wayne Manor. And as Arthur was older than Batman, arguably he was the heir to Wayne Industries.'

Ratio said nothing. It was Ty, instead, who spoke. 'Are you saying . . . ? Are you telling us that Ratio is the heir to Longcross? And the earldom?'

'I'm not the actual heir.' Ratio spoke at last, almost with a sigh, as if a secret he had been holding close for so long could finally be released. 'Rightful heir, maybe. But, like the Joker, I'm a bastard. An illegitimate child.'

'Rollo didn't hunt your mother,' I said gently. 'He seduced her.'

'That's putting it politely,' he said shortly. 'I'd call it rape.' We all flinched at the brutal word.

'That's why you went after them, for all those years,' breathed Ty.

'Yes,' said Ratio. 'My mother was dazzled by Rollo. When she went to work at Longcross in the late nineties she was only sixteen.' I thought about the woman we'd met at Ratio's house; Lorna Rennie must be in her early forties now and was still beautiful – when she was sixteen she must have been stunning. 'He overpowered her,' said Ratio. 'There was nothing she could do. He knew what he'd done, of course.' He looked at Henry. 'When your grandfather Monty sacked Mum, she got in touch with Rollo. She was brave. She made demands, stood up for herself. That's why he agreed to support her, and he sent me to STAGS with his own money.'

'But . . . but . . .' My mind, having connected the dots, now seemed to be having trouble working. 'They didn't put you in the stag . . . the wicker stag, I mean . . . because of who you are?'

He shook his green head. 'They don't know. I think that was my own stupid fault, just like you said. When we sent you the Kevlar vest I signed it: *Ratio and the Peel Tower Rebels*. Just a silly gag really. Cass intercepted it and worked out that someone was living in her childhood den. Since they didn't dare touch you on the day of the Red Hunt, probably because *you* were there –' this to Henry – 'they found a perfect human sacrifice in me – a trespasser, a Savage, a person that could not possibly be of any importance to anyone.' He smiled bitterly. 'But as for knowing who I am – no. No one knows I exist. That was the deal Rollo struck with my mother. He said I was to remain in hiding – "for the time being".' He shrugged his narrow shoulders. 'I know what he meant by that. He meant in case he needed me one day. In case he needed an heir. Then, later in life, he met your mother Caroline,' he said, still addressing Henry, 'and had a legitimate heir. I wouldn't be needed after all.' There was no heat now, no resentment. Now the truth was out, his dislike of Henry seemed to have evaporated with the lies.

'You guessed,' I said, also turning to Henry. 'Didn't you? That morning when I was so desperate to go to the Peel Tower to talk to Shafeen, you wanted to talk to Ratio. Why?'

Henry said, 'It was the morning when we met Louis in the hanging room, over the body of the stag. You talked then about Louis being mad and belonging in that asylum.'

'Arkham,' said Ratio and I together.

'Yes. But that wasn't the bit that was interesting to me. I wasn't struck by the mental-illness part of that conversation, but the half-brother bit. I knew that my father had seduced maids at Longcross, when he was trying so hard to be something he wasn't, when he was trying to prove to himself that he could sire an heir. And I knew my grandfather had sent some of the girls away, and it stood to reason that at least one of them might have been pregnant.'

'And luckily my mother had the gumption not to let him get away with it,' said Ratio. 'She made him support us, and she agreed in return to call me Horatio. He never explained why.'

'I think I could tell you,' said Shafeen, speaking for the first time. 'It was the name he gave to the best version of himself. When he was happy and in love – in love with my father. I think . . . I think the name means he wanted you to be happy.'

Nathaniel stood up. He also hadn't spoken for some time, but he made up for it now. 'If you're the oldest son of Rollo de Warlencourt, we need to get you out of this castle and off this island. Now.'

'Wait – why?' said Nel, catching the urgency in his tone. 'The danger's over. The police are here.'

'I'll explain later.' Nathaniel was already shrugging on his jacket. 'Peel Tower contingent, let's go. There's not a moment to lose.'

'But the police told us to wait here,' I protested.

'It'll be fine,' he said, and I thought then that he had some sort of agreement with the inspector. 'Henry and Greer, get your things and meet us at the Peel Tower too.'

As the Peel Tower Rebels piled out of the library Henry spoke up. 'Ratio.' He corrected himself. 'Horatio. Wait.'

Ratio turned in the doorway. 'I'll be right behind you,' he told Ty.

He came back into the library and the two half-brothers stood facing each other on the hearthrug in front of the fire.

Ratio was a little taller, a little older, but otherwise, now that I knew, the similarities were striking. No wonder he had always reminded me of someone, right from the first moment in his Glasgow bedroom. I wondered now how I'd been so dumb as not to have seen it before. I felt almost as if I shouldn't be here, as though the brothers should be having this moment in private. I looked from one to the other. Who would speak first? What would they say? There was a lifetime of catching up to do. So much in common, and so little.

In the end it was Henry who began. He held out his hand, still clutching the banner of gold. 'Here,' he said. 'I want you to have it. You are the true heir of the family.'

Ratio looked at the Faerie Flag, and then at Henry doubtfully. 'I can't take this.'

Henry, quite unexpectedly, laughed. 'Good Lord. If I can't convince you to take an ancient, bloodied banner, then how on earth am I going to get you on board with the rest of my proposal?'

'Which is?' Ratio looked suspicious.

Henry took a deep breath, as if he was about to dive off a waterfall. 'I want you to have all of it. The earldom, the titles, Longcross. Everything.'

Both Ratio and I stared at Henry, open-mouthed.

'You are my father's eldest son,' said Henry simply. 'It is owed to you. And to your mother. Bring her to live with you. She deserves it.'

Ratio was speechless. For the first time since I'd met him, this sardonic, witty young Scotsman seemed to have nothing to say. Eventually he shook his head, as if he'd just received a blow.

'How could I? How could I become part of the establishment I've spent my whole life hating?'

'Well, you could take that stance, certainly,' said Henry reasonably. 'You could let the hate win, and then this whole cycle begins again and perpetuates itself. Or you could do the hard thing. The brave thing.'

Ratio looked at him warily. 'Which is?'

'You could change the establishment – from within.'

Ratio seemed to consider this. 'But what about you?'

Henry looked at me. 'Once my part in all this comes out, I don't think I'll be stuck for accommodation. I think I'll be housed at Her Majesty's pleasure.'

He meant jail. A cold hand seemed to clutch my heart. 'But, Henry, you've helped blow this whole thing wide open. And the three of us who you hunted, shot and fished, well – we're fine about it now.'

'There's still Gemma Delaney,' said Henry. 'Look. We're talking about atonement. How can I right the wrongs my father did to Ratio's mother if I don't look at myself? You, Nel, even Shafeen have forgiven me for what I did to you at Longcross. The huntin', the shootin' and the fishin', each of you in turn. But the year before you there was Gemma. I seduced her into coming to Longcross.' He caught my expression. 'I *pretended* to be interested in her, made her think there could be something romantic between us. Then, once she was there, we terrorised her for a whole weekend. I deserve to be punished for that. I'll be out of circulation once all this comes out, and *someone* has to inherit the earldom. It won't be Louis now, so who better than the rightful heir?'

Ratio was silent, clearly attempting to process this seismic change in his fortunes.

So I said, 'What about your uncle?'

And just then, loud and unmistakable, the sound of a gunshot.

36

For perhaps a second we looked at each other in horror.

Then we sped out of the library in the direction of the sound. 'The study,' said Henry urgently, and he led us through a nearby door.

It was the ultimate Medieval man cave: leather-bound, gold-tooled books on the shelves, a window with a view of the calm summer sea, a mahogany desk sporting an antique globe, an inkwell.

And a human head, with a hole blasted in it.

Lord Peregrine sat slumped in his chair, forehead on the desk. In one hand was a revolver. In the other, his bottle of whisky.

We stood looking down at this latest Lammas horror. Henry raked his hand agitatedly through his blond hair. 'God, I'm an *idiot*. He went to do the "honourable thing". He even said it.' He began to pace. 'He went into his study with his service revolver and a bottle of whisky. The classic gentleman's way out.'

Ratio, by contrast, was as still as a statue. 'How,' he said softly, 'is this the honourable thing? To leave his wife and daughter, when they've just lost Louis too?'

Henry stopped pacing and looked down at his uncle as

the dark mirror of blood pooled on the desk. 'It isn't. I see that now.'

'What now?' My question seemed intrusive, but it had to be asked.

It was Henry who took charge. 'We go. We were never here. If we get mixed up in this too we'll never get off the island, and Nathaniel seemed pretty clear that we should. Ratio, head to the Peel Tower – we'll follow as soon as we can. Greer, get your stuff and I'll meet you where the pistols used to be.'

We backed out of the room and closed the door on the scene.

Peregrine de Warlencourt had finally done something memorable, and it was destined to be the last thing he ever did.

I didn't have much stuff to pack, so I was ready in less than five minutes. I wondered if Henry was serious about giving his birthright away. I might never again be in a place where everything was provided for you and therefore you pretty much only had to bring a toothbrush. It was such a trivial thing to think at that moment, but then when I got to the bottom of the stairs there was a timely reminder of the horrid reality right in front of my eyes.

The empty brackets on the wall where the flintlocks had once hung.

Presumably the guns were in evidence bags by now.

Henry arrived just after me.

'Got everything?' I asked.

'Almost,' he said. 'Just one more thing. Come with me.'

The castle courts were deserted, and we didn't see a soul as we walked to the mews. Regina was sitting on her hoop perch in the walled garden, shifting and preening in the morning sun. She gave a little throaty chuckle of pleasure when her keen amber eyes lighted on Henry.

Henry went to her and stroked her breast feathers, as he always did, with the back of his scarred fingers. I did the same, assuming that this was goodbye. Our fingers met and about a thousand volts of electricity went through me. Henry took my hand and turned it over, stroking the M for Manslayer brand on my thumb.

I whispered, 'I thought it had come true. I thought I might have been a murderer after all.'

'What do you mean?' His voice was low, to match mine, and I could feel the warmth of his breath.

'I thought I'd killed you.'

'How would *you* have killed me? It would have been Louis. Or the pistol.' For of course by now he knew all about the Judas pistol and its lethal trick mechanism.

I pulled my hand away. Being that close to him was dangerous. 'There's this great film called *Léon*,' I said, as airily as I could, 'about an assassin who always works alone. Then he meets this girl called Mathilda, and from then on – spoiler alert – he's doomed. That's when the police catch up with him.'

'The similarities are striking,' he said, with a certain dark humour.

'The point is, once he let himself love, it made him vulnerable. For one thing, he was less nimble and agile. Before he was always just thinking about himself, but once he loved Mathilda then he had another person to look after. The other thing is . . .'

'Well?'

'He wanted to be a better person. For her. And that made him a less efficient killing machine. Arguably he would have survived if he'd never met her. If he'd been left alone.'

'Like a hawk. A loner and a killer.'

I watched him stroke the peregrine and listened to the hawk's bubbling sounds of pleasure. 'But Regina cares about you. You can see she does.'

'And she's all I have now.' It was a strangely desolate statement.

I shot a glance at him. 'Did you mean what you said in there? That you'd give it all up?'

'Well, let me ask you a question. If I go to prison, who should have the earldom? Ratio or Cass?'

I thought about this. Ratio, the rightful heir with the righteous hair. Or Cass. Cass the enigma, Cass the question mark. Cass who'd had a completely unreadable reaction to her brother's death and hadn't been seen since. 'Wouldn't Cass be in trouble too? She's part of this whole thing, and this weekend I'm starting to think she isn't as innocent as we thought.'

'She's done nothing that can be proven, I don't think. She opened the bulletproof vest, and didn't give it to you right away. She possibly gave Ratio's whereabouts to the Order, so they could capture him, but that would be difficult to prove, particularly if she told her father and he's now dead. But what else?'

'I don't know,' I said. 'I just get the feeling she's been a bit more central to things than we thought. I used to think, Cass Good, Louis Bad, but now I'm not so sure.'

'Well, if you're right then you're just making my point

for me. Ratio should inherit. We can't doubt that he'd be an honourable steward, and also that there'd be an end to the death hunts once and for all.'

He was right, of course. 'Well, look, we should hurry up and join them.' I didn't want to rush the farewell, but we had priorities.

To my surprise Henry didn't answer but ran into the mews and emerged with a hawk basket. He hooded Regina, untied her leash and settled her in the basket with one of her beloved chicken necks as a packed lunch. 'She was my last piece of luggage,' he said. '*Now* we can go.' Then, quickly and quietly, we left the walled garden.

Again, I was surprised at just how easy it was to leave the castle. I'd expected two cops on the door at least. But no one stopped us going anywhere. I supposed by that time Peregrine's body had been discovered and all the police attention was elsewhere. We walked right out of the courtyard and beyond the castle walls. No hand reached out to stop us and no voice stopped us in our tracks.

But once we were a safe distance away some nameless instinct made me look back.

From the top of the North Tower, where I'd met Henry on the night of The Gathering, the one remaining heir of the MacLeods watched the interloping MacDonald leave her castle.

Her cropped blonde hair was blowing in the wind, her expression too far away to see.

37

On the ferry back to the mainland we all stood at the rail at the back – the bow, I guess – like extras on *Titanic*.

We watched the black island recede into the distance across the silver sea. No one had stopped us as we'd hurried to the Peel Tower to meet the rebels and tell them the news of Peregrine's end. And we'd had no trouble getting onto the boat – no spot checks, no questions, no nothing. I'd worried all the way on the drive from the Peel Tower to the terminal that we would be stopped at one of the checkpoints Nathaniel had threatened the Order with on Lammas Eve. The island, he'd said, was surrounded by an iron ring of police. But the reality was very different. The village of Armadale was full of happy summer tourists, traffic was moving as normal, and I didn't see a single policeman anywhere. And so a little band of brothers (and sisters) who had flown the scene of two crimes walked onto the ferry like a group of day-trippers. As I didn't want to jinx things I waited until we were safely on the ferry, and there was a broad channel of water between us and Skye, to ask Nathaniel just what exactly was going on.

'We had to get Ratio off the island as soon as possible,' he said bluntly. 'There was a real threat of a further attempt on his life, particularly once his identity was revealed.'

'But the police?' I said. 'Surely he would've been safe with all those Feds around?'

'There were no policemen on Skye,' he said, looking back at the island we'd left, brown curls stirring in the wind. 'Either on it or surrounding it.' I could swear he smiled a little.

'*What?*' we all chorused. All except Nel, who kept quiet. She'd known, of course. Nathaniel explained. 'I – we – the FOXES, that is – do have significant contacts at Scotland Yard,' he said, 'but they said there was nothing they could do on a hunch. They couldn't sanction the massive amount of manpower we needed to patrol the whole of Skye for the Lammas weekend. They told us to do some evidence gathering and come to them with a case. So that's what we've done.'

'But . . . but all the officers,' said Shafeen, 'the ones that turned up on Lammas Eve . . .'

'All FOXES,' Nathaniel said. 'There's a good chance that the local plods are in the pockets of the family. We couldn't risk it.'

'You're right,' I said. 'At Longcross the family definitely had tame policemen – they were the ones who questioned us about the murder of –' it felt crazy saying it now, with him standing there – 'Henry.

'There you go,' said Nathaniel. 'My colleagues – the FOXES agents on the island – were there primarily to keep you all safe. For instance, there were two "officers" guarding your staircase, Greer, and another four at the Peel Tower. But they've also been conducting interviews. They already have a number of signed and recorded confessions, elicited from perpetrators who believed that they are actual police. It seems that the Order have been very ready to testify against each other, in return for promises of anonymity that the real police couldn't possibly give.'

'So much for honour,' muttered Ratio, and Henry shot him a look.

'But they are racing against time. There's not one single genuine detective on the island. But there will be soon. This morning, at some point, the *real* police will arrive, and the coroner too. They probably got off this very boat, travelling the other way.'

'How did they know to come?' said Ty.

'Oh, we called them. Once Louis died, and then his father, we couldn't not report that. We had to involve the authorities. But we already have enough evidence to build our case.'

'And what will the FOXES do now?' asked Shafeen with obvious concern. 'The ones playing the police inspector and all the officers?'

'Leave the castle before the real police arrive, change their clothes so they look like tourists. We'll all meet in a day or two on the mainland and build a rock-solid portfolio of evidence to take to my friends at Scotland Yard. Ratio – I'll need that footage as soon as possible.'

'I'll be back home by this evening,' said Ratio. 'You'll have it by the end of the day.'

I looked down the line of people leaning on the rail. My dear, dear friends: some old, some new. It felt like things were breaking up – not just Shafeen and me, but the whole group. Ty echoed my thoughts. 'Will we even see each other again?'

she said. 'You guys have left STAGS and are heading to uni. And I guess the Surroyal Ball won't be happening now . . .'

'Oh, I think it should,' said Nathaniel very definitely, 'and for a very good reason. The kids who are at STAGS now are the next generation who will be ruling this country. Captains of industry, politicians, the great and the good in every area of society. They need to know what the cult that runs the school has done. The evidence we've gathered will secure a good number of convictions of the old guard – the grown-ups, if you will, and the leaders of the Order. But the case may take a while to come to trial, and we want to stop this thing at source – with the young. We have a chance to turn them onto the right path.'

'So what are you thinking?' asked Henry.

'As far as the governors are concerned, I'm still the headmaster of STAGS,' said Nathaniel. 'I haven't yet given my notice. I am still nominally in charge of the ball. I could, in my valedictory address, tell the students exactly what has been going on.'

Maybe it was because I could see the ruins of Armadale Castle across the silver strait, where I'd treated Henry to a night at the movies; maybe it was because we were heading back to Glasgow where it had first occurred to me that film was the key to this whole thing. Whatever the reason, I had a sudden notion. 'Why don't we *show* them?'

'What do you mean?' asked Henry.

'We show them,' I repeated. 'We *show* them the drone footage. Everyone. All the students. We show them exactly what happened to you, Ratio, so they can no longer turn away.' We needed something much more high tech than my screening to Henry. I turned to the man in the know. 'We'd need cinematic resolution, pin-sharp sound, a big-screen look. But projected onto a wall. Is that possible?'

'Perfectly.' Ratio perked up at the thought of his beloved tech, blue eyes shining. His green hair was riffling in the sea breeze, showing about an inch of blond roots. 'You'll need a Barco projector – a good one, high spec. You could even do some projection mapping – that would be really cool.'

'But is it a plug-and-play thing?' asked Ty.

'Yes. I'll edit the footage like a film. Why?'

She clasped his arm fondly. 'Because you want to *be* at the ball, don't you? *I* want you to be there. You *should* be there.'

He looked at Nathaniel. 'Am I even invited?'

'Invited?' laughed Nathaniel. 'You're the guest of honour. And you are, strictly speaking, an alumnus of the school.'

'Jesus. I've never been to anything like that.' I could see him processing it – that after so long being an observer, on the outside looking in, he was now going to be a VIP. 'See how the other half live, eh?' He looked at Henry, in an almost friendly fashion. I thought then, if he was going to be the Earl of Longcross, he'd better get used to fancy balls, but I didn't say anything out loud, as the others didn't yet know.

Then Henry spoke up. 'Can I make a special request?' He sounded humbler than I'd ever heard him.

'After the help you've given us?' said Nathaniel. 'I should think you can.'

'It's about a special guest of my own. You were talking about alumni. Would you let me invite another former pupil?'

'I don't see why not,' said Nathaniel.

'I'd like to invite a girl called Gemma Delaney.'

The guilt about what he'd done to Gemma was obviously really playing on Henry's mind. He didn't just want to pay for his crimes with a prison sentence – he wanted to apologise to Gemma in person. I said, gently, 'But, Henry, Gemma will never accept an invitation from you. Not again.'

'I know.' For the first time since I'd known him, he looked at me almost pleadingly. 'But she would accept one from *you*.'

38

And so it was to end where it all began.

St Aidan the Great School.

Aka STAGS.

The taxi dropped me at the gates, the gates where I'd first stood as a scholarship applicant, over two years ago now.

I remembered, like it was a scene in a movie, the first time I'd clapped eyes on the school. It was when I'd come here for my interview. It had been one of those sunny midwinter days, all glittering frosty fields and long, low shadows. Dad had driven me through the gates and up this long driveway through lush green grounds in his ten-year-old Mini Cooper. And at the end of the drive we'd got out and just stared and stared at this beautiful, vast medieval manor house, with a sort of moat and a little bridge to the entrance. It didn't look, then or now, at all like the headquarters of a disturbing cult, which is what it actually was. The only clue, if I'd been looking for it, might have been the pair of antlers over the great door.

The weather was different this time. There were no frosty fields or long shadows. It had been a glorious late-August day, and it was a beautifully warm summer's evening, which was a good thing because I was actually wearing a pretty lightweight dress. A very special dress indeed. It was the one my mother had made especially for me, one of the only things she had *ever* given me. The dress was perfection – silver-grey, strapless, with thousands of tiny jet-black beads swirling and clustering down the front like a murmuration of starlings. My mother might not have been much of a mother, but she sure as hell could make a dress, and I respected her for that. There was a lot of work in it, every bead sewn on by hand. Every time I wore it I thought that she must have loved me a little, to make this dress for me, and the thought gave me courage. I raised my chin a fraction and walked under the antlered gates, to the Surroyal Ball.

The school itself looked different. It too was dressed up for a party. The gates were woven with flowers and unlit torches lined the drive and the drawbridge, ready to be kindled when darkness came. Flags and banners of the five houses – the yellow of Honorius, the blue of Bede, the silver of Lightfoot, the green of Oswald and the purple of Paulinus – streamed and flapped from the gatehouse. I took a deep breath. The one thing I had to do tonight – the *one thing* – was make sure I wasn't alone with Henry. But, of course, no sooner had I walked through the gates than I heard a car pull up behind me and Henry was getting out of one of the Longcross Estate Land Rovers, looking incredible. I tried to ignore how great he looked in white tie and tails; no one wore this very British uniform of the privileged like him. He was carrying a large basket in his right hand. Regina, hooded and chirruping gratefully to be out of the car, shifted inside.

'She your date?' I said, by way of a greeting. I had to keep things trivial, because things between us were just too serious. He looked me up and down appreciatively. 'I was rather hoping that *you* would be my partner. Especially looking like that.'

I eyed him sternly. 'I'm here with Shafeen.'

He looked about him, comically. 'Where is he?'

'He'll be here,' I said, with a confidence I didn't feel. In fact, things were far from back to normal, but we'd been working on it over the past weeks. Shafeen had gone back to India, so we'd had several unsatisfactory FaceTimes and phone calls hampered by different time zones, but we were working on our relationship, slowly building trust again, and he'd promised to be back to take me to the Surroyal Ball.

The other Peel Tower Rebels had scattered to the four winds since Lammas too. I'd been in Manchester with my dad, enjoying a bit of normality for once and watching a buttload of films with him. Nel had gone home to her bougie mansion in Cheshire. Henry had gone to Longcross Lodge, to oversee the nearly completed rebuilding of the hall after the fire. Ty had been at Ratio's in Glasgow, and I knew that Nathaniel had been there for a time too, collating all the data from the HAWK and the dossier of evidence on the Order of the Stag that Ratio had been collecting for the last few years. Then Nathaniel had taken the whole lot to his contact at Scotland Yard, and according to Nel arrests were imminent. It was inevitable that the net was closing on Henry, and I wondered how many nights of freedom he had left.

'Well, look,' said Henry as though he had read my mind,

266

'since we may not have another moment together like this, will you help me do something?'

'I suppose,' I said warily.

'Nothing untoward,' he said. 'It's just that you've been hawking and you can help me with Regina. I'm going to let her rake away.'

'What does that mean?'

'Free her. Return her to the wild.'

I felt a lump gather in my throat. It seemed so, so . . . final, and a strange foreshadowing of all the other endings to come. 'Will she survive?'

'Yes,' said Henry. 'All that stooping to the lure has a function, you know. It mimics hunting in the wild. And you saw her take a gull on the Dunvegan cliffs. She'll be fine.'

'Why didn't you free her on Skye?'

He hesitated. 'You'll laugh.'

'Try me.'

He sighed a little. 'I want her to be under the same skies as me. If you're incarcerated, you're usually tried in your county and put in a facility close to your home. If I'm in Frankland Prison in Durham, I might be able to look out of my barred windows and see Regina flying free.'

I'd never felt less like laughing in my life. 'OK.'

He checked his watch – this was typical Henry; he was the only person our age I knew who used a watch. Everyone else used phones. 'We're a bit early. The welcome reception is in the Honorius Quad at seven. Let's find somewhere away from everyone to let her go. The water meadows should do it.'

We walked down by the river to the flat meadows beyond

the playing fields. Despite their name, the water meadows had been drained centuries ago and reclaimed by wildflowers and bees. I helped Henry extract Regina from her basket, and she settled herself happily on his gauntlet. Henry unhooded her and let her take in her surroundings. Then we walked a little so he could have a few last moments with her. With the hawk on his wrist and those ancient buildings in the background beyond the evening summer haze, I felt, as I had before, so Medieval I could burst.

'Let's wait for a sparrow or something to fly her at. That'll start her off,' said Henry breezily. But then he stroked her breast feathers one last time and said, in a very different voice, 'Goodbye, old girl.'

In the next moment, a songbird, disturbed by our footsteps, burst from the meadow grass and fluttered skywards. Henry flung Regina off his wrist in pursuit, and she was away, speeding into the infinite blue like a bullet. He watched, eyes as blue as the sky, as she became a dot, then disappeared. He blinked once, stooped and collected the basket. 'That's that then,' he said briskly. 'Come on.'

But that wasn't that. We'd barely gone the length of a field when we became aware of a presence. Regina, bored of the chase, was following us. She was fluttering from tree to gatepost to drystone wall, never letting her beloved master out of her sight. She obviously thought this was some sort of game and was going to play it to the last. It was heartbreaking. Henry studiously ignored her, but I could see how much it cost him. 'She'll clear off eventually,' he said. 'Once we go into the ball. There will be too many people, too much noise.' This sounded offhand, even callous, but his tone was in complete opposition to his words. If I hadn't known that Shafeen would materialise the instant I touched Henry, I would have squeezed his hand. For the first time since I'd known him, he seemed perilously near to tears.

As he'd guessed, once we were inside the precincts of the school we lost sight of Regina. And as we walked the familiar grounds I forgot the hawk. There were too many memories crowding her out. To our left, Lightfoot House, where I'd received the original Invitation to Longcross. In the distance, the swimming pool, which I'd pounded up and down every morning, in unwitting preparation for my fishin' ordeal in Longmere. Next to that, the De Warlencourt Playhouse, where I'd put on *The Isle of Dogs*, been hanged by the neck in a noose and been tried for manslaughter by the Dark Order of the Grand Stag. And to our right the chapel, where I'd first realised that the Old Abbot was the Grand Master of a cult that centred on this very school, and underneath it the Crypt where we'd finally plotted to bring the Order down. So many dark memories – and now it was time to let the light in and make an ending. Henry and I walked through Honorius House to the White Quad.

39

The big square space, surrounded on four sides by beautiful medieval buildings, was crowded with girls in bright ballgowns and guys in white tie and tails.

White-clad staff moved around with trays of champagne and fruit punch, and the friars, in their ceremonial white habits, chatted with the leavers, who were destined for Oxbridge, St Andrews or Durham. A string quartet, parked unobtrusively in one corner, played genteel chamber music. The Jerusalem tree, the enormous cedar that was supposed to have been grown from a seed which the crusader Conrad de Warlencourt brought back from the Holy Land, provided shade from the low evening sun.

And underneath it stood Shafeen.

He was on his phone, and I thought then what a Savage he had become since I'd first known him. A guy on a phone – especially a guy in white tie and tails on a phone – was an odd sight in the middle of this ancient quad. Time was when having a phone out in the open at STAGS would be an offence that would get you expelled, just like Ratio had been.

I turned to Henry, but he hadn't noticed Shafeen. His blue eyes were scanning the crowd anxiously. 'She's not here.'

'Who?' I asked, thinking for a moment he meant Regina.

'Gemma Delaney.' He seemed agitated. 'Why didn't she come?'

'It was always a long shot,' I said. 'Maybe the school didn't have the right address. Or maybe she just couldn't face coming back here. It wasn't exactly a happy place for her.'

'I just wanted . . . I wanted to see her before I go.'

'Wait, you're not planning to do a Cinderella, are you?' I said, suddenly worried. 'You are going to stick around to see the projection?'

'Yes, of course. I want to see this thing through to the end.'

I looked at him. 'Couldn't you do some sort of deal? I mean, you helped us bring everyone to trial. Can't you get . . .' I searched for the phrase I'd heard in mafia movies. 'Immunity from prosecution?'

'Don't you see?' he said, raising his eyes to mine. 'I don't *want* that. I *deserve* what's coming to me, for what I did to Gemma, and I'll take my punishment.'

'Well, if that's how you feel about it.' It came out harsher than I meant, and I took a little nervous breath, as I was about to deal him another blow. 'Probably best if we don't arrive together,' I said, feeling utterly shit.

I didn't need to explain; Henry stood back at once. 'Of course,' he said, giving me this courteous little bow. I walked ahead, feeling like a total bitch. He'd lost Regina and now I was abandoning him – but I knew if I walked into the Surroyal Ball on Henry de Warlencourt's arm, Shafeen would do his nut.

As it turned out, I got right up to Shafeen before he noticed me, so intent was he on his phone. 'Playing Candy Crush?' I said lightly. I wasn't at all sure how to greet him after all this time – were we still boyfriend and girlfriend? – so as usual I took refuge in a joke.

Shafeen looked up from the screen. At least he smiled. 'No,' he said. 'I'm flying the HAWK. We thought it was a good idea to film the evening.'

'A film within a film,' I said. 'Very meta. Didn't Ratio want to do it?'

'He's busy sorting out the projection. Besides, he gave the drone to me.'

'He *gave* you the HAWK?'

'Yes. Said I'd saved his life with it on Lammas Eve, and he wanted me to have it. So I got my drone licence and took it out to India. Got some amazing shots of the Aravalli Hills. We thought that tonight it would be good to have some footage of the students' reaction to the projection. It's an insurance policy too – no one can plead deniability later.'

'How do you mean?'

'No one can say they haven't seen it,' he explained. He waved his arm in a sweeping gesture at all the privileged kids crowding the quad. 'All these golden lads and girls, no one can deny after today that they are aware of the full extent of the Order's cruelty and criminality. I'm just doing a quick test, plotting the flight path, before tonight.'

He lowered the phone and looked at me properly for the first time. 'You look amazing.'

'Right back atcha.' It was true. He was in what I called his Prince Caspian mode and looked just the way I'd seen him at

272

Longcross Hall the very first time, when I'd realised that I was not the only misfit to be invited to their little Hunger Game. Now we almost seemed as much strangers as we were then; he was back to being an unknown quantity, as if we had gone full circle. Did he even want to get back together? And the bigger question: did I? We had one of those awkward, bumpy hugs where you're not sure whether to go in for the kiss or not and ended up clashing cheekbones. Then, luckily, Nel bounded up like some beautiful golden Labrador and hugged both of us at once with no awkwardness at all. In her presence we were able to chat about the last month – what we'd been doing, how everyone's parents were; comforting small talk, leaving the bigger things unsaid. After a bit Shafeen excused himself to go and land the drone.

Nel and I turned to each other, best friends together, almost with relief. But the relief didn't last for long because she was on my case straight away.

'Did you tell him?'

I didn't need to ask what she meant. She and I had had multiple lengthy phone conversations in the intervening month about the love triangle I'd found myself in. 'Not yet.'

'*Greer.*'

'I *know*. But he nearly killed Henry when it had just been a kiss. Imagine what he'd do if he knew I'd slept with him.'

'Doesn't matter,' she said, china-blue eyes wide. 'You've *got* to tell him. If you're going to get back together he's got to have all the information. It's only fair. You need a clean slate.' This was an oddly Medieval thing for the Savage Nel to say. She was right, of course. But I feared that if Shafeen knew the sordid details, there would be no way back for us. I changed the subject. 'How about you and Nathaniel?' I asked. 'Everything OK?'

'More than OK,' she said, with a cat-that-got-the-cream smile. 'He's going back to Oxford, did you know?'

'I didn't know.'

'Yes. As a postgrad. Doing his doctorate – a DPhil, they call it there. In Renaissance and Revolution.'

'Pretty apt for one of the FOXES,' I said. 'That's great, Nel. That means you can finally be together.'

'Yes,' she said. 'We'll just be two students then, so there's nothing to keep us apart.' She practically hugged herself. 'I'll be in college for the first year, just like you, but if things go well we might get a place together.'

'Big stuff,' I said, but I was really pleased for her. My own love life might be egg salad, but it was great to see her so happy. Shafeen came back, carrying the HAWK, checking the rotors almost as tenderly as Henry would check Regina's prime feathers after a flight. Then, as if just thinking about him could conjure him, Henry appeared. He kissed Nel and me in exactly the same way, coolly on each cheek, and shook Shafeen's hand. It was all perfectly civil, but it was a relief when Nathaniel joined us.

He looked so different to the half-man, half-fox I'd seen on Lammas Eve. He was pristine in his ceremonial white habit, his brown curls ruffled in the breeze, every inch the correct young Abbot, a gifted teacher promoted beyond his years. I could see that this evening he and Nel were maintaining a certain distance. Tonight, he was her headmaster again, and there could be no intimacy for now. Low-voiced, he filled us in on the progress of the Scotland Yard investigation into the Order of the Stag. 'The bigger fish are already on the hook,' he said. 'My predecessor, Gideon Villiers, the Old Abbot, as well as a number of the other dignitaries who were unmasked as DOGS on Lammas Eve, are already in custody. Next, they'll be going after the minnows,' he said, 'the peripheral actors who colluded in the death hunts.'

I couldn't look at Henry; that meant him.

'And for my last night in the teaching profession,' the Abbot went on, 'there's one more group to educate. The young are the future, and we have to teach these sons and daughters of STAGS exactly where privilege can lead.'

He borrowed a spoon from one of the waiters and began to tap his glass until the whole quad fell quiet, including the string quartet. 'Welcome, graduates of St Aidan the Great School, to the Surroyal Ball,' he said. 'This evening represents the end of your school journey. And because here at STAGS we take your education very seriously, we would like to continue the teaching up until the very last minute. Therefore, on the stroke of midnight, we will gather in the Chapel Quad for a very special presentation. Knowledge is the greatest gift you can give, and we have something to impart to you that we hope you will carry forward into your lives. It is particularly important for you to leave with this knowledge, as you are destined to be the men and women who will lead this nation, and with knowledge comes responsibility.' He clapped his hands. 'That's enough of the serious stuff. To paraphrase Epicurus: eat, drink and be merry, and we'll all meet again at midnight.'

I looked about nervously. The Abbot had set the scene for this big screening at midnight, like some *Cinema Paradiso* movie night. But there was one crucial player missing: the projectionist. 'Where's Ratio?' I whispered.

Then, like an actor picking up his cue, Ratio entered the White Quad.

40

In the silence that followed the Abbot's announcement, Rollo de Warlencourt's eldest son walked under the Honorius arch, with Ty on his arm.

He looked almost entirely different to the Ratio we'd come to know on Skye. His hair had been cut so all the green had gone, and there was just a glittering blond crop. He wore a black tailcoat, which fitted his long, rangy frame remarkably well.

'*Jesus*.' I kissed his cheek. 'You look so . . . *unlike* yourself,' I said, the surprise making me even less articulate than usual.

He extended his arms and turned around 360 degrees. 'Do I fit in?' he asked, somewhat sardonically.

I considered. 'You look like a de Warlencourt.'

'So, yes then.' He grinned. 'But some things are the same. Look.' He rolled up his sleeves, *Miami Vice* style, to show his forearm tattoo of the deer hunt. And in his right ear he wore the antler earring we'd last seen in the Lammas Circle around the wicker stag. 'Nathaniel got it back from the "police",' said Ratio, flicking his earlobe and regarding the Abbot gratefully.

'It's your family crest now,' said Henry.

Ratio smiled at him – a proper, fraternal smile. 'Yes, I suppose it is. And look.' He opened his tailcoat to show us that underneath he was wearing, not a shirt with a wing collar, but a faded old T-shirt emblazoned with the words 'OH, FOR FOX SAKE'.

'Your favourite.' I smiled too. 'Classic Ratio.'

'Actually,' he said somewhat shyly, 'it's *Ho*ratio now.' He looked at Shafeen. 'I decided to go back to my given name once I realised what it meant. My father didn't give me much, but he did give me something really precious, and I'm not going to throw it away. And speaking of precious things . . .' He took something from the pocket of his jacket. It was a small book with orange leather covers, and a long tie of the same leather wrapped around it. I recognised it at once: It was Aadhish Jadeja's diary, the one we'd found in the tiger-skin rug's mouth and read from cover to cover in Jaipur. Ratio handed it reverently to Shafeen, as if it were the Dead Sea Scrolls. 'I should return this to you. Thanks a million.'

Shafeen took the book and looked around at the rest of us. 'I sent it to him from India,' he explained. 'I thought he should know who his father used to be, once.'

Henry put out his hand. 'May I?' he asked. 'For the same reason.'

Shafeen regarded him, then passed him the book. 'Of course,' he said. 'You have a right to know him too.'

This was so typically Shafeen. Kind, considerate. Not something I would ever have said about Henry. Surely that was why I would be better off with Shafeen? But I couldn't process all that stuff right now. 'What's it like to be back at STAGS?' I asked Horatio.

'Weird,' he said, closing his tailcoat again. 'I hated it so much back then, every stone of the place, and couldn't wait to leave. But now I'm back, I have to admit, it is beautiful. It was just the people . . .' He grimaced and didn't have to finish the sentence.

'All set for the projection?' Shafeen asked.

'Yes. I've been here since yesterday. Nathaniel and I did a recce and found the ideal place to screen the film.'

'It's the chapel wall,' said Nathaniel. 'The Gospel side is flat and undecorated – the oldest bit before everything got all gothic. It's rather fitting because it would have been here when St Aidan was alive, one of the first parts of the foundation to be built. Actually . . . you must excuse me – lots to do. I'll see you all later.'

And, with a fond but discreet glance at Nel, he strode off, presumably to organise his final act as STAGS's Abbot.

I turned back to Horatio. 'And how does it feel to be an earl of the realm?' The others, of course, now knew all about Horatio's identity and his change of fortune. 'You'll have to see your new home, Longcross Hall.'

'I've been,' he said.

I looked at Henry with surprise.

'I invited them,' he explained. 'And I had the great pleasure of meeting Horatio's mother, Lorna.'

'She came too?' asked Nel.

'Yes. They were my guests at Longcross Lodge. I hope that the estate can become a happy place for her now, instead of one filled with bad memories.'

Horatio looked at him more fondly than he'd ever done, in a way that was almost . . . well . . . *brotherly*. 'We had quite a few conversations about Henry's father. *Our* father,' he corrected himself. 'I found out from Mum that their . . . relationship . . . was more of a seduction than an attack. Still totally unacceptable, of course, but we figured that he must have loved my mother and me just a *little* bit to have agreed to her request to fund me. The short version,' he said grudgingly, 'is that he wasn't *all* bad.'

'No one is,' I said, looking at Henry.

'We had quite a few conversations about the future of the estate too,' said Henry. 'I wanted Lorna to have some say in it all.' He smiled. 'What you Savages would no doubt call "agency".'

I stared at him, trying to process this new Henry. There was hardly anything that I recognised. This was Shafeen levels of kindness and consideration.

'We've been talking about outward-bound weekends for inner-city kids,' said Horatio. 'Computer camp for kids who can't afford tech. Stuff like that.'

'Sounds very Savage,' I said jokingly. I turned to Henry. 'What do you think of all this?'

'I think it's a capital idea,' he said, a very Medieval endorsement.

'And what about you?' I said to Ty. 'Countess of Longcross? How funny if you become **mrs_de_warlencourt** after all.'

She laughed. 'It's not Jane Austen! I'm only eighteen. I've still got a year at STAGS, if it stays open. But if things go well –' she looked fondly at Horatio – 'then one day, who knows? There's no reason why I shouldn't be a very good lady of the manor.'

'No reason at all,' I said, smiling.

'So funny,' she said, smiling too. 'From east London to Northumberland. We used to call Limehouse Estate "The Manor". The irony, hey?'

I laughed. Then I bumped on something she'd said. 'Hold on, back up. What d'you mean, *if* STAGS stays open?'

Henry said, 'A bigger question than what to do with the estate is what to do with this school. STAGS is on the earldom's land and the de Warlencourts have always had a controlling interest in the running of the school. Didn't you know that?'

'No,' I said. 'Just *how* much land belongs to you?'

'Belongs to him,' he corrected, nodding his head at Horatio. 'You can walk from here to Longcross without ever leaving de Warlencourt land.'

'So what are you thinking?' said Shafeen to Horatio. 'About the school, I mean.'

'I think it should be a state school,' said Horatio, without hesitation. 'The facilities are great – theatre, pool, all that.'

'No more lordlings and ladies?' asked Nel. 'No more Honourable this or that?'

'Don't get me wrong,' said Horatio. 'There's no reason why privileged kids can't come here – it's not their fault they were born rich, any more than it is a poor kid's fault that they're born poor. The wealthy can apply like everyone else. I just think local kids should have access to all this stuff. It should be for *everyone*. The only way to get rid of the cancer of class that rots this country is if rich kids and poor kids mix together, become friends.'

I looked from one brother to the other – the one who'd been brought up in a mansion and the one who'd been brought up in a council flat. 'I hope it happens.'

'Who can stop it?' Henry asked. 'If we both agree?'

And then, as if she'd been waiting for *her* cue too, Cass walked into the quad.

41

She looked amazing, and was wearing, as was her style, male evening dress.

With her cropped blonde hair and slight frame, she carried off the white tie and tails as well as either one of her cousins. She marched right up to them, as if she were joining some sort of gentlemen's club. She, Henry and Horatio stood in a triangle looking at each other, like the three Spider-Men meeting each other in the Multiverse.

I was so fascinated by their similarities and differences that it took me a second to register that Cass wasn't alone.

At her back were a couple of the snottiest-looking, *Mean Girls*-esque resting bitch-faces you couldn't wish to meet. A little behind them were three guys who looked like Burberry models. All six of them looked us all up and down as if we were dirt on their handmade shoes.

'Let me introduce my friends,' said Cass, all politeness. 'This is Athena, India, Jock, Will and Christof.'

I heard her with something like despair. Was there no end to this cycle? Was history destined to repeat itself? Not one of her little cohort smiled; they all looked down their noses at us. My heart sank. I didn't need any introductions. I knew who they were.

They were the New Medievals.

Cass smiled pleasantly at Nel. 'I hear our dear Abbot is leaving,' she said, cocking her head on one side. 'That's so sad.' She pouted her lips like a little girl. 'But don't worry. Some of us will still be here to keep the home fires burning.' She looked at Horatio pointedly. 'I'm sure we can . . . *guide* the new Abbot and acquaint him with the rules. Luckily, *some* members of the de Warlencourt family can be relied upon to keep the old traditions alive.' Now she shot a poisonous blue glance at Henry. That one look conveyed that she felt utterly betrayed by him and now hated him as much as she'd once loved him.

He ignored the look and smiled tightly. 'How's your mother?'

'Perfectly fine, thank you,' she almost snapped. 'We're entering a new age at Castle MacLeod. The age of the matriarchy. Mama, me, and Nanny of course. Things are running like clockwork.' I shivered, thinking of those three up in the remote Highlands, like some weird multigenerational reboot of *Macbeth*'s witches.

'Going to be quite something, being top of the school, isn't it, Ty, darling?' she cooed. 'Great that you've got another year too. We are thinking about putting on a revival of *The Isle of Dogs* in the Michaelmas term. Such a shame just to act it once, don't you think, when it was lost for 400 years? Maybe you'd like to reprise your role as Queen Cynthia?'

Suddenly, tragically, I realised where she was going with this. 'Cass,' I said, low-voiced, clutching her arm. 'You're not actually planning to try to bring Louis back from the dead, are you? Because that's . . .' I searched for the words. 'Breathtaking in its batshittery.' I was appealing to the girl we'd all liked, the girl who'd acted with us in the first production of *The Isle of Dogs*, who'd taken us all to Longcross, who'd helped us find the lost play in the tomb of her ancestors. I knew she was in there somewhere. And she was. She looked at me, quite like the old Cass. 'Why not?' she asked plaintively, tears standing in her eyes. 'It worked before.'

Now I felt real pity. I toyed with the idea of reminding her that Henry had been alive all along, that he'd done the Dead Man's Drop dive from the top of the waterfall, the dive they'd both practised as kids. But there was no arguing with Cass's skewed logic, and I was relieved when the dinner gong sounded and we all made our way to the Refectory to eat.

42

There was the most sumptuous banquet laid on in the Refectory, but we rebels picked at our food.

I sat next to Shafeen, as technically we had come to the ball together, but we had this weird, stilted conversation. He told me about his time in India with his parents, and I told him about my three weeks in Manchester with my dad. I'd been to India with him before, and he'd been to Manchester with me, but the differences between the two experiences only served to emphasise the new gulf between us. I wondered if it could ever be crossed.

There was one person, though, who was more miserable than us. I looked over at Henry, who was tactfully sitting a good distance away from me. Morosely, he was pushing his food around his plate. I think I knew the reason for his misery. He had escaped death a second time only to feel the prison bars clanging shut on him, but I thought an even bigger issue for him was that Gemma Delaney had not turned up. He hadn't been given the opportunity to apologise or atone, which he so desperately needed to give himself peace before he took his punishment.

After the meal we all went to the Paulinus Quad, where the ball proper was to be held. The string quartet struck up once more, and Shafeen led me onto the dance floor, which had been laid down across the quad. As we whirled around I was always aware of Henry, drinking heavily, standing on his own. As the night wore on his isolation was compounded by the fact that Ty was dancing cheek to cheek with Horatio, I was constantly in Shafeen's arms and even Nel managed to have a discreet dance with Nathaniel. There were loads of distractions – an ice-cream cart, fireworks, traditional fairground games like a coconut shy and a strongman's hammer, but nothing seemed to divert Henry. He stuck by the Paulinus well where the Medievals traditionally gathered, as if glued, chain-smoking and dropping his cigarette butts down the shaft. He'd obviously started smoking again, but I thought under the circumstances it was understandable.

I carefully danced every dance with Shafeen, and throughout the evening we became closer and closer, relaxing into each other's arms as if the ice between us was melting. But it felt all wrong; I was weighed down with guilt. I longed for us to get back together, but I knew that Nel was right. I couldn't rebuild a relationship on a lie. I had to tell Shafeen the truth about that night in Castle MacLeod. Of course, Shafeen and I had officially broken up when I'd spent the night with Henry, but I wasn't about to offer up the *FRIENDS* defence. Being 'on a break' didn't excuse what was, in fact, a massive betrayal.

'Shafeen?'

'Yes?' He sounded so kind, so gentle.

'There's something you should know.'

'I think I know already.'

I looked up at him guiltily.

'You slept with Henry. The night before the duel.'

I couldn't believe he had known all this time. 'Don't you . . . *mind?*'

'I mind less about you sleeping with him than the fact that you're in love with him. You *do* love him, don't you?'

I didn't deny it – I couldn't. But I answered with a question. *The* question, which I now knew had been buzzing around my head like a trapped bluebottle since Henry had confessed his feelings for me in a hospital corridor in India. No – before that – since he'd shivered in my arms in Cumberland Place, telling me how his father had trapped him in a boot room with a fox when he was a little boy. Or even before that, when he'd kissed me on the silver midnight roofs of Longcross Hall. 'Is it possible to love two people?'

Shafeen smiled sadly, and somehow that was so much worse than if he'd frowned. 'Not for me. But I'm sure there are people that do.'

'I think I might be one of those people.' I looked up at him. 'How long have you known?'

'I saw how you reacted after the duel,' he said. 'When you thought he might have been shot. It was the way you held him.'

'I'm sorry,' I said.

'Me too.'

'I don't deserve you,' I said, quite truthfully.

'Probably not,' he said, with a half-laugh. 'But I'd take you back, Greer. I'd like to try, despite all this. If you want to, that is.'

I opened my mouth to answer, but my treacherous gaze

landed on Henry one last time. I caught sight of him just as he looked up from his glass and did a double take, the colour draining from his face. He looked like a ghost at that moment, or at least as if he'd seen one. His complexion was paper white, mouth agape, blue eyes staring. He turned the wide eyes on me, pointed towards the archway and mouthed two words.

She's here.

A young woman walked into the quad. She was alone and looked unsure. I remembered her being in the year above me at Bewley Park Comprehensive, before I'd even heard of STAGS. She was one of those pretty, popular girls, one of those girls you look up to, that you wish you could be. Then I remembered her here at STAGS, the day she gave me the warning, that heartfelt, unheeded warning not to go to Longcross. Then she'd been a shadow of herself, a thin, grey ghost, almost transparent with terror.

Now she looked shy but determined. She was wearing a sky-blue ballgown and a defiant expression. 'Sorry,' I said to Shafeen, breaking our grasp. 'I'm *so* sorry. We will get to this. But I've *got* to go and talk to someone.'

He followed my gaze. 'Who's that?'

'That,' I said, 'is Gemma Delaney.'

43

Henry tossed his cigarette away and joined me, and we weaved through the dancers to meet Gemma.

He gave her a little bow. 'Thank you for coming.'

She looked from Henry to me, the fragile self-possession gone, once more hollow-eyed and afraid. 'Greer? What's going on? Is this another trap?' Her Manchester accent was like home to me. 'I only came because you invited me. But you didn't say *he'd* be here.'

'Because you wouldn't have come,' I said, unrepentant. 'But it's not a trap,' I reassured her. 'This is the night that the Order of the Stag will finally be defeated, and I thought you'd want to be here for it.'

'I'd like nothing better,' she said. 'But . . .' Her eyes had not left Henry.

He said, 'And I . . . I would like to talk to you, if you'd allow me. There's something I want to say, something long overdue.'

She raised her chin an inch. 'Well, go on then,' she said, very northern. 'I'm here. What do you what to say?'

I looked around. People were looking over with interest, and there were too many prying eyes and flapping ears. 'Not here,' I said. 'Let's go somewhere private.'

I led them out of the Refectory to the Hundred Steps, the stone staircase between Paulinus and Lightfoot. It was fully dark now, as it was almost midnight, but the stairs were beautifully lit with torches at intervals, and you could see someone coming from a mile away, either up or down. We talked a little as we walked. Gemma was at Newcastle University, so not far away, and over the summer vacation was working part-time for a children's charity. I wondered if her experiences at Longcross had motivated her to work with other young children who'd been bullied and abused, and I felt both humbled and impressed that she'd been able to turn such a negative experience into a positive one.

Henry and Gemma sat together halfway up the steps. I hovered, unsure of what to do. This really had nothing to do with me, but I didn't want to leave Gemma alone with Henry if she felt vulnerable. 'Shall I stay?'

Henry looked to Gemma. This had to be her call. She shook her head and looked up at me, clear-eyed. 'No, it's all right,' she said. 'I was afraid of him once. I'm not now.'

So I wandered away, giving them some space and privacy. I wasn't sure where to go. There would be more dancing in the Paulinus Quad, and I definitely had unfinished business with Shafeen, but today had been a *lot* and I didn't really feel like being with anyone for a bit. I just wanted to go somewhere to sit and breathe. I thought about what Cass had said about putting on *The Isle of Dogs* again. I'd always known that she was pretty out there, but to actually buy into Ben Jonson's black magic and think she could raise Louis from the dead was positively unhinged. Unbidden, my feet made their way across Bede's Piece to the De Warlencourt Playhouse. A low mist clung to the grass, and the replica theatre rose above the playing fields like a mirage, its timbered walls and thatched roof glowing in the moonlight. As I reached the entrance I read the plaque above the door. It said:

THE DE WARLENCOURT PLAYHOUSE
BY KIND DONATION OF THE
DE WARLENCOURT FAMILY
OPENED ON 24th JULY 1969
AND DEDICATED TO
'GABRIEL SPENSER'
PLAYER

Cass's voice came back to me.

It worked before.

Maybe she hadn't been talking about Henry being brought back from the dead. Maybe she'd been talking about another family member from the seventeenth century: Nazereth de Warlencourt, who'd acted under the name Gabriel Spenser, and had been killed in a duel with Ben Jonson. His body was missing from his tomb in the Longcross crypt, and legend said that he lived his second life out on his secluded Northumberland estate. I put my hand on the timber of the door. I didn't really expect the theatre to be open, but the door gave way at once. The theatre still scared me – I'd nearly lost my own life here – but I thought to myself that I should go inside. If I was never to return to STAGS, it would be good to face my demons, just as Gemma was doing now. So I walked in through the timbered doors underneath the de Warlencourts' commemorative plaque, out of the summer evening sunshine, into the candlelit dark.

For a moment I couldn't see a thing, but my eyes slowly adjusted to the light of wavering candles. I mounted the steps and climbed to the middle of the stage, to the very spot where I'd spoken my epilogue as Poetaster, with the noose around my neck. I remembered the rope growing tighter and winching me upwards until my feet no longer touched the boards. Even the memory made my throat feel tight. But I took a few deep breaths. There was nothing to fear here. It was just an empty theatre.

Except, it was not empty.

'Hello, Greer.'

44

Abbot Ridley was suddenly there in the aisle, lighting the candles around the proscenium with a taper.

The flames flowered under his hand like he was some wizard from *Fantastic Beasts* or something. Obviously the candles had not just been left burning in an empty theatre. He'd lit them, and for a reason. Some nameless instinct told me he was here to meet someone. That someone clearly wasn't me, but he greeted me without surprise. I almost expected him to say, *I've been expecting you*, like some Bond villain.

'Hi,' I said uncertainly. 'Do . . . do you need the room?'

'No, no,' he said. 'Actually, it's good you're here. I've come to meet a mutual acquaintance.'

Now, this puzzled and began to frighten me, because pretty much the only people we both knew were all partying in the Paulinus Quad. Then I heard footsteps in the aisle and a figure emerged from the dark. 'You remember Professor Jennifer Nashe?'

Of course I did. I remembered her pretty well. You don't tend to forget a woman who witnessed your hanging at the end of a revival of a play that was lost for 400 years. Not when that same woman subsequently interviewed and admitted you to her Oxford college. She looked just the same – strong Professor McGonagall energy with her iron-grey hair escaping from a messy bun, penetrating green gaze and fine, flaring nostrils. She was wearing a greeny-black gown, which added to the *Harry Potter* vibe, and it rustled as she walked.

'You might have heard that I'm returning to Oxford to complete my doctorate,' said Nathaniel. 'Jennifer will be my tutor, and yours.'

She smiled, and I recalled that strange combination of a young face and old hair. 'Hello again, Greer.'

'Hello, Professor.'

She inclined her grey head. 'I think we can dispense with formalities, since we are going to be working so closely together. All FOXES in the same den.' She looked at Nathaniel, who gave her a tiny nod. 'I think it's time you called me something else.'

'Well,' I said shyly, uncertain of where this was going, and babbling as I always did when I was uncomfortable, 'I mean, you're still my tutor. I don't think I'd feel comfortable calling you "Jennifer". I mean, I was always pretty creeped out by those teachers who were all like, *Call me Kevin*. Always seems to be English teachers, doesn't it, although I don't know why. Maybe all that poetry makes them feel like they are freewheeling, unfettered dudes who are down with the kids. But I don't –'

'Greer,' she interrupted gently, 'I didn't mean you should address me by my first name. It was another name I was referring to. Or rather, an alias.' She looked at me significantly. 'You received my reading list, did you not?'

This seemed like a dizzying change of subject, but I tried to focus. I'd all but forgotten about the reading list she'd sent – the page of books I was supposed to chew through before starting uni in October. 'Yes. That is, I don't have it *on* me . . .'

'Then allow me to furnish you with a copy.' She took a paper from her sleeve and handed it to me. It read:

Renaissance and Revolution – Joseph Anthony Mazzeo
European Theories of the Drama – Barrett Harper Clark
Youth Revolution – Anthony Esler
Notion of the State – Alexander Passerin D'Entreves
All's Well That Ends Well: The Problem Plays – Simon Barker
Rebel Women – Stephen Wilmer
Dramas of the Revolution – Mikhail Shatrov

'I think I wrote, at the time, that you would find this list very revealing,' she said. 'Look more closely.'

I did.

And this is what I saw:

Renaissance and Revolution – Joseph Anthony Mazzeo
European Theories of the Drama – Barrett Harper Clark
Youth Revolution – Anthony Esler
Notion of the State – Alexander Passerin D'Entreves
All's Well That Ends Well: The Problem Plays – Simon Barker
Rebel Women – Stephen Wilmer
Dramas of the Revolution – Mikhail Shatrov

'Reynard,' I croaked. 'Reynard . . . is *you*?'

She bent close and whispered, 'Yes,' before drawing back

and giving me a significant green gaze. I opened my mouth, and shut it again, the world revolving around me.

'I have to go . . .' I muttered, backing away. 'Sorry . . . nice to see you . . . see you in October . . . got somewhere to be . . .'

I hurried out of the theatre and her voice drifted after me. *'To be continued . . . I'll see you in Oxford . . .'*

As I stumbled away from the playhouse I tried to process what I'd just heard. *Professor Nashe* was the mastermind behind the rebels who had sworn since the days of Guy Fawkes to bring down the elite? No wonder she'd come to the Surroyal Ball. Of *course* the head of the FOXES would want to see the final act – this was the boss-level battle and ultimate rout of the Order of the Stag. How singular that it was a Queen's Gambit at the end, a face-off between two women: Cass for the STAGS and Professor Nashe for the FOXES.

My synapses firing with the implications of what I'd just learned, I hurried back to the Hundred Steps, where Gemma and Henry were still deep in conversation. To a casual observer they might have looked like friends, or even, I thought, with a little pang, a couple. The truth was, they were the hunter and the hunted. But the question now was: which was which?

I climbed halfway to reach them, breathless with exertion and revelation. I noticed that Henry was still clutching the little orange book like a totem – Aadhish Jadeja's diary. 'Everything all right?'

Gemma looked up and gave me a small, tight smile. 'Yes,' she said. 'It is now. I've accepted Henry's apology. Not just for his sake, but for mine. I've been carrying this around a long time. Now I think I'll be able to try to forget.'

Henry looked troubled. 'About that – I have to tell you that there is now an active police investigation. You should contact them as soon as possible, because you'll be the key witness. Only you can press charges against me for what I did to you that Justitium weekend.'

She looked down at her hands for what seemed like a long, long time. 'No,' she said at last. 'I can't.' She looked up. 'They will ask me to relive it. All of it. And I can't go back there.' She began nervously pleating the silken folds of her skirt. 'Before you talked to me I would have sung it from the rooftops. I would have happily seen you rot in jail. But now . . .' She looked directly at him, suddenly stronger. 'I've never had power before. Certainly not over someone like you.'

I knew now that I'd been right to ask myself the question as I'd approached them. Gemma was now the hunter and Henry the hunted. Her testimony would be what jailed him. The tables had well and truly turned.

'But I'm better than you.'

'I know,' he said, seemingly with absolute honesty.

'So I choose *not* to exercise that power. I'm not going to the police.'

Now we both looked at her, gobsmacked.

'Are you *sure*?' said Henry.

'Yes.' She stood and smoothed down her skirts decisively. 'I ask just one thing of you.' She looked down at Henry, now his superior. 'Be *better*.'

'I will,' he said humbly. 'That I promise you.'

'And now,' she said, 'I need a drink.'

I smiled. 'We'll be right behind you.'

We watched her go, walking down the Hundred Steps, straight-backed as a princess.

I took her place next to Henry on the warm stone, suddenly feeling ridiculously happy. I nudged his shoulder with mine. 'So I guess this changes everything,' I said. 'You're not going to jail. And you don't have to give away the earldom.'

He folded my hand in his, and I let it lie there. It was just for a moment. Just because it was the last time. 'Greer,' he said seriously, 'I didn't give everything up because I was going to jail. I gave it up because of *you*.'

'*What?*' I couldn't quite believe what I was hearing. That seemed like such a huge thing to do – such a sacrifice. 'Are you joking?'

'Not at all,' he said. 'Ever since I first began going out with girls they were always bedazzled by Longcross and the title. They could see themselves as the next countess. You were the only one who didn't care about all that. You could look past it and see who I really was. And I was a shit, Greer. An absolute shit.'

'You won't get any argument from me,' I said with half a smile. As usual, I had to joke when things got serious.

'But you made me want to be better. And to do that, I have to get rid of all the trappings and the privilege. I *like* Horatio's vision for the future of Longcross – I think he'll be a fine custodian of the estate. I'm the younger brother now and with that comes a certain measure of freedom.' He looked into the dark, as if he could see his future. 'I want to see if I can make my way in the world on my wits. If I'm to have money, I want to be the one to make it – pull myself up by my bootstraps like

Nel's dad. I looked down on that kind of money once. Now I know it's the only kind worth having.'

I tried to absorb all this. 'So what will you do?'

'I don't know. Maybe uni. Against all the odds I did get some fairly decent marks in my Probitiones.' He smiled. 'But it hardly matters. The point is that you once said we were worlds apart. This can bring us closer together. If I give it all away, then we are the same.'

He'd never let go of my hand, and now he wiggled it until I looked into his eyes.

'So, what do you say?'

I blinked once, as if that would somehow reset my spinning brain. My world had turned upside down in a matter of minutes. I'd discovered the identity of Reynard, learned that Henry was not going to jail after all, and now I was on the business end of – not a proposal, that would be ridiculous, but the most serious piece of wooing I'd ever heard. It was every Hallmark Christmas movie about the prince and the chalet girl, it was King Cophetua and the Beggar Maid on acid. This was courtship on a whole new set of terms. I'd been so sure that the right thing to do was to rebuild things with Shafeen, to make things right after cheating on him. But this evening I'd seen the gulf between me and him too – the distance, not just physical, between a palace in Jaipur and a rented flat in Manchester. I'd never really pictured myself – well, not more than momentarily – as the lady of the manor, the Elizabeth Bennet at Darcy's Pemberley. My secret fantasies were far more focused on being a film director and winning a hatful of Oscars. But I'd never expected anyone to make such a colossal sacrifice for me as the one being laid at my feet now. Henry was offering himself to me as nothing more than a fellow university student, in the name of that Holy Grail of the movies: True Love.

What the hell was I supposed to do now?

Just as I opened my mouth to reply, the chapel bell began to strike midnight.

45

Literally saved by the bell, I jumped to my feet, hauling Henry up by the hand I still held. 'Come on,' I said. 'We'll miss the main feature.'

Together we ran to the Chapel Quad, where the half-pissed but obedient students were gathering. I could see by the numbers that pretty much all the guests were here, obviously expecting a valedictory speech, or maybe some sort of comic awards ceremony. The huge harvest moon made the night as bright as day.

Horatio and Nathaniel had chosen well with the long, plain Gospel wall. It was the ideal setting for my projection idea – trialled in the ruins of Armadale Castle. At the back of the walled garden was a square white tent a bit like a Punch and Judy show, with a hole in the top. This, I knew, concealed the projector and the projectionist – Horatio.

Henry and I walked up to Nathaniel – he was already flanked by Ty and Nel, and also Shafeen, who eyed Henry and me warily.

But I couldn't focus on Shafeen now, despite everything. This was more important than any of us. 'Are you going to introduce the film?' I said to Nathaniel.

He smiled down at me. 'Well, actually I thought *you* might.'

'Me?' I brayed like a donkey.

'Yes,' he said, quite seriously. 'Film is your thing, isn't it? And it was when you came to this school that this whole edifice began to crumble. You've brought us to this moment. To use a fishin' metaphor, this is your catch.'

They were all looking at me, all smiling. Nathaniel, kind and clerical. Beautiful blonde Nel. Brave and brilliant Ty. Even Professor Nashe stood with us, a little apart, smiling benevolently. And, on either side of me, Shafeen and Henry. 'Go on,' urged Shafeen. 'You can do it,' said Henry. And with those two in agreement, there was really no choice.

I walked to the front of the crowd, a ticker tape of word salad spooling through my brain. But as I got to the front and turned, my back to the chapel wall, I suddenly knew exactly what I was going to say.

'You're about to see the first film that's ever been shown at St Aidan the Great School,' I began. 'When I first came to this school I noticed something that you all know only too well: that technology – smartphones, laptops, even TV and film – is considered "Savage". I began to realise that this policy was borne out of fear. Fear of change. Books, and the things of the past, were considered "Medieval" – comfortable and safe. I hope to show you tonight that there's no need to fear change. Embracing tech doesn't mean getting rid of the good bits of the past. Books, traditions, they will always be with us. But some traditions need to end.' I looked around the faces that watched me – the drunk, the bored, the attentive, the arrogant, the amused. 'Tonight.' I took a breath. 'Technology

303

can be a force for good, as I'm about to demonstrate. And so I'm introducing the very first film to be shown at STAGS. But this isn't a Bond or *Star Wars* or Marvel or even a black-and-white classic. This is a film about an ex-STAGS student. His name is Horatio Rennie, but his story might as well have been that of any number of other alumni.' I looked at Ty. 'Leon Morgan.' Then my gaze shifted to Shafeen. 'Aadhish Jadeja. Or Gemma Delaney.' Gemma herself stood tall and brave, looking straight at me, willing me on. 'They were all students at this very school. But they were all made to feel that they were lesser beings, that they didn't matter, that no one would miss them when they were gone. You may have heard these stories. These are dark rumours, urban myths and school legends. They could be the plots of horror films. But they are not. They are *real*.' I gestured to the screen behind me. 'This film is not a feature but a documentary. A testimony. Thanks to the Savage technology that this school has long feared, we actually have documentary evidence of one of these atrocities, happening in real time. What you are about to see did not take place in the fifties or sixties. These events can't be dismissed as "different times". They happened *three weeks* ago. This film is in the hands of the police. Arrests have been made, and those involved who have not yet been apprehended will be soon. Watch and learn.'

I stood back from the screen as Horatio – the Punch and Judy man – emerged from the white box and looked at Shafeen. He gave the thumbs-up sign. 'Ready?'

Shafeen nodded. 'Ready.'

The two Savages, working in tandem, activated their devices. Shafeen tapped his phone and the HAWK rose, whirring, from behind the garden wall and soared above us, its red cyclops eye ruby bright. At the same moment Horatio activated the projector and the entire chapel wall was transformed into a cinema screen. *Son et lumière*, Industrial Light & Magic. This was the silver screen as I'd never seen it before. This wasn't an iPhone in an old ruin. I was amazed at the breadth and clarity of the image – it was like 16:9 or even IMAX. We might as well have been in the Odeon Leicester Square.

And there we were, transported from this warm and balmy summer night to a different summer night – Lammas Eve on the Isle of Skye. Horatio had done a masterful job with the film. It was cut together like an award-worthy short. He set up the action beautifully. There were even cutaways of all the animal heads. Then the turning point of the film, the march of the stag-headed Order to the top of the hill, and the lighting of the stag. The flames licking up the vast effigy, the *Midsommar*-type procession under the legs of the stag. The punishment of the Lammas Fool with eggs and milk. And then, the horror of the realisation that there was someone in the head of the stag: a human sacrifice. The drone had captured everything in chilling detail – Ratio writhing in the stag's head, Nathaniel in his fox mask climbing the burning wicker to free Ratio, and the two figures falling to the ground. Then, in the aftermath, the arrival of the 'police', the unmasking of the STAGS, and the drone lingering on every single guilty face. The fathers, mothers, aunts and uncles, godfathers and godmothers, second cousins, MPs and church acquaintances of the very students standing watching here.

The film faded to black and there was utter, utter silence.

In the sudden darkness I stepped forward. I wasn't shy any more. There had to be an ending. Abandoned by the Savagery of electric light, and lit only by the Medieval moon, I spoke again. 'You'll go from here,' I said softly but clearly, 'into the country's finest universities and to massively successful careers. You'll be running the civil service, government, schools and hospitals. I want you to be *good*. I want you to treat those who have less than you with respect. I never want you to forget that they are people just like you. Their lives do not have less worth than yours. No one is born bad.' I looked at Henry. 'Everyone is the victim of their circumstances, and the product of their upbringing – even kids like you.' I was faltering, suddenly deathly tired. 'I'll shut up now. But at the very beginning I said you don't have to fear change. Be *part* of that change. I *know* you can do it.'

There was a silence that I couldn't interpret. Was it hostile, or had my message sunk in? Then something really odd happened. Someone – and not any of my allies or Gemma, but someone from Cass's little group (I think his name was Will) – started to clap. And then the people around him joined in. And then *everyone* else started to clap, until a giant roar of applause echoed around the midnight garden.

Red-faced and grateful for the darkness, I ducked my head and ran back to the safety of my friends. They all converged on me, the Peel Tower Rebels, the FOXES, my dear, dear friends – whatever you like to call them. I was at the centre of a rugby scrum of back patting, hugging and kissing.

'It's over,' gasped Henry, when he could speak.

'The ball or the Order?' I asked.

'Both, I think,' said Shafeen. 'Look.'

People were drifting away in small and sober groups. Only Cass stood alone, as her little coterie of Medievals turned away from her. 'Guys? Guys!' she appealed to them, hands spread wide, but those haughty teens seemed not to hear her – they walked away, unhalting, their heads now down, their expressions quite changed. The rest of the students streamed away, utterly subdued, to the smart fleet of cars that had arrived to take them back to their stately homes. These sprigs of nobility, these privileged young Britons, had something to think about as they bowled home through the midnight miles of English dark.

Our own little group began to break up too. Ty went off with Horatio, Nel with Nathaniel. Professor Nashe disappeared into the night. Soon there was only me, Shafeen and Henry in the moonlit garden, standing, rather poetically, in a triangle.

'Well.' Henry looked at me. 'What now, Greer?'

I looked at Henry. Medieval, blond and beautiful, holding a book. Then I looked at Shafeen. Savage, dark and handsome, clutching a phone.

'What he said.' Shafeen gave a slight smile. 'I think the moment has come. I think it's been coming for a long time. I think you have to choose.'

I looked from one to the other. Henry or Shafeen? Medieval or Savage? Then there was a shriek from above; something primal and predatory. I looked to the heavens as if they somehow had the answer.

And they did.

There, high in the midnight sky, a shadow crossed the moon, just like in *E.T.* Regina, wings spread like a dark angel, starlike talons poised to strike, and the HAWK, rotors spinning like blades.

And as I watched, the hawk pounced on the drone with its curling talons, knocking it clean out of the sky.

THE END.

HISTORY OF S.T.A.G.S.

S.T.A.G.S. was founded in the seventh century by St Aidan the Great. The name Aidan means 'fire' in Gaelic, and he is considered to be a protector against fire. He was dubbed 'the Great' in order to distinguish him from the lesser saint St Aidan of Ferns. Our St Aidan was born in Ireland, and became a monk on the Scottish island of Iona. He travelled to Northumbria, where he was made Bishop of Lindisfarne. Realising the value of education, he founded a school in the hope that he would train the next generation of Christian leaders. The school began with just twelve boys as pupils, but it grew into a centre of education and a jewelhouse of scholarly knowledge.

Aidan was canonised upon the performance of a miracle; he saved a stag from the hunt by turning him invisible. That stag gave the school an emblem, and a name. Today, after a thousand years of exceptional scholarship, S.T.A.G.S. has educated a dozen British prime ministers and countless members of both houses of parliament. St Aidan's dream that he would train the future leaders of men has become a reality.

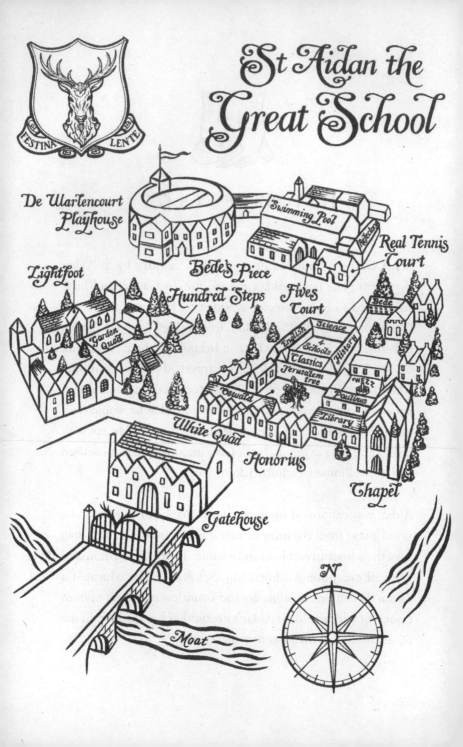

- **DE WARLENCOURT PLAYHOUSE** – built in 1969, the theatre is an exact replica of the sixteenth-century Swan Theatre which used to stand on London's bankside.

- **BEDE LIBRARY** (incorporating the Scriptorium) – named after the Venerable Bede, the library has several notable architectural features, including the medieval Scriptorium, a remnant of the original monastery school, and the Tudor Reading Room.

- **GATEHOUSE** – the gatehouse forms the entrance to the school, reached by crossing the medieval moat. In the days of the monastery school, the drawbridge was raised at night to keep marauding Scots away from the treasures of the chapel.

- **BEDE'S PIECE** – STAGS boasts extensive playing fields, named for a piece of common land enclosed by the school during the eighteenth century.

- **CHAPEL** – Founded in 683, the chapel is the oldest surviving building of the first monastery school. The stained-glass window of Aidan and the stag is original.

- **REFECTORY** – This long building with vaulted ceilings was rebuilt at the time of the Civil War after a fire. The wooden benches and tables on which the students dine are the original ones from the monastery, on which the monks ate their breakfast of bread and beer.

- **ENGLISH SCHOOLS** – In the reign of Edward VI, New Quad –a quadrangle of exquisite Tudor buildings – was built at STAGS to represent the four pillars of learning. The first of the schools (always referred to in the plural) is the English Schools, and the original sign still remains carved above the door.

- **HISTORY SCHOOLS** – The second side of the quad, the History Schools houses the original copy of Bede's work.

- **CLASSICS SCHOOLS** – The third side of the quad, the Classics Schools still fulfills its function of teaching Latin, the language of law and learning.

- **SCIENCE LABS** – Originally the Theology Schools, the fourth side of the quad, despite its Tudor appearance and theological sign carved in stone, now houses STAGS' extensive science laboratories.

- **THE HUNDRED STEPS** – this ancient stone stairway connects the upper and lower schools. Legend has it that in 1348 Edmund de Warlencourt rode up the hundred steps on his horse for a wager.

- **POOL** – The STAGS swimming pool is Olympic-sized and fully compliant with the regulations of the Fédération Internationale de Natation. It is 164 feet long, 82 feet wide and 6 feet deep, with eight swimming lanes marked with rope and buoys.

- **FIVES AND REAL TENNIS COURTS** – Both courts are fully enclosed, and constructed of their original timbers. The Real Tennis court is fashioned after Charles II's court at Hampton Court Palace. The Fives court is designed to replicate one of the exterior bays of the chapel, where the game was first played after Mass.

HOUSES AT S.T.A.G.S.

HONORIUS

Honorius was Archbishop of Canterbury in the seventh century. His is the oldest and grandest house at STAGS. The White Quad, dating from the tweltfh century, features at its centre the Jerusalem Tree, a cedar tree grown from a seed brought home from the Crusades by Conrad de Warlencourt.

Honorius house colours: a white stag's head on a ground of red and gold with a cedar tree as a charge.

BEDE

The Venerable Bede was an English Benedictine monk who wrote The Ecclesiastical History of the English People, a draft of which survives in the Scriptorium at STAGS. Bede house incorporates the extensive playing fields known as Bede's Piece.

Bede house colours: a white stag's head on a ground of red and blue, with a book as a charge.

OSWALD

Oswald was king of Northumbria from 634, uniting the kingdoms of Bernicia and Deira to become the most powerful ruler in Britain. Oswald did much to promote the spread of Christianity in the north, and fittingly the school chapel can be found in his house.

Oswald house colours: a white stag's head on a ground of red and green with a crown as a charge.

PAULINUS

Paulinus was a Roman missionary and the first Bishop of York. The Paulinus Well, built during the bishop's mission to Northumbria in the seventh century, stands in the middle of Paulinus quad. The waters at its depths were said, upon drinking, to turn a sinful man to God.

Paulinus house colours: a white stag's head on a ground of red and purple with a well as a charge.

LIGHTFOOT

Lightfoot is the girls' house at STAGS, and is the newest of all the houses, built originally as a dwelling for masters in 1550. It is a handsome Tudor building with its own Garden Quad, and it was first named Aidan's House. The name was changed when Bishop Joseph Lightfoot of Durham successfully lobbied for the admission of girls in 1880. Since then, Lightfoot House has borne his name.

Lightfoot house colours: a white stag's head on a ground of red and silver, with a bishop's mitre as a charge.

UNIFORM POLICY

By the first day of Michaelmas Term, all students must be equipped with the following uniform

Black Tudor coat
Scarlet stockings (unless you are a Medieval, in which case you may wear knee-high stockings of a design of your choosing)
Narrow brown deer-leather belt
Plain white wing-collar shirt
White clerical tie
Black knee breeches
Black deer-leather lace-up shoes
Regulation black PE kit with STAGS crest

Uniform may be purchased from our suppliers: Keytes of Berwick-upon-Tweed.

The STAGS uniform must be strictly observed year round. A scarf in the colours of one's house may be worn during Michaelmas and Hilary Terms.

⤺ GLOSSARY ⤻

JUSTITIUM – a short holiday that falls roughly in the middle of each term, when students are permitted to return home if they wish

MEDIEVALS – the prefects, usually between three and six in number, chosen from among the final-year students at STAGS

PROBITIONES – final examinations at STAGS, set in the final year

FESTINA LENTE – the STAGS school motto: 'Make Haste Slowly'

MEDIEVAL – anything traditional or historical, in line with the highly prized values of the school

SAVAGE – anything modern or technological, considered not in keeping with the ethos of STAGS

Acknowledgements

There are so many thank-yous to say, and this time they are particularly heartfelt, as this book marks the end of the long STAGS journey.

This series began with a meeting between two extraordinary women who have been instrumental in bringing these books to life. One was my wonderful agent Teresa Chris, and the other was publishing powerhouse Jane Harris, who saw something in the *STAGS* idea on the strength of just one conversation.

One book became three, became five; and on every one I was privileged to have the same expert editing team of two more terrific women, Emma Matthewson and Talya Baker.

I must also thank Holly Kyte for her copy-editing skills, Tia Albertson for her series bible, everyone at Easypress for the typesetting and Sally Taylor for making STAGS school a reality with her beautiful artwork.

Alexandra Allden gave the series the most striking and eye-catching covers I could have wished for.

I'm grateful to the whole team at Hot Key Books for their hard work and support for the STAGS series.

And now to some *HAWKS* specifics . . .

Firstly my apologies to Barry Hines for bastardising the first line of *Kes* to begin this book.

I had a wonderful time visiting Skye to research *HAWKS*, particularly the twin wonders of Dunvegan and Armadale castles. Armadale in the south, the hearth of the MacDonalds, and Dunvegan in the far north, the stronghold of the MacLeods, bookend what is an absolutely stunning island.

Thank you to my own Highlander Sacha Bennett, for being a 'MacLeod of the Clan Macleod'.

Thank you to Conrad Bennett and Lyndon Fisher for clueing me in about high-end drones and their capabilities.

Thank you to Ruby Bennett for the 'marshmallows and rainbows and unicorns and bunny rabbits' mantra, which always brings restful sleep in our house, and worked for Greer too.

Much of my writing comes from reading, and three books in particular informed this one. I first fell in love with Skye in the pages of a book by the incomparable Mary Stewart, called *Wildfire at Midnight*. In it she cites James George Fraser's *Golden Bough*, which became my reference for all the strange black magic in *HAWKS*. The other book is *Falconer's Lure*, by Antonia Forest, who, incidentally, wrote the *Kingscote* books (my own favourite school series). *Falconer's Lure* is the story of one glorious summer of hawking, and I've borrowed aspects of Patrick and Nicola's adventures for this book, together with the name of Henry's hawk, Regina.

My tricky duelling pistols were inspired by the ones in *The Judas Pair*, by Jonathan Gash. Apparently it wasn't unknown for the gunmakers of the past to stack the odds in one combatant's favour. Something to bear in mind if you're ever fighting a duel.

The bits of my writing that don't come from books, come from movies. *Kes* (1969, dir. Ken Loach) is a wonderful film, and well worth a watch.

Lastly but not leastly, I must thank Sacha, Conrad and Ruby, not just for *HAWKS*, and the whole of the STAGS series, but for everything.

And now we really have come to:
THE END
?

THE END

M. A. Bennett

M. A. Bennett is half Venetian and was born in Manchester, England, and raised in the Yorkshire Dales. She is a history graduate of Oxford University and the University of Venice, where she specialised in the study of Shakespeare's plays as a historical source. After university she studied art and has since worked as an illustrator, an actress and a film reviewer. She also designed tour visuals for rock bands, including U2 and the Rolling Stones. She was married on the Grand Canal in Venice and lives in north London with her husband, son and daughter. Her first YA novel, *S.T.A.G.S.*, was published in 2017, shortlisted for the YA BOOK PRIZE 2018 and won the Great Reads 'Most Read' 2018 Senior Award.

@MABennettAuthor
@mabennettauthor

Thank you for choosing a Hot Key book.

If you want to know more about our authors
and what we publish, you can find us online.

You can start at our website

www.hotkeybooks.com

And you can also find us on:

We hope to see you soon!